PUSHKIN PR
In association
WALTER PRES

T0021016

THE SCORPION'S HEAD

In a world where we have so much choice, curation is becoming increasingly key. Walter Presents was first set up to champion brilliant drama from around the world and bring it to a wider audience.

Now, in collaboration with Pushkin Press, we're hoping to do the same thing for foreign literature: translating brilliant books into English, introducing them to readers who are hungry for quality fiction.

I've always been a huge fan of Belgian drama, so exploring Flemish literature was high up on my list of priorities. Even the title of this book, *The Scorpion's Head*, is a bit off-kilter and perfectly sums up what I love about this country – they specialise in producing the slightly unusual, the unexpected, the surprising. This book will grab you by the throat from the very first page – a family with a young child, in a forest, with a serial killer – but it's not what you think it's going to be. It doesn't get any more high-octane than this thriller with the action zipping through Germany, Poland, Paris and Tuscany. Get ready for a rollercoaster ride of emotions which will leave you gasping for breath until the very last page.

Walter

HILDE VANDERMEEREN wrote a wide range of books for children and young adults before becoming a thriller writer. Within a short space of time she has become a major voice within Flemish crime writing: her third crime novel was shortlisted for the Gouden Strop prize and her fifth won the Hercule Poirot prize. A trained psychologist, she specialises in psychological thrillers that are tightly and cinematically structured.

LAURA WATKINSON studied medieval and modern languages at Oxford, and taught English around the world before returning to the UK to take a Masters in English and Applied Linguistics and a postgraduate certificate in literary translation. She is now a full-time translator from Dutch, Italian and German, and for Pushkin Press she has translated titles by Tonke Dragt, Annet Schaap, Benny Lindelauf and Jan Terlouw. She lives in Amsterdam.

THE
SCORPION'S
HEAD

HILDE
VANDERMEEREN

TRANSLATED FROM THE DUTCH
BY LAURA WATKINSON

PUSHKIN PRESS
In association with
WALTER PRESENTS

Pushkin Press
71–75 Shelton Street
London WC2H 9JQ

Copyright © 2016 by Hilde Vandermeeren

Original title *Scorpio*

English translation © 2021 Laura Watkinson

First published in 2016 by Uitgeverij Volt, Amsterdam

First published by Pushkin Press in 2021

This book was published with the support of
Flanders Literature (flandersliterature.be)

1 3 5 7 9 8 6 4 2

ISBN 13: 978-1-78227-748-4

Designed and typeset by Tetragon, London
Printed and bound by CPI Group (UK) Ltd, Croydon, CR0 4YY

www.pushkinpress.com

For my stepping stones

PENSEZ LE MATIN QUE VOUS N'IREZ PEUT-ÊTRE PAS
JUSQUES AU SOIR, ET AU SOIR QUE VOUS N'IREZ
PEUT-ÊTRE PAS JUSQUES AU MATIN

Think every morning that you might not
make it until evening, and think every evening
that you might not make it until morning

An inscription in the Catacombs of Paris

Prologue

S HE WAS WOKEN by a high-pitched, piercing sound. It was like a warning that penetrated her brain.

Run.

She wanted to sit up, but her body was too heavy. The same lethargy kept her eyes closed and stopped her from screaming. She tried to swallow the sour taste in her mouth, but it was no good.

She had no idea where she was. She could still hear that pulsing note, like an alarm. Gradually, more sounds seeped in. Voices that came from far away. A door closing.

And that smell.

She tried to think what the smell reminded her of. Medicine. A child. That smell made her think of a child.

Something bad had happened to that child.

Again, she tried to sit up, but a sharp pain shot up her neck to the back of her head. The pain was new. She took it as a sign that her body was slowly waking up. It was probably going to be a few minutes before she could open her eyes and feel strong enough to escape.

Because that was what she had to do. The child needed her.

The heaviness that held her captive came in waves. She could feel herself getting sleepy again. The voices faded into the background, and even the repetitive high-pitched notes became duller, until they were no more than the dripping of a tap.

She struggled not to drift off.

Or she would be too late.

She repeated the thoughts that had passed through her mind.

There was a child.

Something bad had happened to that child.

Suddenly a voice came out of the darkness, no more than a whisper.

And it was because of you.

Four days earlier

S HE SHOULD HAVE KNOWN that Bernd's stubbornness would send them in the wrong direction. This was only the first morning of a weekend in Altensteig, an idyllic old town in Baden-Württemberg, close to the Black Forest Natural Park, and Gaelle's mood was at rock bottom. She was following Bernd along a narrow forest path and swatting yet another horsefly off her arm. One had just taken a bite out of her calf, making her shriek. Which had made Bernd angry. He had stopped and turned to glare at her. The foliage on both sides of the path was so dense that the sun couldn't get through.

"Stop making a fuss, Gaelle. What's Lukas going to think?"

Her son had just looked seriously at her from behind his glasses. He was likely wondering if seven was the age when you were supposed to start protecting your mother from nasty bugs or if he could assume she would be the one to protect herself.

A swelling had appeared on the back of her leg with a drop of blood, which she had wiped away.

"It's okay, Lukas."

She'd smiled as she said it. But Lukas hadn't batted an eyelid. *He looks tired*, thought Gaelle. Dark hair, pale face, too slight for his age. His severe asthma didn't make travelling easy. The supposedly dust-free room they'd booked at the hotel especially for him hadn't lived up to expectations. There were some rugs on the floor, which she'd had to remove on arrival last night. The duvet wasn't made of synthetic material, and she suspected that the previous guests – against the hotel rules – had smuggled a dog into the room. Who else could have left behind the black hairs she'd found in the corner?

She'd heard Lukas coughing in the adjoining room last night. Combined with Bernd's snoring and the hard mattress, it hadn't exactly been conducive to a good night's sleep.

She looked at her watch. The short, child-friendly walk that Bernd had mapped out this morning at the hotel had already taken an hour and a half. Twice as long as he'd promised. His promises often had to be taken with a grain of salt.

"Will you be home by six for dinner?"

"Yep, sure."

That had been a week ago. When he still wasn't home by eleven that night and hadn't answered her text messages, she'd thrown the rest of the casserole in the bin.

She looked at Bernd's back over the top of Lukas's head. Her gaze slid over his black hair and his powerful neck. His hair was always neat, parallel to the collars of the shirts he wore as an investment advisor at a bank. There were patches of sweat on his T-shirt, as if the "child-friendly" walk had been too much for him, even though he worked out three times a week at the biggest fitness centre in Potsdam – before coming home and collapsing on the sofa in front of the TV with a beer.

The walk didn't pose any physical challenge for Gaelle – except for the blasted insects. As a former European running champion, she had to hold herself back so they didn't end up going too fast, which was why, as usual, she was bringing up the rear.

The undergrowth on either side was becoming denser, so there was less room to walk on the path. Too late, she noticed the thorny branches of a bush sticking out, and they scratched her leg. As she warned Lukas to watch his step, she realised she hadn't seen any markings on the tree trunks for a while.

"Are you sure we're following the right route, Bernd?" she said.

Not even turning around, he replied that he'd never lost his way yet. That wasn't true, though. Ten years ago, before they were married, they'd got lost on a sweltering summer's day while hiking in the Eifel Mountains. Rather than worrying, they'd spent the time kissing and cuddling on a rock near a waterfall, until they were caught by an elderly couple.

She looked again at Bernd's back and wondered exactly when it had gone wrong. She couldn't think of a single tipping point.

But maybe she could. Lukas's birth.

She didn't want to think back to that period. Never again. The therapist had said it could happen to anyone and that she shouldn't blame herself. The irritations between her and Bernd had accumulated over the years, Gaelle realised, like a pile of stones that might suddenly cause an avalanche.

Startled by a sudden noise to her left, a snapping branch, she looked up, but she couldn't see anything through all the trees. She knew there were boars in the forest. A hiker had been attacked here last year after getting too close to a wild sow with piglets.

"Did you hear that, Bernd?" she asked.

He turned around.

"You mean that rushing sound? There must be a river nearby," he said. He sounded considerably more cheerful than a few minutes ago. "We should be able to see it after we turn the corner. It's probably the river I saw on the map."

The same map he'd left at the hotel because he wouldn't need it for such a short walk. As she'd already pointed out a couple of times in the past hour, which hadn't improved the atmosphere.

Now she could hear the running water too. She stopped. The splashing sound was soothing. But not soothing enough.

She felt like she was being watched.

She looked at the tall trees surrounding her, at the dense foliage and the undergrowth on both sides of the path. The vegetation formed dark walls behind which all kinds of dangers might be lurking.

"You always act like life is out to get you."

Bernd had said that to her recently when she'd woken him up one night because she thought she could hear burglars downstairs. The sound turned out to be a door that wasn't shut properly.

In spite of the heat, a shiver ran through her body.

She looked ahead.

The path was empty.

She was alone.

2

H IS NAME WAS MICHAEL, but they called him the Chameleon. In his line of business, no one used their full identity. For the services he provided, leaving a calling card could mean his death or at least ensure a long spell behind bars. It had never come to that. Like the other Scorpio assassins, he lived his life in the shadows. He was a master at blending in. He was everyone and no one. He spoke eight languages fluently. In recent years he'd specialised in the latest tech, such as microchips that distorted his voice. He used prosthetics and professional make-up techniques that allowed him to assume other identities. Future victims had ignored the beggar holding out his hand at the railway station, unaware that this same beggar would kill them a couple of hours later. He was the foreign waiter whose female customers thought he had that typical Mediterranean flair. He was the sickly old man for whom young people with skateboards willingly gave up their seats in the crowded underground train. He lived everywhere and nowhere.

At the moment he was staying at a campsite in Altensteig, near his next target.

He had another four days to carry out his job.

He looked at the forest floor beneath his sturdy walking boots. Today he was a middle-aged British tourist with red hair, a beer belly and a cap to keep off the sun. The sort of person you'd give directions to the nearest pub and automatically offer them your sunscreen.

With the tip of his shoe, he pushed aside a snapped branch. He'd just broken one of his own rules. He had to be not only invisible, but also silent. When he'd caught sight of his target through the leaves, he had taken one step too many. The woman on the path had probably heard something, but he was certain she hadn't seen him. He'd stopped to observe her through the trees. At first sight, the thirty-six-year-old looked athletic, with her light-brown hair in a ponytail and her toned body in skimpy shorts. But there was a weariness in the way she walked along the path. This didn't look like the same woman who had thrown her arms in the air when she'd been the first to cross the finish line in the 100 metres at the European athletics championships. He'd watched the footage of her victory on YouTube as part of his preparation. It wasn't the only medal she'd won in her sporting career, but it had been the last. Her son was born the following year, when she was twenty-nine. After that, she'd never taken part in another athletics competition.

He'd done his research.

His modus operandi was always the same. First stage: information and observation. Second stage: on the basis of that information, formulate a strategy for a natural death, an accident or suicide. Third stage: carry out the hit. And all of that had to happen by the deadline that was given to him by the woman who led Scorpio. He'd never seen her in person. He only knew the name she used to sign her messages: Dolores. Maybe it really was her first name, he suspected, as the rest of her identity was impossible to track down online anyway. She sent her assignments via the Dark Web, the term used for the collection of websites that could only be visited using special tools, with the IP address or the server they were running on remaining hidden. Future clients could visit the Scorpio website via the Dark Web. The Dark Web was a small part of the Deep Web, the invisible side of the internet, which couldn't be detected by ordinary search engines. During an information session he'd attended years ago, the instructor had said that the Dark Web was as much of a mystery as the dark side of the moon. Michael thought that was an insult to the celestial body in question. The Dark Web was more than just a place where no light shone. It was a hiding place for paedophiles, contract killers and other criminals.

The messages Dolores sent never said anything about contract killers. Scorpio was her firm, and she was a businesswoman who dealt in murder to order. There were customers, assignments and staff. But there was also competition.

There were other organisations promoting their services on the Dark Web's hitman market, with excellent results and lower fees.

And so Dolores had decided to expand her operations, as Michael had discovered when he'd received his current assignment.

From now on, children were valid targets too.

3

GAELLE WAS STILL STANDING motionless on the path, wondering what she wanted to do with her life. She thought about the fork they'd just encountered on their route. It seemed symbolic of their relationship, with Bernd wanting to go left and Gaelle wanting to go right.

A heated argument had ensued.

In the end, Bernd had got his way.

As usual.

She only gave in because she wanted to spare Lukas the arguing.

She looked around at the trees and the impenetrable undergrowth blocking her view. They were lost and Bernd would never want to admit that. That, too, felt symbolic of their relationship. When she'd suggested going to marriage counselling last summer, he'd just said he didn't want some shrink sticking their nose into their business.

They would work it out – every marriage had its ups and downs. He'd sounded as if he believed it himself. *And he probably does*, thought Gaelle.

But the problems didn't go away. The distance between them had only increased, as had been proven again on this two-day trip.

She tilted her head.

In the distance, she could hear Lukas's voice.

And then Bernd's. He was calling her name.

Something had happened.

She started running, as fast as she could, the thorny bushes along the path scratching her legs.

As she turned the bend, she saw them. The undergrowth wasn't as thick here, and Lukas lay on the ground in one of the small clearings, with Bernd crouching beside him. Water raced under the nearby wooden bridge and around the boulders.

Gaelle was panting when she reached Lukas and Bernd. She took off her backpack, threw it to the ground and sat down beside her son.

She immediately saw what was wrong. As she heard the rasping sound of Lukas's breath, she read the panic in his eyes and saw the colour draining from his face.

The doctor might have said that forest air was good for asthma patients, but that didn't apply to a gruelling hike in the heat along a route that didn't exist.

"Why did you have to insist on having things your way again?" she snapped at Bernd, as she opened her backpack to look for Lukas's inhaler. "If we'd gone right at that fork, we'd have been back at our hotel ages ago."

Bernd fell silent and hugged Lukas to him, trying to calm him down.

Her hands ran over the contents of the backpack: the bottles of water, the sandwiches in aluminium foil, the first-aid kit and the useless anti-insect spray.

But she didn't find an inhaler.

Lukas's face had turned even greyer and his whole body was shaking.

"Where's the damn thing got to?" asked Bernd, looking at his mobile phone.

His voice sounded much more shrill than usual when he told her there was no signal here.

She turned the backpack upside down, tipping everything onto the ground, and then inspected every item in turn, not wanting to believe her eyes. As she searched inside the pocket of the backpack again, she felt her breath catching in her throat.

"The inhaler's back at the hotel," she said.

"What?" replied Bernd. "How the hell did that happen? I reminded you about it before we left the room!"

Gaelle had never forgotten the inhaler before. She wasn't looking for excuses. It was her mistake. Maybe it was because she was so exhausted after the almost sleepless night. She remembered putting the inhaler on the bathroom cabinet that morning, ready to take with them, and then leaving the hotel, certain that it was in her backpack.

"You forgot the inhaler? How stupid can you get?" yelled Bernd.

"About as stupid as wandering around without a map," she said. "Or did you think I hadn't noticed that we're lost?"

Lukas was still in Bernd's arms, whimpering like an animal in agony. All around them, the forest rustled away as if nothing were wrong. For a fraction of a second, Gaelle closed her eyes and absorbed the silence.

Then she calmly asked Bernd if she could take Lukas from him. Bernd seemed to hesitate for a moment, but then he gave him to her.

The boy flailed around in panic. Gaelle held him and rocked him.

Stroking his head, she told him he was going to manage fine without his inhaler. She said it without a trace of hesitation in her voice. The hand she stroked Lukas's head with was cool, not clammy. She hummed the lullaby that had always soothed him as a baby and said everything was going to be okay. She told him that the doctor had said that in an emergency it was possible to beat an asthma attack without an inhaler.

Every sentence, every calming gesture gradually eased Lukas's panic. She didn't know how long the attack had lasted, but it seemed like an eternity until his breathing calmed down and a healthy colour returned to his face.

She wiped away his tears.

"You did a fantastic job, Lukas," she said quietly.

"So did you," Bernd said to her.

He stroked her cheek, just as she had done with Lukas. The gesture was as fleeting as the wind, but she could still feel it when they got back to the hotel half an hour later.

4

MICHAEL HAD SEEN IT ALL. He'd observed from a distance as the boy had become desperately short of breath, as if the air had been poisoned by the man who'd been watching them for some time.

For a moment, he thought half the job was already done even though he hadn't lifted a finger. That had happened to him only once in recent years. His target had been a wealthy eighty-year-old, who went to the golf course almost every day. The name of the client – the person who had requested the hit – was never disclosed to Scorpio's contract killers. Dolores was the only one who knew their identities. In the case of the elderly man, Michael suspected that one or more heirs were starting to get impatient. One evening he'd followed his target as he drove off in his Jaguar after playing golf. To his surprise, the old man didn't head directly to his well-protected home with its security systems in a street with a local neighbourhood watch, whose members kept a close eye on everything. Instead, he drove to a bar where the red lights in the windows indicated that there was more on sale than just alcohol.

The old man never came back out again. An ambulance pulled up an hour later, with no sirens, as if the paramedics knew there was no need to hurry. Hidden in a doorway, he'd seen another car stop outside the bar a while later. A woman with a black bag got out of the car, presumably a medical examiner. And still later a hearse appeared. Throwing his cigarette away, he'd turned and gone back to his hotel. Using a non-traceable phone, he'd then called the bar in question, pretending to be a police inspector and said he wouldn't make a fuss about any suspicious work permits as long as the manageress would answer a few questions. Her voice shaking, the woman had confirmed that the old man had suffered a heart attack during a sex show. She'd added, through her sobs, that it had been a wonderful way to go. Then Michael had turned on his laptop and logged in to his personal page via the Scorpio website.

The goods have been delivered.

It took just a few seconds for a reply to appear.

It was businesslike, as always.

The payment due will be transferred soon.

The money Michael had made over the years was in a Swiss bank account. It was enough for him to be able to retire for the rest of his life – at forty-six, he should still have a good few years ahead of him. He knew, though, that Dolores would not let him retire before fifty-five. That was the average age at which hitmen were allowed to leave Scorpio after a completed career. There were some who wanted to stay longer, but Dolores thought employees began to lose their edge after fifty-five for a job that was, after all, extremely demanding.

Michael wondered if he was already starting to lose that edge. Although he would never admit that to Dolores. Something strange had happened just now. As the boy lay there, gasping for breath, Michael had thought he'd feel liberated, as if he'd been let off the hook.

If the boy died now, here in the middle of the forest, he wouldn't have to kill him. No child's blood would be on his hands. He'd seen the woman desperately searching for something in her backpack and then heard the couple arguing.

All that time, the boy lay beside the river, gasping for air like a fish on dry land.

He'd watched the woman taking the boy in her arms and the two of them sitting there, mother and son. It reminded him of Michelangelo's *Pietà*. But unlike the marble statue, the mother had not been mourning her dead son. She'd been doing everything she could to bring him back to life.

And she'd succeeded.

At that moment something strange had happened.

A feeling had passed through him that he couldn't immediately identify, and it had confused him. If he'd wanted the boy to die, he should have felt disappointed. But he wasn't.

Lukas – that was the boy's name.

The name shooting through his mind at that moment only added to his confusion. As soon as he knew the identity of the person he was supposed to kill, he erased their name from his thoughts. They became an object, a neutral target that had to be eliminated. The delicate boy who had just fought for his life in his mother's arms had awoken something deep within Michael. A memory he'd tried to suppress for over thirty years, which had been buried under a layer of dust and blood as the years passed.

Janek had been counting on him. And he'd failed him.

As soon as he'd seen that the boy was back on his feet, he'd turned around and left the forest. On the way to his campsite, he'd met a friendly German tourist who had brought out her best English to have a conversation with him. Weren't they having good luck with the weather? It had rained all last week, far too gloomy for June. Did he know there was a nice pub near the campsite? Finally she'd looked at his puffy red face and advised him to apply an extra layer of sunscreen.

He'd promised to bear that in mind and had said goodbye awkwardly, as befitted a middle-aged British man who looked very much like a single.

As soon as he got back into his tent, he started his laptop.

He travelled the dark paths of the Dark Web to the Scorpio website and logged in with the code, which only he knew.

Janekbfleur83

Outside, he heard a child laughing.

His hands paused over the keyboard. If he decided to do this now, there was no way back. There were dozens of clauses in the contract that Dolores agreed with her contract killers. Most of them were specific demands whereby the signatory undertook to continue training throughout their entire career, in the use of high-tech equipment, non-traceable toxins, weapons, combat techniques and languages. But one of the clauses was a favour.

Just one time, only once in their career, a contract killer could refuse, for whatever reason, to accept a particular job.

Michael put his fingers on the keys and started typing.

5

Dolores Bartosz looked out of her office window. Her workspace was on the first floor of her safe house, a cube-shaped building that looked like a bunker. Her private domain was hidden in the dense woodland of the vast Knyszyn Forest, in the northeast of Poland. The window of her office took up the entire façade and was made of bulletproof glass. If someone were to try to fire a bullet at her now, she wouldn't even flinch, but watch with a smirk as the bullet bounced off the outside, like a bird smashing into the glass.

Above the forest, dark clouds were gathering. She didn't like the tapping of raindrops on the windows. If it started to rain heavily, she'd log into her home automation system and press the button for a complete lockdown. That meant the concrete panels on either side of the windows, the garage door and the front door would automatically slide shut. The panels were a metre thick, as were the walls of her house. She'd visited the test space of the Danish architect who'd designed her house, and she'd seen for herself that these walls could withstand grenades and Kalashnikovs. The same architect had also constructed safe houses for movie stars, drugs barons and Russian oil magnates. She'd paid him enough money to keep his mouth shut about this job and so far the man had been wise enough to do so. She knew that because she'd had his computer hacked and secretly kept an eye on his online communication.

She looked out at the rosebush in the garden. It was the only plant growing on the perfectly manicured lawn, which was surrounded by a high wall with motion sensors. The wall was the first major obstacle for anyone who wanted to get inside without an invitation. The entrance gate was not an alternative for any would-be intruders. It wouldn't open until the computer had confirmed the visitor's identity with a fingerprint scan. Her only regular visitor, the man who delivered her groceries every month, reluctantly had to have his finger scanned every time to get onto the property.

The man, who left the goods in the garage and then drove away in his van, had never seen her. As far as he knew, some reclusive elderly businessman lived in the house.

She looked at the sky again and decided she had just enough time to go into the garden before it started raining. She left her office and headed for the stairs.

In the garden, she stood beside the rosebush, breathing in the sweet scent of the unique variety and looking at the red petals, which were folded together to make what she considered a natural work of art. Every flower was different. If it weren't about to start raining, she could have stood and looked at it forever.

The bush was blooming beautifully. That was because of the fertiliser, which had been of an exceptional quality this spring.

Three months ago, she'd instructed Cédric to mix a pot of ash with fertiliser and to scatter that mixture under the bush. She hadn't mentioned that the ash was the burnt remains of a former employee who had dared to join the competition. It had not ended well. At least, not for him. The ashes had been parcelled up and sent to her by Vasili, one of her employees who specialised in torture techniques and had disposed of the man at her request.

She'd watched as Cédric pushed the full wheelbarrow with a shovel in it across the lawn. Dark-brown hair, medium height, with his eternal sunglasses, which he took off only at night, and a solemn air, as if he were not transporting fertiliser but serving caviar. His serious expression made him look a little older than he was, thirty-eight. Cédric hadn't needed his white stick and had headed straight for his goal. It was March and the roses were not yet blooming, but the wind playing in the rosebush must have shown him the way, or perhaps he could smell the chicken manure that had been spread under the bush the week before. Over the past few years, she'd been surprised by his sense of hearing and smell, which were keen even for a blind person. Maybe he'd also smelt that the ash he was told to mix with the fertiliser came from a corpse.

As usual, he had not asked any questions. Dolores thought he was a good butler. Even though she was almost a quarter of a century older than him, he always knew exactly what she needed. The sugar in her tea was perfectly dosed to the milligram, he cooked healthy meals, which they ate separately, and with electronic help, he succeeded in keeping the house spotless, even though he could never see for himself how the floors were shining.

She stroked the velvet-soft rose petals with her fingertips and then slid her hand down the stem. *Semper Dolor.* The name of the rose variety with the most beautiful flowers and the largest thorns in the world.

Clenching her right hand around the stem, she didn't flinch as the thorns entered her flesh. A few drops of blood ran down her fingers. They were almost the same colour as the roses.

Semper Dolor.

No life without pain.

The first drops of rain began to fall. Dolores turned around and went back inside. In her living room, she operated the panel to initiate the lockdown. It took a couple of minutes for all of the sliding doors to close completely.

Seeing her reflection in the window, she quickly turned away.

She heard Cédric walking down the corridor. When the lockdown system started up, it was his job to check that everything went smoothly. He did so using a device that reflected ultrasonic sounds and then indicated whether the panel in question was shut properly. Her thoughts lingered on Cédric. He probably thought she'd initially employed him out of pity, because, as a poor, blind eighteen-year-old orphan, he had no future. But he was mistaken. She, Dolores Bartosz, showed no pity.

She tolerated a blind man in her presence for the same reason there were no mirrors in the entire house.

As the sliding doors gradually dimmed the office, she thought about the message Michael had sent her today. The Chameleon had presented himself in a guise she'd never seen before. Clause 48 was not a favour, as her employees believed – it was a test of loyalty. No one had ever tried to use it before.

And Michael shouldn't have done so either.

She'd already passed his job on to Vasili, who would take out the two targets within four days, as agreed with the client. That wasn't what was worrying Dolores.

She was concerned about Michael.

She wondered if she had been wrong about him.

6

G AELLE SAT WITH LUKAS and Bernd at one of the wooden tables on the hotel terrace. A breeze made the yellow parasols flutter gently. It was busy. The restaurant had a reputation for its simple food and generous portions, and it also attracted people who weren't hotel guests. Gaelle stroked her hair. It still wasn't completely dry after her shower. As Bernd studied the menu, she glanced sideways at Lukas. He was reading a comic that he'd taken from the kids' corner in the restaurant.

Lukas looked so much fresher than the heap of misery she'd held in her arms that morning. When they'd got back to the hotel after the walk, which had been anything but child-friendly, Lukas wanted to lie down for a while. Which had given Bernd the idea that the two of them could retire to their own room for a quickie. They could lock the connecting door for as long as it took.

The entire time he lay on top of her, Gaelle had looked at the door to make sure the handle wasn't moving. That would mean Lukas needed them for some reason. She'd turned her head away from Bernd's panting so she could hear if Lukas was calling her. She'd put his inhaler on his bedside table, but if he had an attack he wouldn't be able to shout loudly.

For a moment she thought she heard something.

Bernd apparently felt her stiffen and asked her if she'd come. She said yes and, satisfied, he'd slipped out of her. Then she'd got out of bed, quickly pulled on some clothes and went to Lukas's room to check that everything was okay.

He was still asleep.

When they'd booked this hotel, Bernd had insisted that Lukas wouldn't sleep in the same room as them, as he always had before when the three of them had gone on holiday. A boy of seven was old enough to sleep alone, Bernd had said. Or had she forgotten that Bernd had to help out on his parents' farm when he was that age? As a seven-year-old, he'd even helped with the calving.

She was startled out of her thoughts.

"Steak with pepper sauce and fries," she suddenly heard Bernd say, "and a beer."

A waitress had turned up at their table, and she was looking at them as if she didn't have a second to spare. Somewhere on the terrace, a toddler started whining about being hungry, and a baby was crying a few tables away.

"How do you like your steak?" the waitress asked Bernd.

"Extra rare. Have you made a note of that? I hope I'm not going to need my beer to wash my steak down," said Bernd.

The waitress didn't even smile. Pen and notebook at the ready, she turned to the other side of the table.

"Do you know what you want?" Gaelle asked Lukas.

They hadn't even had the chance to have a proper look at the menu.

"I'd like spaghetti bolognaise," said Lukas. "And a big glass of Coke."

"And I'll have a salad with goat's cheese, please," said Gaelle. "And a white wine."

The waitress nodded, picked up the menus and left. Lukas went back to his comic.

Bernd took his phone out of his pocket.

"You promised to leave your work at home," said Gaelle.

"Just want to check my messages."

Gaelle's gaze wandered to the other tables. To the left, a rather portly man with reddish hair and an unhealthy flush sat reading his newspaper. Gaelle assumed he was a British tourist, as he was reading an English newspaper. There was something sad about the way he was sitting there by himself, thought Gaelle. Most of the tables were occupied by couples and families with children.

Gaelle looked at Bernd again. He was tapping out a message on his mobile, a look of irritation flashing across his face.

"I just need to deal with this," he said without looking up.

Gaelle felt something flare up deep inside her. She always seemed to be waiting for him to give her the go-ahead. About another child. About her plans to convert their spacious home in Potsdam, on the outskirts of Berlin, into a guesthouse. It was a project she'd been dreaming about for a long time, the ideal way to combine work and family. After years of sitting at home, she finally felt like doing something productive again, now that Lukas was becoming more independent and caring for her sick mother was definitely a thing of the past. But Bernd didn't think much of her plans for a guesthouse.

He swore under his breath at something he'd just read on his phone. *More problems at work*, thought Gaelle. Everything always revolved around him.

She'd waited long enough.

Sometime soon, the money from the investment fund she'd inherited from her mother would be released. She didn't know the exact date. That was something Bernd kept an eye on at the bank where he worked. It was a nice amount at any rate. The door to the future was opening up.

"I want to use the money from the investment fund to convert the house into a guesthouse," Gaelle suddenly announced.

Bernd looked up from his mobile.

The waitress came over with the drinks. When she put down the glass of Coke for Lukas, she did it so quickly that it splashed onto the table. Without saying a word, she disappeared.

"But I've told you time and again that it makes much more sense to reinvest the money," he said.

He'd just taken a swig of his beer and there was a line of foam on his top lip.

"I inherited that money from my mum. It's only fair that I get to decide what happens with it, isn't it?"

"Are you actually trying to wind me up?" said Bernd. "We're in a public place here. Maybe you've forgotten we're having a weekend away. You know, most people would try their best to keep things nice and friendly."

Lukas looked up from his comic.

"Is something wrong, Mum?" he asked.

"No, of course not," said Gaelle. "We're away for the weekend. We're having a great time, the three of us."

Bernd threw her an evil glare.

A little later, the waitress brought their food. As Gaelle was about to start her salad, Lukas began coughing. It turned into his typical asthmatic cough, which made it impossible for him to eat. Gaelle soon identified the cause. Someone at the next table was smoking, even though no smoking was allowed on the terrace. The breeze blew the cloud of smoke in their direction.

Before she could mention it to Bernd, he put down his knife and fork and waved at the waitress.

So apparently he does pay as much attention to his family as he does to his mobile, thought Gaelle.

"Can I help you?" the waitress asked.

Bernd pointed at his plate.

"This steak is completely inedible," he said.

7

A FTER LUNCH on the hotel terrace, Michael had walked back to his campsite so quickly that his hair was sticking to his temples with sweat. He wasn't concerned about the drops of sweat leaving trails on his seemingly sensitive, sunburnt skin. The professional make-up he'd used was water-resistant.

He was in a hurry because he'd realised during lunch that he'd made a bad decision.

It was because of that boy, Lukas. Their eyes had met during the meal and the boy had given him a quick smile, with the innocent look of a child who trusted that another day would simply follow this one. The slender boy reminded him of Janek. Janek had been about five years older than Lukas was now when they'd first met at the detention centre over thirty years ago.

Janek had been counting on him.

But he'd been too late.

And that was something he could never put right.

Not that.

He sat down at his table and turned on his laptop. He looked at the winged insect that was slowly walking down his leg and raised his hand to swat it dead.

If he abandoned Lukas and his mother to their fates now, neither one of them would survive. Even if he warned Gaelle that she and her son were in danger, chances were that she wouldn't believe him, certainly not when he told her that the anonymous client – as was often the case with contract killings – must be someone she knew well. He thought about Gaelle's love and patience as she'd calmed Lukas during his asthma attack. It was hard to believe someone wanted to get rid of them. He wondered why he was worried about it though. He didn't know them. He didn't want to know them.

Look what's become of you, son.

He tried to tell himself that his mother's tone didn't sound like an accusation. Just as he tried to kid himself that, for thirty years, he'd had no time to visit her grave.

Look what's become of you.

He was holding his hand right above the insect now.

Maybe, somewhere deep inside, something still remained of the boy he'd been before they'd sent him to the detention centre. He lowered his hand, bent forward and blew the insect off his leg.

He waited, rather than logging in at once. He knew he shouldn't be too hasty. Every word he typed had to be carefully considered. Even a comma in the wrong place might betray his real intentions. His message needed to have exactly the right tone: self-confident, decisive, without forgetting what his place was within the organisation.

The message was starting to take shape inside his head.

He would let Dolores know that he'd changed his mind. He would write that, upon further consideration, he wanted to take this job after all. But because of the complexity – which was why he'd brought up Clause 48 – he wanted to enlist the help of another hitman. This job did involve two targets, after all.

He logged in and read the message twice before sending it.

Dolores would probably read the message right away. She seemed to be focused on her work day and night. He looked at the screen and tried to imagine how she'd react. He assumed she'd already contacted someone else by now. The hitman was probably already on the way here. He had no idea about his colleague's identity. All communication went directly via Dolores. The contract killers weren't able to send one another messages. She was the only one who knew their encrypted email addresses.

If he wanted to prevent Gaelle and Lukas being killed, he first had to eliminate whoever was planning to do it. The best way to do that would be to seek out the hitman himself, instead of blindly waiting for him to strike. That was step one. Warning the targets now would be pointless. That would only cause panic and the hitman would find them soon enough anyway. Step one was clear. As long as Dolores agreed. As for step two, creating a smokescreen so that it would appear to the outside world and the client that mother and son were dead, he'd think about that later.

He picked up a bottle of water and took a swig. It was a bit tricky with the latex skin, which made his face look puffy. He felt like peeling it off, standing up, leaving all this behind, breaking away from Scorpio and disappearing into the anonymity of some big city.

But he did none of that. He wiped his mouth, put down the bottle of water and looked at the screen. He had enough money to disappear, but he knew Dolores had more than enough money to get back at him.

He wasn't afraid of dying. Except for Bellefleur, no one would mourn his passing. She would lie, sad and lonely, in the satin sheets of her apartment near the Quai d'Orsay in Paris for a few nights. Then it would be business as usual as she returned to offering her affections to her other clients.

Michael shifted in his chair, which creaked under his weight.

What he was doing now wasn't for Gaelle or for Lukas.

He was doing it for Janek.

As if, by doing this, he might be able to make up for not saving his friend.

8

Poland, January 1982

*B*efore that first winter they had to get through without his father, his mother had never lied to him. Even though Michael was only thirteen, she told him everything he needed to know. She'd told him that his father, who was a miner, had been killed the previous year during one of the many strikes against the Communist regime, which were violently suppressed. That hard times were coming now that Jaruzelski, the leader of the military junta, had declared martial law. And that it was hard to make ends meet as a widow in a remote village without water and electricity, but still she managed to put food on the table every day. She told him his father would have been proud because he was doing so well at school and because he'd never missed a lesson, even when he was sick or had to walk for an hour through the snow in patched-up shoes to get there.

She'd never lied to him – until that day. It was the end of January and exceptionally cold. A bitter wind blew around their house. The roof creaked under the snow and there were flowers of ice on the inside of the windows. Michael was lying on the sofa in the living room so that the woodstove could keep him warm.

He had a fever. His mother could tell as soon as she placed her hand on his forehead. They'd had very little to eat for a few days now. Their supply of potatoes had run out a while ago. The heavy snowfall of recent weeks had made it impossible for the promised food that was supposed to get them through the winter to be delivered. Yesterday his mother had cooked a handful of tough carrots, which he'd struggled to get down.

"They have enough flour and potatoes for our whole village in the military food depot down by the railway line," Michael growled. "Dad once told me about it. So why don't they come and help us?"

"The roads are blocked with snow, Michael."

"It's not just the snow, Mum. They probably don't even want to help us. There are still people living here who are against the government, like my father."

His mother was silent. Her eyes were hollow, her cheeks sunken, but her hands were as soft as ever when she stroked his head.

"But everything's going to be fine, Michael."

His mother coughed and then took out a handkerchief and spat into it. Her spit was mixed with blood. She'd told him before that it was nothing serious, just inflamed gums, and that it would get better when spring came.

Michael wondered how she was going to make it to spring if they had nothing to eat.

Becoming drowsy, he turned over and went to sleep. His feverish dreams were a welcome distraction.

A long time later, he woke up, feeling a little better. On the table in the living room, he saw two bowls. He stood up. He was hungry, it was noon, and his stomach was so empty it hurt.

"Did you have a good sleep?" his mother asked. "I've already had my lunch."

He sat down at the table. His mother's bowl, opposite, still had a few traces of green soup in it. He gulped down his bread, spooned up his soup, licked his bowl clean and put it back down on the table.

The fire of the woodstove cast shadows over his mother's face. She'd grown so thin that she no longer had the strength to fetch a bucket of water from the pump. Michael did everything for her, even before she had to ask him.

After eating, he went back to lie on the sofa and pulled the blanket over himself.

It was dark by the time he woke up. Through his eyelashes, he saw his mother putting the last meal of the day on the table. She stuck a spoon into what looked like a kind of mash and scooped some out. Then she took her plate and rubbed the vegetable mash around it, without taking a bite.

She placed the plates opposite each other on the table, just as she'd done yesterday and the days before.

He sat up straight.

"You lied to me," he said quietly.

His mother turned to look at him.

"I thought you were still asleep, Michael."

"When did you last eat?" he asked.

His mother started coughing up blood again.

He jumped up from the sofa and went over to the chair where his winter coat was hanging. His mother had made it as thick as possible by sewing layers of old clothing into the lining.

"Where are you going, Michael?" his mother asked.

"To the military food depot. I'm going to ask if they can spare any food and medicine."

"But it's four villages away. Everything's snowed under."

"I'll get through."

"Don't do it."

"We have no choice, Mum. You're coughing up blood. There could be something wrong with your lungs. My teacher said it can kill people."

He put his gloves on.

"I'm sure they'll help us."

His mother came towards him. She grabbed his hands and begged him to stay at home. But they both knew she wouldn't be able to stop her thirteen-year-old son, who was stronger than she was and, in his head at least, already a man.

He kissed his mother on the cheek and made her promise to eat his portion, which was still on the table, right away.

He opened the door and walked out into the dusk.

41

A few metres on, he turned around to look.
His mother was standing at the window, watching him go.
It was the last time he ever saw her.

9

*T*HIS IS TURNING INTO *a weekend to forget*, thought Gaelle. That Sunday afternoon she sat with Bernd and Lukas in a noisy bistro in the old part of Altensteig, at a small table near the toilets. They'd dived into the nearest café to escape a cloudburst. Unfortunately, a lot of other people had had the same idea, and the customers were squeezed in like a pack of wet dogs. And they smelt just as bad too. Or maybe the smell was coming from the toilets, as the door swung open and shut.

The bistro wasn't equipped for the number of tourists streaming in to avoid the downpour, and the staff couldn't handle the rush. Gaelle looked at her watch. They'd placed their lunch order over an hour ago, and the two young waiters seemed to be avoiding their table since Bernd had angrily asked if they'd had to go out and slaughter the cow.

Gaelle was fiddling with the beermat in her hands. All around her, people were talking so loudly that she could barely hear the music coming from the speaker right above her head. Lukas was sitting beside her, playing a game on Gaelle's phone. Bernd sat opposite, his face even darker than the clouds outside. He was drumming his fingers on the table, ready to pounce on a waiter as soon as they ventured into the vicinity of the toilets.

Gaelle's thoughts drifted to their home in Potsdam, a large, solid house, built fifteen years ago, the first floor and attic of which could be converted into eight guestrooms with bathroom facilities. The breakfast room could be set up downstairs. They could have an extension built on the back of the house, with a nice view of the garden. Maybe there would be some money left over for a terrace. She took a pen from her handbag and started sketching a design on the back of the beermat.

She pushed the beermat towards Bernd.

"This is just an initial idea," she said.

He glanced at it.

"What's that supposed to be?"

"The breakfast room for our guesthouse," Gaelle replied. "With a terrace outside."

"What's a guesthouse?" asked Lukas, looking up.

"A house with rooms where guests can pay to spend the night and have breakfast," said Gaelle. "Not as big as a hotel."

Bernd pushed the beermat away.

"For God's sake, don't start going on about that again," he said with a sigh. "Not now." After that, they hadn't spoken to each other for a long time. Gaelle had memorised the menu and daily specials by heart.

Her glass was empty.

She leant forward and pointed at Bernd's beer glass.

"Do you want another one too?" she asked.

"What?"

"Did you want another beer?"

"Of course I want another beer. I've been wanting another drink for half an hour now, but those two idiots don't appear to get it."

He waved at a waiter again, who deliberately looked the other way.

"Right. I've had enough of this," said Bernd, standing up.

He walked over to the bar and Gaelle saw him gesticulating at the woman behind the counter.

The toilet door opened, and a girl waited patiently until a plump woman came out. Gaelle was starting to feel queasy.

Maybe it was the noise, the crowd, the smell of the toilet cleaner and Bernd, who seemed to be getting increasingly angry over at the bar. She stood up.

"I'm going to get some fresh air," she said to Lukas.

She asked for her phone back. He finished his game and handed it to her. Then he took the inhaler out of his pocket and brought it to his mouth.

"You okay, Lukas?" asked Gaelle.

He nodded and, after a couple of puffs, put the inhaler away.

"I like the idea of people sleeping in our house," he said. "As long as it's not in my room."

She smiled, turned around and walked across the room. As she passed one of the tables, a man suddenly pushed back his chair without looking – and without apologising. As she approached the door, she had to squeeze her way through a group of dripping-wet tourists who had just come in, hoping to find a free table.

She pushed open the door, the window of which was completely fogged up.

Finally – air!

Gaelle stood outside under the bistro's awning. The rain poured over the edge of the canvas, a few cold drops blowing into her face. She shivered. She hadn't thought to bring her coat with her. On the other side of the street, a couple in their fifties walked past under an umbrella. Their arms were entwined, as if they wanted to protect each other from the rain. A little further on, a man in a black raincoat stood with his back towards her, looking in the display window of a souvenir shop.

Gaelle took her phone out of her pocket.

She wondered if she and Bernd would be walking together under an umbrella in twenty years' time.

Ebba was the only one who would understand. They'd known each other for over thirty years now. They'd lost their first teeth together, laughed, argued and learnt that sadness is just a part of life. The couple with the umbrella had disappeared. The man in the black raincoat was still there.

Gaelle looked for Ebba's number in her list of contacts and called her. As she waited for her to answer, she glanced back into the bistro. Bernd was still at the bar, talking to an older man now.

An automatic voice told Gaelle to leave a message after the tone. Gaelle looked at the puddles on the road and decided that a voicemail message was not the right way to let your best friend know you had doubts about your marriage.

"Hey, it's Gaelle, can you pop round on Monday afternoon? There's something… I'd like to talk to you, Ebba. See you soon."

She hung up.

Taking a deep breath, she opened the door and then ignored the dripping-wet tourists who were still waiting in vain for a free spot and walked through to the back.

Their plates were on the table. Bernd and Lukas were already eating.

"You should have seen the look on the manager's face," Bernd said between two bites of food. "The guy didn't know what had hit him."

Standing under the awning of the souvenir shop, Michael looked over at the bistro that Gaelle had just come out of and then gone back inside. He'd seen her phoning someone and, judging by the length of the call, she'd probably left a message.

He took one last look at the bistro across the street. Today the family was going to leave Altensteig and return to their home in Potsdam. They'd only booked two nights at the hotel. It hadn't been hard to find that out after he'd hacked the hotel's computer system.

What was in store for Gaelle and Lukas was not going to happen in Altensteig.

Dolores had informed him that it would happen on the first Tuesday after their return home.

Tomorrow he had a meeting with the other hitman, whose codename was Vasili. Dolores had arranged for them to meet at Potsdam Hauptbahnhof.

S ITTING IN THE LIVING ROOM, Gaelle could hear the familiar sounds of Monday morning in an empty house: the washing machine spinning, the coffee machine in the kitchen bubbling away. She looked through the window at the large front garden and pictured the lawn giving way to eight parking spaces for guests. She'd also done a quick sketch of the car park, which she kept with her other designs in a folder labelled GUESTHOUSE MADELYN. The name was a tribute to her mother, Maddy, who, even in the last few weeks of her life, had applauded her plans to start a guesthouse. It was about time she left the sketching phase behind, Gaelle decided, and took the first real steps towards making her dream come true. She'd start soon, by finding out about the required permits, putting together a business plan, getting in touch with the bank to discuss the financial situation, consulting an architect and, last but not least, persuading Bernd.

Even though she'd be able to finance most of the renovation and furnishing costs with the money released from her mother's investment fund, she couldn't do this without his support. After all, they shared both the house and the mortgage.

She walked out of the living room and to the kitchen, put the dirty cups from breakfast in the dishwasher and turned it on. For a Monday morning – after a rainy weekend in Altensteig – Bernd had been in a remarkably good mood. He'd made scrambled eggs for everyone and hot chocolate for Lukas, just the way he liked it, with plain chocolate and two sugar cubes. While she'd cycled to school with Lukas, Bernd had apparently had the time to clear the table – he'd forgotten the cups, of course, but he didn't have an eye for detail. She'd never made an issue of it.

There had been other issues though. That was what she wanted to talk to Ebba about today. She expected that her friend would pop round in her lunchbreak. The transport company where Ebba worked in the office was nearby. She often drove back and forth at lunchtime, and sometimes the two of them met for lunch in Potsdam.

Gaelle checked her phone for new messages.

Still nothing from Ebba.

She thought it was kind of strange that Ebba hadn't been in touch after the message she'd left her yesterday afternoon. She thought about sending her a text, but decided against it. Gaelle couldn't stand it herself when people were too pushy. She put her phone down on the kitchen counter.

Ebba would soon turn up. Distracted as she was, she must have just forgotten to let Gaelle know.

Half an hour later, her phone rang.

It was an unknown number.

"Hello. This is Gaelle." Silence.

"Hello, who's there?"

The caller didn't say a word. All she could hear was a sound that reminded her of a train going past.

She hung up.

When she went upstairs to air the rooms, she soon forgot about the phone call.

This was a Monday just like any other.

Vasili slipped his phone into his inside pocket, grabbed the briefcase at his feet and walked into the railway restaurant at Potsdam

Hauptbahnhof. It was pretty quiet, with only a quarter of the tables occupied. At the beginning of June, the tourist season was not yet in full swing, the children were at school – or that was where they were supposed to be – and the commuters were travelling to work, counting the days until their summer holidays.

Vasili never went on holiday. He thought there was no need when your work was your hobby. He looked around the café and chose the table that seemed most suitable. With his back to the wall, in a corner where he'd be able to keep an eye on everyone and everything and close to the exit, ready to run in a split second. Before sitting down, he inspected himself in the mirror on the wall. Not for too long, just the glance of a businessman checking that he'd shaved properly that morning. His black hair was combed into a side parting, and the wig was so well made that no one would ever suspect it wasn't natural. It even had a few flakes of fake dandruff. People would remember him as a well-dressed businessman somewhere in his early forties, over one metre eighty, bright-blue eyes with frameless glasses, dark hair and a bit of a scalp problem.

When the waiter came, he ordered a coffee. He looked at the clock above the entrance: half nine. His appointment with the man who was known as the Chameleon wasn't for another thirty minutes, but Vasili liked to arrive in good time. He took pleasure in sneaking into the habitats of his prey, sniffing out scents, tracking movements.

And hearing voices.

He had just had the woman on the phone. Gaelle.

He looked at the clock again. Time was ticking for Gaelle. And for her son.

Tomorrow they would die.

T HE MORNING WAS almost halfway through by the time Gaelle sat down at her laptop in the living room. The more time she spent looking up information about permits and regulations for setting up a guesthouse, the more she realised that she urgently needed expert advice. Maybe she could ask Rolf. Ebba's husband wasn't much of a talker, but as an estate agent he'd be able to help her through this legal merry-go-round.

She focused on the screen again, studying an expert's tips for starting your own business. A couple of minutes later, she was startled by the sound of a car tearing up the driveway and coming to a stop, its brakes shrieking. She stood up and walked to the window.

It was Ebba. She got out of the car and hurried to the front door.

Gaelle walked to the hallway and opened the door before her friend had pressed the doorbell.

Ebba was a mess. Her long, dyed-blond hair hadn't been brushed, her eyes were red, her mascara was smeared, and her blouse was crumpled.

"He's gone," said Ebba.

And when Gaelle didn't react immediately, she said, "Rolf's left me."

It was five to ten, and Michael looked around the station restaurant. He'd been sitting at a table directly opposite the entrance for ten minutes and he'd checked out all the people in there. There were two possible candidates for Vasili. All Dolores had told him was to look out for a businessman type with dark hair and glasses, who would be drinking coffee and would place his laptop on his table at ten o'clock sharp. At that moment, Michael was to go up to him and address him with the words, "It's been a long time since we last saw each other." To which the only correct response was, "High time we caught up."

Two men answered to the right description, but Michael would have dared to bet his entire arsenal of weapons on Vasili being the man in the corner.

It was the spot he would have chosen himself if the table hadn't been occupied. He looked at the other people: an elderly woman with a child, a couple in love, travellers with backpacks and business people. Michael wondered if their food would taste as good if they knew there were two hitmen in the room.

The clock said it was ten.

He stood up. Today he was a businessman in his late fifties, with silver hair and a brown leather briefcase full of documents about deals that would never be made.

The only deal he wanted to make was the one inside his head. He had to prevent a woman and a child from being killed the next day.

The man in the corner had placed his laptop on the table. Michael walked over to him.

"It's been a long time since we last saw each other."

The blue eyes behind the glasses expressed not a trace of emotion when Vasili replied, "High time we caught up."

It took two cups of coffee before Ebba was able to tell Gaelle what had happened. This morning at breakfast Ebba had asked Rolf if there was something they needed to say to each other. She'd meant it half as a joke, just to break the silence. Rolf was about to leave for the south of France for a week, where he was looking for a place in the countryside on behalf of a wealthy client. He'd looked at her with a serious expression on his face and said that he was relieved she'd brought it up. They'd been leading separate lives for so long, he'd said, and it'd be easier to separate as friends, if she was thinking the same way too. He'd also added that there was no one else involved. It was just over.

He'd sort out the practical matters, such as moving his personal belongings and settling the mortgage, with Ebba when he got back from France.

She'd started yelling and pleading, and she'd hurled a cup at his head, but he'd just stood up and said he'd made his decision and that Ebba making such a fuss wasn't helping anyone. Then he'd left. She was so upset that she'd called in sick to work.

"He's not coming back," said Ebba, rubbing her right eye and smudging her mascara even more.

That's maybe just as well, thought Gaelle. But saying something like that out loud would be inappropriate, and so would the other thought that crossed her mind: *It's a good job you don't have children.*

She said nothing and poured Ebba a third cup of coffee. Ebba's hand was shaking as she brought the cup to her mouth.

"I'm all alone now, Gaelle," she sobbed. "Maybe for the rest of my life."

"You mustn't think like that, Ebba. I'm still here for you." Ebba's phone rang and she answered it.

"No, Lore, I'm not at home," she said in a nasal voice, wiping her nose.

Ebba had better not ask her sister to come round here, thought Gaelle. She wasn't in the mood for pretending that Ebba's sister and mother were welcome. Anyway, that'd be rather hypocritical after Ebba's last birthday party when – after a few too many – Gaelle had described the two of them to Ebba as leeches and parasites. The volume of her voice had been so out of control that the two women in question had been able to hear her from the adjacent room. Unfortunately, she hadn't realised that until afterwards. In the heat of the moment, Gaelle had described in detail how Lore, a woman who called herself a "job hopper" but in fact lived on benefits, always came bursting into Ebba's house and grabbing whatever she could: pieces of fresh fruit, make-up, a second-hand designer dress that Ebba had picked up. Not even a packet of smoked salmon in the fridge was safe from her grasping, manicured hands. Not to mention Ebba's mother, who drained everyone dry with her stories about her bad back, bunions and other people dying of cancer. That too had been clearly audible in the next room, Gaelle had learnt afterwards. It had been two weeks before Ebba was on speaking terms with her again.

"See you later," said Ebba, and she hung up. "Mum and Lore are coming round to my place this afternoon."

"Okay," said Gaelle, trying to hide her relief that she wouldn't have to set eyes on the younger, prettier and also more arrogant version of Ebba – or her moaning mother.

There was a silence. Gaelle looked at her framed wedding photo on the wall. If she pulled the plug on her marriage, as she'd been contemplating this weekend, it would be over for good.

Ebba put her handkerchief away.

"You left a message on my voicemail yesterday," she said. "Said you wanted to talk to me about something. Sorry, it completely slipped my mind. Why did you want to see me so urgently?"

"Never mind," said Gaelle. "It really doesn't matter anymore. All that counts now is what happens next with you."

There was something about Vasili that Michael found disturbing. They'd been sitting at the table in the corner of the restaurant for about ten minutes now. They talked calmly, without whispering, but there was no need to keep the volume down. To any casual – or less casual – listeners, they'd been talking the entire time in fluent German about a possible deal with a textile factory in Hungary.

It was all code. The deal they were discussing didn't involve carpets, but human lives.

The previous night, Michael had come up with a plan to save Gaelle's and Lukas's lives while creating a smokescreen to ensure that Scorpio would never go in search of them. Dolores would think the targets had been eliminated, and the anonymous client would be satisfied that he'd got his money's worth. Then Michael would help Gaelle and Lukas to start a new life elsewhere under fake identities. The two of them would be safe there – far away from the person who had taken out a hit on them – whoever he or she might be. Then Michael would disappear from the radar. His plan was daring, but he'd taken bigger risks before.

The first hurdle would be convincing Vasili that the scenario of a depressed mother killing first her son and then committing suicide was the most logical option in this situation. He leant forward and informed Vasili about what was going to happen tomorrow.

To Michael's surprise, Vasili just nodded. He didn't even ask any questions. Michael tried to fathom the man who was sitting in front of him. Perhaps he was the kind of man who never asked questions and who did whatever was expected of him without stopping to think about it. Murdering a child, for instance. Maybe he was never troubled by his conscience simply because he didn't have one.

They drank their coffees and said goodbye.

As Michael walked out of the station, it struck him that everything had gone very smoothly.

Maybe too smoothly.

Poland, January 1982

*H*idden in the undergrowth and surrounded by darkness, Michael looked at the bigger of the two soldiers who was just beginning his rounds of the food depot. It had taken him almost three hours to reach the site. He thought back to the moment he'd arrived here. He'd been shivering as he walked up to the two soldiers, partly because of the cold, partly because of his fever, which was probably rising again.

They hadn't even let him finish speaking. After they'd heard which village he came from and had questioned him about why he was growing up without a father, they'd laughed in his face and said that he and his mother would have enough to eat if his father hadn't been so stupid as to go against the government.

They'd chased him away like a stray dog.

But as soon as he was out of their sight, he'd turned around and crept back through the undergrowth.

At the front of the building was a crackling fire, which the two guards occasionally warmed their hands at. The depot was a simple red-brick building with a door that was firmly bolted and secured with chains and padlocks. There were no windows on the left and rear walls of the building. His heart had sunk, but when he crept through the undergrowth to investigate the wall on the right, he spotted a way he might be able to get inside.

The only way.

To the right of the depot was an adjoining wooden shed with a flat roof that was about a metre lower than the roof of the depot. If he climbed onto the shed roof, he'd be able to reach the depot's side window. It wasn't entirely *without risk. First he had to get rid of the glass without making too much noise and then he'd have to squeeze through the opening. The window was just large enough for a child to get through. He could only hope he didn't freeze to death before he could get inside the depot, because he would have to leave his thick winter coat behind in the bushes.*

Shivering, he tried to ignore the cold climbing up his soaking trouser legs. To prevent the snow from crunching under his feet, he stood perfectly still. He held his padded gloves to his face to protect his skin from the biting wind.

The bigger soldier was by the fire again. Michael could see another building nearby, presumably the barracks, where the rest of the soldiers were asleep. He hoped the two soldiers who were on guard wouldn't be relieved any time soon. They clearly preferred standing by the fire to exploring the area.

But they were both armed.

He looked up. The moon was lonely in the sky. This was not a night for stars. Silently, he took off his coat and hid it under the snowy bushes. He looked at the shed. He was nimble enough to hoist himself up on the planks of the wooden wall. Then it would all have to happen very quickly. From where he was standing, he could no longer see the two soldiers, but he could hear the crackling of the fire and the sound of their voices.

One slow step at a time, he moved through the snow. Luckily, it was no more than a few metres from the bushes to the shed. After each step, he turned and tried to erase his footprint with his gloves. Then he placed his feet in the trail that the patrolling soldiers had left around the depot. When he reached the shed, he found spots for his hands and right foot in the boards of the wall and pulled himself up. But as he tried to stand on a protruding board halfway up, his foot shot free and he landed in the snow.

A dull thud, like snow falling from the roof.

He could only hope the two soldiers would think the same. Scrambling quickly to his feet, he found another foothold and stopped to listen.

He could no longer hear voices coming from the front of the depot.

Perhaps they'd been alerted after all.

He pulled himself up, scraping his knee on a protruding nail, ignored the pain and hoisted himself onto the flat roof, where he lay in a thick layer of snow.

Just in time.

He heard one of the two soldiers coughing as he walked past the shed. The crunching footsteps stopped close to the wall he'd just climbed up.

He heard a sound coming from nearby but didn't dare to move. Maybe the soldier was aiming his rifle.

Michael's cheeks were ice-cold and he was shaking all over. Without a coat, he wouldn't last long.

Down below, he heard the snow crunching. It sounded like footsteps moving away. A while later, he peered over the edge of the roof. The smaller soldier was disappearing around the corner, smoke swirling around his head.

Nothing had happened. The man had just stopped to light a cigarette.

Michael crept to the window high on the wall of the depot. The shed roof creaked beneath him.

Or maybe it was the snow down below.

He was close to the window now.

He could hear the soldiers laughing.

Clenching his fist, he gave the window a tap with his thick glove.

It smashed.

He heard the soldiers laughing even louder. Moving quickly, he removed the rest of the glass from the frame. One of the shards pierced his glove, but he pulled the piece of glass from his hand without flinching.

Drops of his blood dripped into the snow on the roof. He would have to bandage his hand before he went back down, so that he wouldn't leave a trail.

Michael squeezed his way into the building. He stood on a platform and lowered himself to the ground floor. Then he took off his gloves and took the lighter that had belonged to his father out of his pocket. He lit it, cupping the flame with his hand. He couldn't believe his eyes. The room was crammed with food. There were whole shelves full of tins, sacks of potatoes and packet upon packet of grain, rice and flour. There was enough food here to keep several villages going through the winter. He took the sack he'd been carrying on his back and quickly filled it with everything he could grab.

On one of the top shelves, he spotted tinned peaches in syrup.

As far as he could remember, he had eaten them only once in his life. It had been his father's last present for his mother's birthday.

She'd thought they were delicious.

A tin of peaches would be sure to make her feel better.

With his left hand, he lit up the shelf and stood on tiptoe to take the tin. He could just reach it.

Outside, the talking had stopped.

He had to hurry.

As he lifted the tin of peaches from the shelf, it caught on another tin.

Before he could grab it, it clattered to the floor.

For a fraction of a second, he froze.

Then he picked up his sack of food and hurried to the platform so he could climb back out of the window.

I can do this, he thought. I'm the smartest boy in the class. And the best at climbing.

They were waiting for him by the shed, their faces next to the barrels of their guns, their expressions grim.

He raised his arms in the air and watched as his injured hand slowly turned the snow red.

M ICHAEL LEFT HIS HOTEL near Schloss Sanssouci, the most famous of all the palaces in Potsdam, as the receptionist had just enthusiastically informed him without any prompting. There was some irony, thought Michael, to those words today: SANS SOUCI, without worries, which the Prussian king Frederick the Great had had written on the façade of his palace in the eighteenth century.

Michael had never felt more worried before. The night hadn't brought any rest, only the bad dream that recurred far too often. Again and again, it threw him back into the past and once more he became that scared little boy in the snow. Bellefleur said that he screamed in the night. He'd never wanted to tell her why.

It was nine in the morning, and the sun was shining away in the sky, with the promise of a nice day. Michael walked along the pavement behind a group of Japanese tourists heading towards the palace. He'd exchanged his business suit from the previous day for a pair of jeans, a grey polo shirt and comfortable shoes. He walked into the park of Schloss Sanssouci and sat down on a bench by the large pond with the fountain, surrounded by statues of the twelve Titans. The sight of those powerful giants only added to his unease.

In his head, he went over what was going to happen in about three hours' time.

They were going to strike on the route Gaelle cycled every afternoon when she went to pick Lukas up from school. She only took the car when the weather was really bad, as Michael had ascertained when he'd followed her every day last week. Their bike route ran alongside the canal, a secluded road with one-way traffic for cars. There was a bend in the road – and it was going to happen after that bend. While Vasili stood guard to stop any cyclists or drivers and ask them where the nearest garage was, Michael would be around the corner, carrying out the job as quickly as possible. He would lie in wait for Gaelle and Lukas, while his van, with false number plates, stood at the side of the road. He'd told Vasili yesterday that it would all happen quickly: he'd stop the two of them with some excuse about a breakdown, and then knock Gaelle out with ether, deposit her son and their bikes on the verge and put the antidepressants in her handbag, along with a note saying SORRY in the hasty scrawl of a woman saying farewell to a world she can no longer face, a woman who wants to spare her son that same misery. Then he would throw the two unconscious bodies into the canal. As the drowning process takes a couple of minutes at most, death would come quickly. That, at least, was what he'd told Vasili.

From that last point, his actual plan went differently. The van, which Michael had hired from a company that could be found only on the Dark Web, had a false base. The vehicle was designed to conceal weapons, contraband and/or a maximum of two people. Michael would place the unconscious Gaelle and Lukas in that space and tell Vasili and Scorpio that he'd thrown the bodies into the water and that the strong current meant they might never be found. He would drop off Vasili in the centre of Potsdam at the spot where he'd picked him up and then they'd go their separate ways. As soon as Gaelle woke up, Michael would explain to her that his intentions were good.

It was doable, Michael thought. He couldn't make any mistakes, but the plan was not impossible.

As he listened to the splashing of the fountain and the twittering of the birds in the trees, an old woman took out a bag of bread and scattered crumbs on the ground. She smiled as the first birds descended. The group of Japanese people came past, following the guide who was steering them through history and through the park towards the monumental steps to the palace. All of them people without a worry.

Michael thought back to the previous day. He could have followed Vasili to his hotel room, killed him there and made sure no one found the body. But Vasili's sudden disappearance would alert Dolores and she wouldn't rest until she got her hands on him, Gaelle and Lukas. He might be able to save his own skin, even if it meant he'd be on the run for the rest of his life, but it wouldn't take Scorpio's contract killers long to track down Gaelle and Lukas. Not everyone had the camouflage skills of a chameleon.

Another thought occurred to him: for the first time in years, he was going to do something that would make his mother proud. Perhaps that would give him the courage to visit her grave in Poland after all this time.

The woman with the bread had gone and a jackdaw had landed on the ground, chasing all the sparrows away. "Might is right" – a universal law, thought Michael.

He stood up, left the Titans behind and walked out of the park.

M ICHAEL'S HUNCH hadn't deceived him. Something was wrong.

It had started when he'd stopped his white van beside Vasili at the agreed meeting place, a supermarket car park in the centre of Potsdam. Vasili, who had blond hair today, no glasses, and was dressed like an average family man, didn't climb in on the passenger side. Carrying a plastic shopping bag, he walked around the vehicle and opened Michael's door.

"Get out," he said. "I'm driving."

Michael stayed where he was. "You've no need to doubt my driving skills," he said. "I can manoeuvre a truck down the narrowest of streets without any accidents."

Vasili didn't budge.

"Instructions from Dolores," he said.

At that moment, Michael's phone beeped. He took his mobile from his pocket. The message was from Dolores, confirming what Vasili had just said. Michael got out and, as he walked round to the other side of the van, he tried to work out what was going on.

He sat down, and Vasili started the car. Without saying a word, they drove out of the car park. Michael focused on his own body language. He knew Vasili would be able to read his anxiety and suspicion in the smallest of gestures: a nervous cough, tensing up in his seat, checking his safety belt a few times and looking around too much.

He tried to avoid doing any of those things, but when Vasili turned left at a junction instead of right and towards the canal where they were going to wait for Gaelle, he whipped his head around to look at him.

"What are you doing?"

"Instructions from Dolores," Vasili said again, staring ahead. "The plan has changed."

Michael swore to himself. That was why it had gone so smoothly yesterday. While he was revealing his plan, Vasili had known all along that Dolores would come up with a different one. It was a test, and nothing he did or said now could suggest he was anything but obedient.

"Fine," he said. "But it'd be nice if you could tell me what *is* going to happen."

Vasili told him, emotionlessly, as if he was reciting a shopping list. They weren't on their way to the canal but to a dead end near where Gaelle lived. Vasili would park the van there, and then they'd walk to the vacant plot of land at the back of Gaelle's garden. To anyone who walked by, they'd be potential purchasers interested in the wooded land, which had been for sale for some time now. They would climb over Gaelle's garden fence, and no one would see them because of the dense trees and undergrowth. Then they'd enter the house through her back door without leaving any signs of entry and wait for her there. Overpowering Gaelle and Lukas before either of them had a chance to escape, they'd knock them out with ether. As soon as they were unconscious, they would inject first Lukas and then Gaelle with a lethal dose of the anaesthetic propofol. It was all in the plastic bag Vasili had brought with him. They'd leave the empty syringe next to Gaelle's body with only her fingerprints on it. They'd also plant a box of antidepressants in the drawer of her bedside table, in such a way that it would be found quickly. The note saying SORRY would be left beside her body before they silently made off through the back door. Their gossamer-thin gloves would ensure they didn't leave any fingerprints.

They were getting closer to the neighbourhood where Gaelle lived. Michael glanced to one side, his gaze sliding over Vasili's hands on the steering wheel. He knew there was an athletic body concealed beneath the family man's simple attire. The man was a murder weapon in his own right.

But so was Michael. He and Vasili were the same size, over one metre eighty, and both were equally fit and equally capable of finishing each other without hesitation. Michael thought back to the jackdaw in the park and wondered in whose favour the universal law of "might is right" would decide.

Michael was not carrying any weapons today. Vasili didn't appear to have any either, and Michael realised he'd made an error of judgement. They'd agreed yesterday that they wouldn't go in packing guns. No weapons meant they wouldn't have any trouble in the event that they got stopped by the police. It was something Dolores insisted on with operations that didn't require weapons.

Vasili drove into the dead end, parked the van and took the keys out of the ignition.

"What explanation did Dolores give you when she asked you to change the original plan?" Michael asked in as neutral a voice as possible. "And why didn't she inform me?"

"Someone like Dolores doesn't owe us any explanations," said Vasili. "Never. You should know that by now."

15

M ICHAEL LOOKED at the carving knives in the wooden block a metre and a half away from him. Like Vasili, he was standing ready against the wall, hidden behind the open door that connected the kitchen and the living room. He didn't have much time. In a few minutes, Gaelle and Lukas would come into the kitchen either through this entrance or through the door into the hallway. Either way, before they realised what was happening, they'd both have an ether-soaked handkerchief pressed to their faces. The boy was for Vasili, and Michael would take care of Gaelle. As soon as Gaelle and Lukas were unconscious, Vasili would carry out the rest of the plan, meticulously and quickly.

Michael weighed up his chances. Vasili was standing just a little closer to the knives on the granite counter. It would come down to a fraction of a second if he dared to be the first to lunge and snatch a knife.

He heard voices outside, coming from the front of the house.

He took another look at the knives in the wooden block.

"Before I forget," whispered Vasili, "Dolores has taken precautions in case anything goes wrong today."

Michael heard the front door opening and thought frantically about the meaning behind those threatening words. He hardly had any time to do so, as Gaelle came first into the kitchen via the living room, followed by Lukas. They were so busy talking that they didn't realise what was going on behind their backs. Vasili darted forward from behind the open door, grabbed the boy and held a cloth over his mouth.

Gaelle screamed. Michael went towards her and grasped her tightly, with his back to Vasili as he whispered in her ear that he could only save her life and her son's if she cooperated by immediately pretending to lose consciousness.

Gaelle stopped screaming, slid out of his arms and onto the floor, where she lay with closed eyes.

By now, Vasili was stooping over the unconscious boy with a syringe.

"Let me finish up here," said Michael, taking the box of antidepressants out of the plastic bag. "Go and put the pills upstairs in the bedroom."

"Why don't you do it?"

"Then you can personally let Dolores know that I don't have a problem doing away with kids."

Vasili looked at him without blinking.

Michael handed him the box of pills.

"Just put them on the counter," said Vasili. "I'll take the pills upstairs in a minute."

As Michael followed his instructions, he saw out of the corner of his eye that Gaelle had something in her hand. She was still pretending to be unconscious and was lying with her face turned away from them, but her fingers were moving over her mobile, which she was holding against the side of her body.

Vasili had seen it too.

He looked at Michael with an ice-cold stare, leant over Lukas and jabbed the needle into the arm of the unconscious boy.

Michael threw himself upon Vasili, pushed him away from Lukas and tried with all his might to prevent Vasili injecting the rest of the propofol into Lukas's arm. In the struggle that followed, the syringe fell onto the floor and rolled away into a corner.

Vasili's hands clenched around Michael's throat, cutting off his air supply. A grin appeared on Vasili's face as he said something Michael couldn't make out.

Gaelle had jumped to her feet and hurried to the counter, where she'd pulled the largest carving knife from the wooden block and was running at Vasili. He'd had to loosen his grip around Michael's throat after receiving a kick in the crotch. Just as Gaelle was about to stab Vasili in the back, Vasili thumped Michael in the stomach, following it up with a blow that took him to his knees. In a single movement, Vasili whirled around and pushed Gaelle backwards with full force. The knife flew from Gaelle's hands and she landed with a dull thud, the back of her head hitting the granite counter. She slumped onto the floor and lay there, her head to one side.

Michael pounced on the syringe in the corner and lunged at Vasili. As the two men struggled, Michael managed to jab the syringe into Vasili's neck and squirt the rest of the propofol into his body. Vasili made one last attempt to attack Michael, but the fast-acting drug knocked him out and he dropped to the floor.

Michael knelt beside Lukas's motionless body. The boy was unconscious, but still breathing. Then he walked over to Gaelle and felt that she still had a weak pulse.

Gaelle's mobile rang. Michael took the phone without answering. He read the text message that she'd sent to someone called Ebba before she'd been caught: AT HOME. HELP.

Then he listened to the voicemail message Ebba had left on Gaelle's mobile when Gaelle hadn't picked up. Ebba said in a panicky voice that she'd be there in ten minutes, and she'd call the emergency services if Gaelle didn't open the door.

Michael put Gaelle's phone down beside her. All he could do now was take Vasili's unconscious body, erase all traces of their presence and disappear before Ebba appeared at the door. He took the empty syringe, pressed Gaelle's fingers onto it and put it on the floor beside her body.

Then he picked up the plastic bag.

Feeling powerless, he looked at the two bodies on the ground. If Gaelle had done as he'd told her and pretended to be out cold, everything would have turned out differently. The fate of Lukas and Gaelle was no longer in his hands. He put the note that said SORRY on the counter, next to the open box of antidepressants. Stooping down, he threw Vasili's unconscious body over his shoulder.

Outside, he took one last look through the kitchen window. Vasili's fingerprints or his own wouldn't be found anywhere.

They had never been here.

The bodies of a supposedly unstable, depressed woman and her son were all the emergency services would find in the kitchen. As the heavy weight pressed down on his right shoulder, he thought about the precautions that Vasili said Dolores had taken. He quickly shoved Vasili's body over the fence and then climbed over it himself. Not long after that, he dumped his load in the hidden space in the van, which was backed up against the trees. Quickly, he closed the doors of the van and got behind the wheel. Just as he was about to start the engine, what Vasili had said to him with a big grin on his face during the fight shot through his mind. This time there were no distractions.

Vasili had said Bellefleur's name. And then he'd said that they knew where she lived.

The hotel bed creaked as Ludka got up to walk to the bathroom. Just to make sure, she checked her phone and saw that there was still no message. Dolores had asked her to be on standby. She knew what she had to do, she was completely ready for it and was waiting impatiently for the signal to go into action.

In the bathroom, she took a piece of dental floss and ran it through her perfect teeth, carefully, to avoid making her gums bleed. She looked contentedly at the result. Her white teeth contrasted nicely with her lightly tanned face and brown eyes. Since deciding, when she was thirty, to wear her dark hair short, she'd noticed how much she resembled her brother, whom she'd called by his codename for years now. Just as he always called her Ludka. Their identities might have been erased, but their relationship had not. When she looked at her face in profile, the resemblance to Vasili was even more striking. The same aquiline nose. Inherited from the same father, who had ended up six feet under after a botched drugs deal. She didn't miss him any more than she missed her mother; neither of them had ever really been there for her.

Vasili had, though. Her brother, ten years her senior, had looked after her in his way. She smiled remembering the time when, as a seventeen-year-old, he'd wanted to make a healthy meal for her because they'd been living on fast food for weeks. His first attempts at cooking burned in the pan, but after that it went better and better. And then there was the time in the car park of a nightclub when he'd put a pushy guy in his place. The guy had fled, leaving half of his teeth behind.

A warm glow always went through her when she thought about Vasili. Maybe that was what was meant by loving someone so much you'd die for them. He was also the one who had introduced her to Scorpio.

She rinsed her mouth and turned off the tap.

When this job was over, they'd finally see each other again. She was looking forward to their reunion.

She sat on the bed, waiting. Her gaze ran over the roofs of the houses in the distance, pausing on the Eiffel Tower up above.

Michael had deposited Vasili's body in the van and driven to an abandoned warehouse on the outskirts of Berlin. As he looked at Vasili's corpse, he'd rubbed his knuckles. He'd hit him hard, but Vasili had died in the knowledge that his killer was in serious trouble. He hadn't revealed anything about Bellefleur or about what Dolores was planning to do with her. Maybe he didn't know.

He'd dumped the body in a place where it wouldn't be found any time soon, had contacted the special hire company to swap his van for a sports car and was now tearing along the motorway towards Paris. He cursed his foolishness in underestimating Dolores. He'd always thought he'd taken all the necessary precautions to stay out of Scorpio's crosshairs whenever he met up with Bellefleur. He'd avoided all modern forms of communication. He didn't even know her mobile number. He wouldn't be able to find it out any time soon either, as he knew she used a secret number after being stalked by an ex-client. So as not to leave any digital traces, he always arranged his meetings with Bellefleur via notes, which he slipped into the doorman's hand at the Hilton, along with a tip, and now he'd endangered the life of the only woman in the world he trusted enough to fall asleep next to.

He looked at the clock on the dashboard. He wouldn't get to Paris until around midnight.

He hoped he wouldn't be too late.

16

DOLORES STARED AT THE CLOCK in her office, waiting for both hands to meet at the top. Although it was nearly midnight, she hadn't closed the shutters yet. At her request, Cédric had installed a special spotlight to illuminate the rosebush beautifully, exactly what a masterpiece needed. Her gaze moved across the lawn to the high wall around her domain and to the trees beyond.

This was her territory, her anonymous kingdom from where she dictated who would die and when. The list of her dead subjects was a long one. There were housewives who'd become superfluous after their children had left home and whose husbands could spare a lot of money to avoid an even more expensive divorce, so they could finally tell their mistresses that they had chosen them. There were politicians from all over the world, including an African dictator who'd died in a plane crash a few years before. The newspapers had reported a particularly tragic accident that had claimed the lives of over a hundred passengers.

She knew better.

She would take the client's name with her to the grave.

When the clock began to strike, her suspicions were confirmed. It was past Vasili's deadline for sending her a message about the outcome of the double hit – and she assumed he would never send another message to anyone again.

And now she would contact the person she considered responsible for that turn of events.

*

According to the navigation system, Michael was a fifteen-minute drive from Quai d'Orsay, the area where Bellefleur had an apartment. He could have been there already if he'd managed to avoid the excruciatingly slow drivers and the congestion around Paris. Ahead of him in the one-way street was a driver who seemed unable to decide where he was going.

Michael blew his horn and drove right up to the bumper of the car in front.

At the next side street, the car turned off.

Michael was about to floor the accelerator when he heard the beep of an incoming message on his mobile. He read it without parking up.

Dolores informed him that she wanted to talk to him right now, via his webcam.

That rarely happened. Which in itself was alarming enough not to ignore the request, thought Michael.

Although all he really wanted to do was drive on to Bellefleur's apartment, he looked for a place to park. He turned off the engine, grabbed his laptop and logged in to contact Dolores via the Dark Web.

As soon as he was connected, he hit the record button. All he heard was her voice. She didn't appear on the screen. Her laptop was positioned so that he could see only a section of white wall and part of a window looking out onto an illuminated lawn, with some kind of bush and a dark forest in the background.

"I haven't heard anything yet," he heard Dolores say. She sounded older than he'd expected. Maybe it was the sharp tone of her voice. "Not from you. And not from Vasili."

The dashboard clock said it was five past midnight. Scorpio's killers were required to contact Dolores before midnight on the day the job was done. He'd hoped she wouldn't think to chase it up until the next morning.

"What happened?" he heard her ask.

"It didn't go to plan. There were some complications."

He added that Vasili hadn't kept to the agreement.

"Where's Vasili now?" asked Dolores.

"It was his fault it went wrong. I did what's expected of us in such circumstances."

Michael knew he didn't explicitly have to refer to Clause 67 of the contract to the woman who had made the rules herself. Clause 67 could be summarised as: Tidy up after yourself. Anyone who didn't keep to the agreement would be liquidated.

"Are you still there?" asked Michael.

Dolores hung up.

Ludka switched on the nightlight when her mobile rang. It was exactly ten past twelve and she'd been asleep for barely an hour, but she was immediately wide awake when she realised who was on the line.

"You need to leave now," said Dolores. "Do what you have to do and then I have a new assignment for you."

That's a shame, thought Ludka. *Now I won't be able to see Vasili for a few days.*

"No slip-ups. Tonight's target is important to your brother's killer."

"*What* did you say?"

Ludka shouted so loud that she thought her voice could probably be heard in the corridor outside.

"Vasili is dead."

"No!"

"He was killed today by the man he thought was his partner. That man has betrayed us all."

Ludka walked into the bathroom, turned on the light and saw her expressionless face in the mirror, with its hard jawline and aquiline nose.

Just like Vasili's.

"Who is it?" asked Ludka.

"He calls himself the Chameleon, but his real name is Michael. And he's your next target."

"My brother's killer is already dead," she said hoarsely. "He just doesn't know it yet."

"Don't underestimate him. He changes his appearance the way a chameleon changes colour. You'll have backup from two men with the codenames of Jorge and Zoltan. They're already on their way. There's a high chance that Michael's somewhere in Paris now."

Ludka watched a tear trickle from the corner of her eye, but she didn't flinch.

She turned off her phone, grabbed the hat that went with her police uniform and left the hotel room.

Bellefleur was standing in the walk-in wardrobe in her luxury third-floor apartment, near Quai d'Orsay. She'd just showered and was standing naked in front of the wall mirror. Drops of water glistened on her skin like the diamonds of the necklace she was about to put on specially for her client.

The room was divided into two parts. When she went to the left side, she was simply Désirée, a girl from Nigeria, whose parents back home were proud of their daughter for having studied philosophy in Paris as a scholarship student and now teaching at the university. She'd never told them that she'd quit in the second year after figuring out that what she could earn as an escort girl didn't compare to the theories of dozens of dead philosophers.

She'd made that decision when she was twenty, eight years ago now, and since then she'd created space in her wardrobe for Bellefleur. It was a name that suited a classy lady who accompanied lonely gentlemen to exclusive dinners, who could hold her own in conversations about globalisation or about the *terroir* of the wine and who was, in addition, prepared to share her client's bed for an extra fee. She usually did so in hotel rooms, but occasionally between the sheets in her own apartment.

She looked in the mirror. Another five years. Then she'd have saved enough to buy a house in Italy, where she could live on sunshine and the produce from the vegetable garden. Bellefleur would vanish from her life for good, and Désirée would finally be able to go in search of a soulmate, someone who didn't necessarily need to know what was meant by the *terroir* of the wine, someone who preferred to drink a cool beer on a bench in front of their house among the Italian hills while the sun went down, someone she could toast the future with as they came up with silly names for children.

So far she'd shared her dream with only one person. She knew him by the name he used when he arranged their meetings via the doorman at the Hilton. He called himself the Chameleon. He always treated her as someone special, a woman he'd invited out, not as an escort whose services he was paying good money for. When they were done, he usually wanted her to spend the night with him, something she allowed her clients only very exceptionally. During those night-time hours, they'd had long conversations, about holidays and exotic destinations, and he'd taught her a few words of Italian, but they'd never talked about their work. She didn't know what he did for a living, and she knew better than to ask.

Bellefleur smiled. She turned and walked to the right-hand side. She had to hurry. She had an appointment in quarter of an hour. The man, in his sixties and the former CEO of a renowned jewellery company, was one of her most loyal clients. For two years now, he'd been coming at least three times a month, usually at around half past midnight, a time when most of his acquaintances would already be in bed. He was always as punctual as the watch he wore. The diamond necklace she was about to put on had been a gift for her twenty-eighth birthday. He asked her to marry him just about every other month, and she always turned him down with a polite smile.

She took a set of lingerie from her wardrobe, a black designer dress and a pair of stilettos. He loved stilettos. It was all she was allowed to wear when she was on top of him.

She slipped into the black dress, zipped it up and had just put on her shoes when someone rang her apartment doorbell. *That's strange*, she thought. He usually announced his arrival via the intercom. Maybe someone else had let him in.

When she opened the door, she found herself looking into the surly face of a dark-eyed policewoman.

Michael left his car in a no-parking zone and hurried towards Bellefleur's apartment. As the shop windows flashed by, an image filled his mind: the beautiful villa in Tuscany with an olive grove that he'd bought last month for Bellefleur. It was a surprise that he wanted to put on her pillow, in the form of a photograph, while she was taking a shower.

This is all for you, he would say.

It was a gift that also contained an unspoken question. Would she let him go with her, so they could spend the rest of their lives in the sun and, there among the Tuscan hills, forget all the dark places they both had been?

He bumped into a man, who swore at him as he ran on.

In a few minutes he would be there, and then they could disappear together.

Out of breath, he reached Bellefleur's apartment complex. Third floor. He opened the door of the porch, quickly ran his finger over the rows of bells – she'd told him her real name after just a few meetings – and pressed the button with the first name Désirée.

No answer.

Not after the second and third attempts either. Just as he was considering trying other bells, he saw someone appear on the other side of the entrance door, heading out of the building.

He slipped in through the door but was shocked to see that it was a police officer. The woman passed him without saying anything.

He walked to the lift and pressed the button for the third floor.

Upstairs, he raced out of the lift, into the hallway and straight to her apartment.

Her front door wasn't closed, as if someone had been in a hurry.

He pushed the door all the way open and saw that he was too late.

Again.

And there, in the hallway on the third floor of a luxury apartment block, he once again became that small, frightened boy in the snow.

17

Poland, January 1982

*T*he two soldiers had locked Michael up for the rest of the night in a shed next to the food depot. When morning came, they led him along a snow-covered path to the military headquarters. They hadn't even given him the chance to put on his winter coat, which was still under the bushes. When he slipped and fell forward in the snow, the bigger of the two soldiers impatiently prodded him in the back with the barrel of his rifle, as a sign that he needed to get up quickly.

He could smell the soldier's bad breath when he hissed in his ear. "The commandant doesn't like thieves. He throws big thieves into a cell for a long time, and he sends small thieves to the juvenile detention centre."

Michael stood shivering on the path.

"What kind of place is that?" he whispered.

"It's ideal for filthy runts like you," said the small soldier, giving Michael a shove. "You'll curse your mother for ever giving birth to you."

The two men laughed.

Just before they came to the entrance of the main building, Michael turned around.

"My mother's very ill," he said. "I'd like to see her one more time before I have to leave."

"Did you hear that?" the big soldier asked his companion. "A thief with an attitude."

"They'll soon knock that out of you at the detention centre," the little one replied.

The soldier tapped on the door. A deep rumbling voice said they could enter.

As Michael stepped across the threshold, he realised his childhood was over forever.

The ride in the back of the army truck had gone on for hours now. Michael was shaken to and fro on the wooden bench, along with the two older boys sitting opposite him. The dreary light fell through the dirty window in one of the back doors.

Hardly any words were spoken during the entire journey. The only one who had made an attempt to speak was the slender boy with spiky black hair who the driver had shoved into the truck at the last stop.

Michael assumed the boy was the same age as him. Thirteen was the minimum age for a detention centre, but the newcomer looked about three years younger than that. His clothes were grubby. After the doors had closed again, the boy stood there for a moment, looking around, as if trying to work out who was the best bet. He moved towards Michael and sat down beside him.

"I'm Janek," said the newcomer.

Michael didn't reply. From now on, it was everyone for himself. That's what the oldest boy had said when the truck had stopped for the first time. All Michael knew about the boy was that his name was Kaz. A strong-looking lad of about fifteen or sixteen, he sat there with a frown on his face.

"I'm Janek," the boy beside him repeated.

Michael didn't feel like wasting his energy on a scrawny kid who looked like a ten-year-old. He was going to have a hard enough time surviving in that hell himself. After those two attempts, Janek stopped trying to strike up a conversation. He was apparently smart enough not to try it with the boys opposite.

A little later, as the truck drove down a bumpy road, Michael, who had just dropped off, was startled awake.

"Do you know what they do there to boys like you two?" Kaz said suddenly. The other boy opposite started to grin.

"First they pull your trousers down and, before you can count to ten, they'll have come for you a hundred times."

Michael pressed his lips together. He thought about his mother, heard her saying that she'd manage without him and that now he just had to focus on making sure he survived. He hadn't got to see his mother again. Right after the conversation with the commandant, he'd been locked up in a cell and then put in the back of this truck heading to the detention centre. They would inform his mother where her son had been sent. They would also tell her that she should be glad that now he would at least receive an education and have the chance to do meaningful work in the service of the state. Because in the detention centre where he was going, he'd learn all about discipline and hard work.

"One year," the commandant had said. "Maybe longer."

Michael glanced aside at Janek, who had moved into the corner. He was sitting with his back to the others and moving his hands across the wooden bench with a strange jerking motion. Michael felt sorry for the pale, fragile boy. Maybe death would have been better than what was in store for him now. He swallowed. He'd barely slept for the past few hours, he was hungry, and his throat was raw with thirst.

Closing his eyes and dozing off again, he heard the voice of his father coming home after a long day at work and calling him. Then he'd throw his son, who had come running, up into the air and catch him in his strong arms.

The truck stopped. The front doors slammed, and the back doors opened.

He blinked in the daylight. In front of him loomed a site on the edge of a forest with a number of grey buildings, surrounded by fences with barbed wire on top and armed guards on lookout towers.

He was standing at the gates of hell.

And there was no one to take care of him.

18

G AELLE FELT AS IF she were floating in the sea, surrounded by the night, with waves that were making her feel sick. Her tongue was stuck to the roof of her mouth and she could taste blood.

Where am I?

Her thoughts were no more than scraps of mist, floating past without her being able to grasp any of one.

Lukas.

Who's Lukas?

Suddenly she was no longer at sea. She was in a kitchen with a granite work surface and a wooden block of carving knives. *Danger.* That was all she could think about. She was in danger. And so was someone else.

The kitchen vanished into the mist, and she was floating at sea again. The more she tried to get her memories clear, the worse her headache became, as if someone were trying to hammer down the thoughts in her head. A rhythmic sound was coming from somewhere in the darkness, some kind of alarm.

She had to get away.

She heard voices.

Help me.

The scream remained inside her head. Not a sound came from her mouth.

The voices were very close now. A woman and a man. The woman was speaking, sounding as if she knew it all. The man's voice seemed young and eager to learn.

Woman: "So you know about her background?"

Man: "I've just been through her medical file."

"Then you know we can't tell her anything about what happened until the police have questioned her."

"I know the rules, Doctor." *Police? Doctor?*

"As you're aware, Franz, she's going to stay here for observation for a while. During that period, you will make up the psychiatric report under my supervision as part of the investigation."

A cough.

"How's the boy doing?"

"The boy is not our concern. He's in Intensive Care at the Charité, the university hospital. I'm sure they know what they're doing."

"Yes, but I just wanted to know if…"

"He's in a coma. His condition is critical. Now let's just focus on *our* client. Don't underestimate what it takes to put together a psychiatric report."

"Of course, Doctor."

More mumbling.

"She may have fallen back against the counter in a confused state – or maybe someone pushed her – the police are still looking into that – but in any case it's left her with a head wound, which has since been stitched. The impact on her memory and the rest of her functions should become apparent as soon as she regains consciousness."

"How long do you think that will be?"

"Hard to say, could be as soon as tomorrow."

The woman's voice headed towards the source of the rhythmic high-pitched sound.

"The readings look good. Including the heart rate."

They exchanged medical terms, which quickly dissolved into the mist.

The voices disappeared. The bleeping of the machine remained.

The headache was getting worse.

So bad that she forgot there was a boy who was in a critical condition at the university hospital in Berlin.

19

MICHAEL HAD NO IDEA how long he'd been wandering around the streets of Paris, numb with pain and grief. After he'd left Bellefleur's apartment, he'd gone back to his car and looked for a place to park. On automatic pilot, he'd taken his laptop, his waterproof backpack and some other important things, including a large amount of cash. Then he'd headed to a hotel where he'd stayed before. It was a dingy twenty-four-hour establishment in a side street, where he paid as much for a single room as you'd pay for a suite at a five-star hotel. There was no Jacuzzi included in the price, no luxurious breakfast, but there was exclusive service for guests like him. It was a place where no one would ask him questions. And all kinds of things were available under the counter. He'd just bought a head torch and two guns, one of which was now in his ankle holster. He'd also got hold of sufficient ammunition and a grenade. He'd stashed everything except the gun in a backpack, along with his laptop and more than ten thousand euros in banknotes, and left it in the safe in his room.

And now he was walking along the street, head bowed to avoid the gazes of the drunken nightclubbers and the garish light of the shop windows.

This wasn't real.

This was not supposed to happen.

He'd had a different outcome in mind, one involving an olive grove in Tuscany, the gift he would never be able to surprise Bellefleur with. They would never walk together among the olive trees on summer evenings, listening to the song of the crickets in the valley.

Dolores had changed that plan forever. Bellefleur would never shine again.

And that was his fault.

In his mind, he saw Bellefleur's body with the gunshot wounds and the blood staining her white floor. It was the fury that brought him back to himself.

He had to get back to Potsdam as soon as possible to prevent any other hitmen finishing what Vasili had failed to do.

That was what Bellefleur would have wanted.

The front desk of the hotel was deserted when he got back. The receptionist, a stocky man with sideburns of the kind that had been fashionable in the nineteenth century, was nowhere to be seen. Michael took it all in as he passed the reception, his brain recording the details in slow motion.

The handkerchief that the man used to wipe the sweat from his forehead lay casually on the counter, and the hotel bell that new guests could ring to announce their arrival was no longer on the red velvet mat but beside it.

His mode shifted from slight suspicion to a state of high alert. If Dolores had been tracking his movements, perhaps she'd also discovered that this was one of his favourite places to stay in Paris.

As he walked up the stairs to his room on the first floor, he pulled his gun from his ankle holster. He held it ready to fire as he stood at the door to his room. He listened. There was no sound coming from the room, no footsteps coming from behind. Maybe he was becoming paranoid, and the fat receptionist had become unwell or had gone to the toilet.

With one hand, he unlocked the door, threw it open and held his gun in front of him. The curtains were shut, so he could turn on the light. The room was just as he'd left it. Nothing had changed about the duvet, which he'd deliberately left askew, exactly ten centimetres longer on the left.

He looked under the bed, checked the wardrobe and opened the door of the bathroom, where there was just enough room for a toilet and a shower.

Empty.

And yet he still felt uneasy. Now that they'd killed Bellefleur, they would come after him.

As he was opening the safe to take out his backpack, he heard voices from the lobby below. Someone screamed. He ran to the door, locked it and barricaded it by pushing his bed against it. Then he put his wallet and telephone with the rest of his things in the backpack and swung it onto his back. Now he could hear the stairs creaking.

He went to the window and opened it. When, as usual, he'd requested this particular room, it hadn't been for the view. He looked down. In the courtyard below, two rubbish bags were arranged to conceal the hatch through which he could go down into the wine cellar.

He crawled out of the window, dropped down onto the terrace of the room below, climbed over the balustrade and was in the courtyard. Hearing a dull thud from above, he suspected they'd used a gun with a silencer to shoot the lock. The bed he'd shoved against the door wouldn't hold them up for long.

He threw the rubbish bags aside, opened the hatch, dropped down through it and closed the hatch above him, before taking the head torch from his backpack and putting it on. The light shone over the low ceiling and the empty shelves of the wine cellar. It smelt of mould and damp. The only useful thing about this room was a well-kept secret: an escape route as an additional perk for the hotel's guests. In the wine cellar was a rotting wooden door that led, via a long, deep staircase, to the subterranean world that lurked beneath the French capital: an ancient network consisting of hundreds of kilometres of tunnels. The corridors, originally limestone quarries, were linked to wine cellars, water cisterns and crypts, some of which were illegally used as nightclubs.

Although descending into this underworld was both prohibited and dangerous, because of floods, cave-ins and the risk of running out of oxygen, this only made it all the more attractive to certain people. They called themselves *cataphiles* and organised illegal parties and exhibitions down there. Tourists were more familiar with the Catacombs, the section of the underground tunnels that was open to visitors, where they could gape at walls of piled-up bones and skulls. Centuries ago, it had been a repository for bones from the overcrowded cemeteries. At the entrance to the Catacombs, there was a warning for the timid, people with heart conditions, and children: STOP – THE REALM OF THE DEAD BEGINS HERE.

He searched on his phone for the map that his contact – an experienced *cataphile* – had sent him some months ago, and descended into the underground labyrinth, with death on his heels.

20

W HEN SHE OPENED HER EYES, the mist had still not completely lifted. She saw the room she was in through a haze.

Where am I?

What am I doing here?

She tried to ignore the thumping headache as the grey veils slowly dissolved. Gaelle. That was her name. She was wearing a paper surgical gown and lying on a bed in some sort of clinical room. There was no one else there. Her right arm was connected to a drip. She had other wires on her chest, attached with plasters, which led to the device that was probably responsible for the constant bleeping.

Carefully, she put her left hand to her head. There was a bandage around it. Her eyes moved over her body, and she lifted the sheet: no broken arms, no splinted legs, no injuries that might indicate a car accident.

But something bad must have happened.

An image flashed through her mind, which she immediately pushed away. *She was standing in a kitchen with a knife in her hand and there was a boy lying on the floor.*

She heard voices in the corridor.

Could someone tell her exactly what had happened? And why wasn't Bernd here? His name suddenly attached itself to her other memories. She lived in a house in Potsdam, and she was married to Bernd. He worked as an investment advisor at a bank and had been doing a lot of overtime lately. Maybe he was at work now, or on his way here with a bunch of flowers. Maybe he'd even have remembered that she preferred white bouquets.

She looked around for a button to call for a nurse to help. *The button's normally somewhere on the edge of the bed*, she thought – at least it had been when her mother was in the palliative care unit.

She felt herself stiffen. Her mother was dead. The chemotherapy hadn't worked, and she'd died of a brain tumour. The memory hurt, like an old wound being torn open. At that moment, fear set in. She felt the bandage on her head again. A brain tumour. Was that why she was lying here and why her memories were coming so slowly?

She'd been operated on for a brain tumour and was now recovering in hospital.

But something about that didn't felt right.

Somewhere among those memories there were gaps, dark pools with things floating around in them that she couldn't see properly.

Finally.

She'd found the button.

Now someone could tell her what she was doing here.

After what seemed like an eternity, there was a quiet knock on the door and a thin man appeared. He looked about thirty and was wearing black-framed glasses. As far as she could remember, she'd never seen him before. But there was something about his voice that seemed familiar. Somehow he reminded her of that overeager classmate who always used to sit in the front row and put his hand up before the teacher had even asked the question.

The man introduced himself as Franz Hanssen, trainee psychiatrist. He pulled up a chair and sat down beside Gaelle.

"So you've woken up," he began.

Maybe the nightmare's just begun, thought Gaelle.

*T*HIS IS HADES, thought Michael, *but without the Styx.* He was walking along an arched corridor, presumably a sewer that had fallen into disuse and was now dry. The dusty floor was uneven, and he'd just stumbled over one of the loose bricks that were scattered all over. There was graffiti on the arches. Some graffiti artists apparently saw it as an extra challenge to leave their mark on this underworld.

He stopped to listen.

It was over an hour since he'd descended into the tunnel system. Dolores's bloodhounds had effective and extremely painful techniques that they could use to obtain the information they needed from the receptionist. By now they probably knew that they wouldn't find any Château Pétrus in the hotel's wine cellar, but a door to the underground. They might already be down here, on his trail, even though he was doing his best to deceive them. Or maybe they were waiting for him by one of the most obvious exits where you might hope to surface unseen from underground Paris.

They'd probably have extracted the information from the receptionist by now, before leaving him dead, the victim of a particularly violent robbery.

He looked at his phone, hoping the battery would last until he got to where he wanted to go.

According to his map, he was somewhere under Montmartre now. It was already deep in the night and, up above, drunken revellers were probably still hanging around Place du Tertre. He had no idea if they were having to hide under umbrellas or if it was still dry – he was so deep underground that he was cut off from everything. There was no sound, no light and, unfortunately, hardly any oxygen.

The air he breathed in was stale. The further he descended into these subterranean caverns, the dizzier he felt and the more the pressure on his chest increased. His contact among the *cataphiles* had warned him that this was not a place to wander around without a guide. But it was too soon to surface. His plan was to look for the dead-end metro line that had never been completed, where he would be able to return to the land of the living via a staircase and a broken grating.

But first he had to go through the Catacombs. At this time of night, the tours that started at Place Denfert-Rochereau had been over for hours, so he didn't need to worry about giving a group of tourists the fright of their lives by suddenly popping up from behind a pile of bones.

Still standing motionless, he listened carefully.

He heard a dull rumbling rising from the belly of the earth. Perhaps it was the vibrations of a nearby metro train, but he dismissed that thought. At half past two in the morning, the trains had stopped running.

He looked up, his head torch shining on the dark arched ceiling, and he saw sand falling down.

He knew that these were dangerous signs.

Since the late nineteenth century, many of the underground tunnels had been systematically filled in to prevent subsidence. But there were still cave-ins in certain parts of the city, including Montmartre.

The rumbling died away.

He walked further along the tunnel, turned a corner and came to an archway that led to a narrow tunnel with a staircase that descended for tens of metres. The thought of fresh air on a spring day with the blossoms in bud was no more than an illusion here. He headed down the stairs, and with each step he took, the air became thinner.

When he reached the bottom, he saw that the last step was underwater. The stairs ended in a gully of dark water that smelt of death. He heard something on a ledge along the side, rustling and then disappearing into the water with a splash – most likely a rat.

So this Hades does have a Styx, thought Michael.

The sewer that was blocking his way wasn't even on his map. To his left and right, all he could see was a dark channel of foul-smelling water, and he had no idea how deep it was. But he was going to have to either crawl or swim, because there was only about half a metre between the surface of the water and the ceiling.

Now and then, he could see movement in the water. And he knew what was doing the swimming.

According to his map, from this point he should have been following a tunnel that went straight on.

Now he had to choose between two directions, both of which would send him the wrong way.

He'd be better off turning around and mapping out a route that, even if it involved a detour, would take him in the right direction, to the place where he wanted to get back to the surface, via the unfinished metro line.

He saw that his phone's battery was almost dead. He was going to have to hurry – a detour meant wasting time. If his battery ran out before he reached his destination, this was not going to end well.

He turned and was about to head back up the stairs.

Just then, the rumbling started again.

Closer and louder than before.

He felt the ground vibrating under his feet.

When he was halfway up the stairs, the earth shook. He heard a dull thundering and cracks appeared overhead in the tunnel. The cracks grew larger, and chunks of concrete fell onto the stairs. Small pieces at first, and then whole blocks.

He realised that the way back up was blocked and that he wouldn't survive if he stayed there in the tunnel. He turned around and went back down the stairs, using his backpack to shield his head from the falling rubble.

As the tunnel collapsed behind him, he stashed his telephone in his waterproof backpack.

Without any hesitation this time, he stepped into the water.

His feet didn't touch the bottom.

He felt something brush past his legs.

He didn't have much time to decide which way to swim.

Wrong decisions could prove fatal.

Janek had taught him that.

22

Poland, January 1982

*M*ichael stood in the courtyard of the detention centre. The fenced-off site had one main building and around ten other grey buildings with flat roofs.

The soldiers who had brought him here with the three other boys ordered them to line up and stand straight, legs together, hands behind their heads.

The bitter wind blew powdery snow into Michael's face, and he felt as if his cheeks were being sandblasted. He thought about the coat he'd had to leave behind at the food depot, the warm winter coat his mother had spent so many evenings sewing, using pieces of old clothing to make all those extra layers, so he'd never be cold. He fought back the tears.

This was a place where you weren't allowed to cry.

"Stay here until Commandant Kaminski arrives," said one of the soldiers.

"And when he gets here, don't say a word," the other one said. "Unless the commandant asks you a question. Got it?" Michael hardly even dared to nod.

The two men turned and headed for the largest building, where smoke curled from the chimney. When the door opened, Michael heard the sound of laughter. It was probably some sort of canteen for the soldiers.

"Psst," he heard Janek whisper beside him. "I still don't know your name." Michael didn't react.

He had to find some way to shake off this little pest as quickly as possible. If he wanted to sleep, to eat – in short, to survive – he didn't need the extra burden of a boy who was sticking to him like a shadow.

"How long do you think they'll keep us waiting here?" said Kaz.

The swagger he'd had when he'd announced in the truck that it was every-one for himself had ebbed away since they'd arrived at the detention centre.

"I've heard bad stories about this place," whispered the fourth boy, who hadn't told them his name yet.

"Well, maybe I don't want to hear your rumours," said Kaz.

The threat in his voice was back. The fourth boy was silent from then on.

Michael had no idea how long they'd been waiting when the canteen door finally opened – half an hour, maybe longer. It had started snowing and he imagined that the snowflakes touching his face were his mother's comforting hands. But what remained was the icy cold biting into his face. He'd lost all feeling in his arms, which he was still holding behind his head, and he thought maybe that was the only way he'd be able to survive here – if he managed to turn off all his feelings.

A frozen heart is invulnerable.

Two soldiers came towards them. The one leading the way was a robust man with a dark moustache. He walked a few steps ahead of the other man, who was a lot shorter and walked so stiffly that he looked like he'd just stepped out of a refrigerator.

The two men stopped in front of the boys.

"I am Commandant Kaminski," said the man with the moustache. Then he pointed at the man standing beside him. "And this is my right-hand man, Sergeant Nowak."

Silently, the commandant paced around the boys, his footsteps crunching in the snow.

He stood in front of them again.

"Let me make this clear. You are a bunch of good-for-nothings, sewer rats, scum. Here you will be given the chance not to sink deeper into the mire."

He paused before continuing.

"I am strict, but fair," said the commandant. "If you follow my rules, you have nothing to fear."

His gaze moved over the newcomers. "But if you break my rules, then watch out."

A grin appeared on Sergeant Nowak's face. Michael would see that grin many times in the months to come – and it was never a good sign.

Michael stood shivering in the room where they'd had to abandon their own clothes and had been ordered to put on some kind of overalls. He'd also been given sturdy shoes, clean underwear and thick socks. It was a bitter thought that his feet had never been so warm in the winter before.

Janek was strutting around as if he'd just made the best purchase of his life. He lifted the legs of his overalls to admire his heavy shoes. They made his legs looked like straws.

"What are you actually in here for?" Michael asked.

It had to be a mistake that a mousy little boy like Janek had been sent here. The police had probably just got the wrong boy.

"You really want to know?" asked Janek.

Michael nodded.

"Then tell me your name."

"It's Michael. And now tell me why you're here."

"Because I murdered someone," said Janek.

If Michael hadn't been in hell, he'd have burst out laughing. He turned his back on Janek.

In the corridor, footsteps were coming closer. The drill exercises would begin in a few minutes, and they'd be taking part for the first time. They'd already become acquainted with one of Commandant Kaminski's rules: anyone who didn't try hard enough during the exercises would not get any dinner. After that, they would be assigned a place to sleep and what was probably going to be the longest night of his life would begin, a night when he could never feel safe. Many more of the same would follow.

"I want to be your friend, Michael. Friends help each other and make sure nothing bad happens to each other."

98

"I don't want a pathetic liar for a friend, Janek." The boy was standing right in front of him now.

"Okay, I haven't murdered anyone," said Janek. "But we can still help each other."

Slowly, Janek opened his palm. Michael saw a long, rusty nail and remembered the strange jerking movements Janek had made in the truck, when he was sitting with his back to everyone else.

He'd underestimated the boy.

In this place, a long, sharp nail might mean the difference between whether you survived the night or not.

The bolt on the door slid open and Sergeant Nowak appeared, with his squint and that strange smile on his face.

"From now on, we're friends," Michael whispered quickly.

It was the best decision he could have made.

Hours later, long after nightfall, Michael crept with Janek through the dormitory to the bed where Kaz was sleeping. At fifteen, Kaz was one of the oldest boys in their dormitory. While Janek put his hands over Kaz's mouth to stop him from yelling, Michael held his homemade weapon to Kaz's throat and whispered in his ear to keep quiet. He'd hammered the nail into a plank – it would be as effective as a knife for slashing someone's artery.

"We want to survive this place as much as you do," Michael whispered in Kaz's ear. "Janek and I aren't the strongest in the group, but we could be the smartest."

"We don't have to be enemies," Janek said quietly.

"Nowak's going to make life difficult enough for us as it is," said Janek, taking his hand from Kaz's mouth.

"What do you want?" asked Kaz.

"To make a deal so we can survive this hell," said Michael.

23

S WIMMING ALONG THE SEWER, Michael had followed the corridor to the left. He hadn't chosen at random but allowed himself to be led by the current. Water always looked for a way out.

He held his head above the stinking sludge, trying to ignore the rats, which were growing in numbers and must have noticed him. He was more concerned about the stench of rotten eggs that was rising from the water, not because – along with the smell of a burnt body – it was one of the most disgusting smells he'd ever encountered, but because it indicated the presence of hydrogen sulphide, one of the most dangerous components of toxic sewer gases. In high concentrations, it could be lethal.

His eyes started to burn, and he coughed and gasped for breath. The sound echoed off the low ceiling, making him even more aware that he was in danger of suffocating in this enclosed place. Further along the tunnel, he had to go through some sort of sluice and, after that, the sewer became narrower. He estimated that there was only twenty centimetres between the water and the ceiling. Just the thought of having to swim underwater to get to the next sluice took his breath away.

As he swam onwards, the smell of rotten eggs disappeared.

That might be good news – perhaps there wasn't much hydrogen sulphide in this part of the sewer. But he knew it could also be very bad news. Hydrogen sulphide is a deceptive gas. They'd warned him about it during his training. Once the gas reaches a certain lethal concentration, the olfactory nerve becomes paralysed, so that the person inhaling it can no longer smell it.

Michael swam to the side and clung to a narrow ledge.

His headache was getting worse. He felt as if his lungs were running out of oxygen and were at risk of collapsing. His eyes were watering so badly now that he couldn't entirely make out his surroundings.

Which is why he didn't believe his eyes at first.

Up ahead, the sewer narrowed to a tube that would be impossible for a human being to get through.

He had chosen the wrong way.

Torch in hand, Fabienne followed Claude, stopping now and then to light up the rows of skulls and bones lining the walls of the Catacombs. Although she'd often gone down to the subterranean burial place before and had conducted guided tours there as a student years ago, she was still as fascinated as ever by this place. She remembered how enthusiastic she'd been, telling her tour groups about the creation of the Catacombs, about the carts full of corpses that moved through the eighteenth-century city at night, accompanied by a priest, to relieve the crowded cemeteries of fermenting bodies and dump them in the quarries under Paris. Over the centuries, millions of human skeletons had been housed here. In some places, it had been a rush job and the bones and skulls had been thrown onto piles, but in others the human remains had been stacked almost lovingly to make works of art. She stopped to illuminate a wall with rows of skulls forming a beautiful cross among the bones.

It was impossible to visit the Catacombs without feeling moved. She knew of few places in the world where death was so present. Even tough teenagers toned down their attitude during the tours. Impressive. That was the word most tourists used when they gave her a tip afterwards. Maybe they were also impressed by her knowledge of history. She was able to tell them stories in vivid detail, such as how the Catacombs became hiding places for the French resistance in the Second World War.

"Are you coming?" she heard Claude ask impatiently. Like her, he was wearing a helmet. He was carrying a small ladder and the ropes they needed to reach this illegal part of the Catacombs.

She sighed.

He was clearly less at home in the Catacombs than she was. At the slightest noise, he thought he was about to be buried alive. The sound they'd heard a while ago did suggest a cave-in somewhere, but it wasn't the first time such a thing had happened while she was down here. And if she met her end here, she'd never be alone.

She stroked the smooth top of the skull that formed the centre of the cross on the wall and regretfully continued on her way. She'd hoped they'd be able to spend longer down here. This was where she found the energy she didn't get from her work. It hadn't been easy to get decent work without a diploma, and she told herself that her job as an attendant at the Louvre was just a temporary necessity to help her gain a foothold in the art world. The highlight of her day was when she was allowed to get up out of her chair and ask visitors not to stand too close to the paintings. Her job was potentially lethal, she often said to Claude. She was in danger of dying of boredom.

His job wasn't much better though. He was the doorman at a branch of Louis Vuitton and stood there every day with a neutral expression and an immaculate tailored suit, waiting until someone who appeared rich enough looked as if they wanted to come in. His professional highlights included receiving an unexpectedly generous tip or – at those moments when he hated the world – denying entry to an American tourist in flowery shorts.

Luckily, they'd found each other among the *cataphiles*, and in the year they'd been together, their lives had become a lot less grey than before.

"I want to go back up now, Fabienne," he yawned. "I'm exhausted."

Sometimes he can be a real whinger, she thought. But the sex was amazing. Now that she thought about it, it had been at least a week since they'd last done it underground. Maybe she could talk him into a quickie before they went back up to the surface.

24

MICHAEL HELD ON to the ledge as he weighed up his chances of survival. The toxic fumes that he couldn't smell but whose effects he could feel were clouding his mind and sucking the strength out of his body. He had to get out of this dead end as quickly as possible, but he didn't know if he was capable of swimming all that way back without losing consciousness.

A big rat appeared on the ledge. Slowly and hungrily, it came closer, and he furiously batted at it.

But then the rat vanished.

Michael looked around. He shone his head torch over the water. He hadn't heard a splash. And the rat hadn't scuttled away from him along the ledge. The creature had simply disappeared.

That was impossible, unless the fumes were making him hallucinate. With the last of his strength, he pulled himself up to the place where the rat had disappeared, and he saw where it had gone. About ten centimetres above the ledge, some of the bricks were loose, and there was a hole that was big enough to stick his arm through. The walls were at least half a metre thick, and the light of the torch was too dim to see where the hole came out. Running the risk of losing a finger to a hungry rat, he slowly put his right arm through the opening, his fingers sliding over the bricks. As he cut the back of his hand on a sharp piece of broken brick, his fingertips brushed against something hairy, which darted away.

Now he could stretch his whole arm. His hand was no longer enclosed by bricks and he could move it around. That freedom of movement gave him hope. He pulled back his arm and held his face to the opening. The air flow was barely perceptible, but enough for him to deduce that there was a room behind the wall, perhaps some kind of passageway, which would take him back to the route he should be following.

His head was about to burst. If he spent any longer in this toxic atmosphere, the rats would have an unexpected feast today. He took off his backpack, supporting himself with his other arm on the ledge, and then rested the bag on the ledge while he took out his grenade. Without hesitating, he pulled out the pin and tossed the grenade into the hole. He moved along the ledge, away from the spot where he hoped the explosion would breach the thick wall.

But old walls were unpredictable.

If the roof above his head collapsed because of the explosion, it was all over.

Ludka, Jorge and Zoltan had followed his trail with the instinct of bloodhounds. His hasty attempts to mislead them by going down one tunnel and then retracing his footsteps had only helped them to close the distance faster. Their army boots marched along the corridors, the receptionist's blood now dry on their steel toecaps. They were wearing night-vision goggles, were heavily armed, and as long as they could follow his trail, they weren't afraid of getting lost in this underworld.

But not long ago they had heard a sound that suggested a cave-in and now they'd come to a place where his footsteps stopped before a collapsed tunnel full of rubble.

"He could be dead," said the man who had introduced himself to Ludka as Zoltan. He was a thickset, hairy man, who reminded her of a bear. Not a good-natured cuddly bear, as the animal was often misrepresented to children, but a predator.

"*Could* be isn't good enough for Dolores," said Ludka.

Or for me, she thought.

"We don't have a map. The only route that'll get us out of here for sure is going back," said the man who was known as Jorge. He was a tall, thin man who for some reason had irritated Ludka right from the beginning. Maybe it was his high-pitched, whining voice. "Just as well we left markers."

"The man we're looking for murdered my brother," said Ludka. "We're not leaving until we've seen his body."

There was a bang. They recognised the sound of an explosion. It could only have been caused by one man.

"Try to locate it," said Ludka. "Let's move in."

"It's going to be hard to find our way around this labyrinth without a map," said Jorge.

Silence.

"If you say that one more time, this place will be your grave," growled Ludka.

They walked off, heading towards where they'd heard the explosion.

Fabienne had talked Claude into a quickie before they disappeared up the ladder and through the manhole, but then they heard the explosion.

"That's it. I've had enough," said Claude.

He pulled up his jeans and put his helmet on.

Fabienne scrambled to her feet, quickly putting her bra and T-shirt back on. But instead of following Claude up the ladder, she went the opposite way, into the illegal part of the Catacombs, which she knew like the back of her hand.

"Where are you going?" she heard Claude shout. "I want to go home!"

"That was no ordinary collapse," said Fabienne.

She heard him swearing and yelling at her to come back. All she could think was that the excitement she felt now was so much more intense than what she'd experienced during their love making.

Michael coughed and wiped away the blood that was running from the wound on his forehead and into his eyes. The explosion had blown away some sections of the walls, and one of the bricks had hit him on the head. He felt sick and dizzy, as if he were about to lose consciousness. The sewer gases had exhausted him to the point where that blow to the head could finish him.

Maybe the breach wasn't even big enough to let him through.

When the dust had settled, he struggled to pull himself along the ledge towards the hole. Just before he reached the spot, he felt his grip on the ledge weaken. His hand let go, he slipped into the stinking water and went under.

He hardly had the strength to fight.

As he sank deeper, he thought maybe it was time to let the water rock him to sleep. Bellefleur was no longer alive. He hadn't made it in time, just like with Janek. Maybe he didn't deserve to live.

Images of his many victims over the years flashed through his mind, mainly men, but also some women. He had cut the thread of their lives on Dolores's orders – and he hadn't felt a thing.

Rotting away in this Styx was no more than he deserved.

But he'd never killed a child.

No one could accuse him of that.

Lukas, that was the boy's name.

Maybe Lukas was still alive.

Like his mother.

They would stay alive until Dolores decided it was time to finish the job. Maybe he needed to resurface one last time and save what could be saved. He made a powerful movement with his arms and, with a scream, he reached the surface of the water. The toxic gases and the dust scorched his lungs. He swam to the place where the grenade had blown a hole in the wall, just big enough to let him through.

He pulled himself up, vomited, felt the throbbing pain in his forehead and squeezed through the opening.

When he reached the other side, his first thought was that he'd found his way into a mass grave. All he could see were bones and skulls in the wall, arranged in the shape of a cross.

He fell to the floor. His head torch was flickering – it had probably been hit by falling debris.

He heard heavy footsteps approaching.

It sounded as if they were marching.

His light went out.

He sat up, looked for his gun and held it ready behind his back.

25

G AELLE TRIED TO SIT UP in the hospital bed. She still had a splitting headache, and she felt sick. Luckily, one of the night nurses had removed the electrodes from her chest and detached her from the drip, so she no longer felt shackled to the bed.

Although…

The thin man sitting on a chair beside her – Franz Hanssen, trainee psychiatrist and on duty tonight – and carefully noting down everything she said, had told her she was not to leave the room. During a strange conversation, he'd tried to find out if she knew who she was, where she lived, what day it was and if she remembered what had happened.

"No, I don't know what happened," said Gaelle when he repeated the question. "Why don't you just tell me?"

"That's the procedure."

"What procedure?"

Hanssen looked intently at his notebook.

"The rules we have to follow in this unit."

"I've never heard of a hospital with such ridiculous rules. As soon as I get out of here, I'm going to make a complaint. Or I'll get my husband to do it – he's good at that kind of thing. Where is Bernd anyway?"

"Try not to become too agitated."

"That's not easy when no one will tell me where I am or what I'm doing here."

He sighed.

"This isn't an ordinary hospital. You're in the secure unit of a psychiatric institution in Berlin, and specific rules apply here."

"Like 'You must drive people to despair by not telling them what's happened to them'?"

"You're becoming agitated again."

"Whose fault is that?"

"Try to keep calm. You have a concussion."

The doctor looked at her.

"If patients are unable to remember certain facts, we're not allowed to supply those memories for them," he said. "It can harm the investigation."

"Investigation? What are you talking about? A brain scan? Do I have a tumour, like my mother?"

Hanssen coughed as he pushed back his chair and stood up.

"I meant the police investigation."

"What?"

"This is an exploratory conversation. The idea is to find out if you're in a fit state to be questioned by the police. As far as I'm concerned, you'll be up to it tomorrow morning, as long as you try to get some sleep first."

Gaelle sat up in bed. She was dizzy, and the whole room was spinning. She could hardly hear what Hanssen was saying to her. She sat on the edge of her bed and saw her white legs sticking out from under the light-blue surgical gown.

"Where are my clothes?" asked Gaelle. "I want to go home."

She slid off the bed and staggered over to Hanssen. She saw the panic in his eyes and the quick movement as he pressed the alarm button.

After taking two steps towards the door, she felt her legs go limp. She collapsed in the middle of the room and fell to the floor.

She heard the door open.

Running footsteps.

Hands lifting her up and laying her on the bed.

A jab in her arm.

And then nothing.

26

MICHAEL WAS WOKEN by the twittering of birds. They seemed so close that he thought he was in the house in the Tuscan hills. Or that somehow he'd gone directly from Hades to Heaven.

When he opened his eyes, he saw that neither assumption was correct.

He was lying in a room in a bed with white sheets, naked except for a pair of black boxer shorts. The decor was neat and tidy, but old-fashioned: roses on the wallpaper, a crystal chandelier, an antique bedside table with a nightlight on a crocheted mat and a large oak wardrobe. On the wall was a framed pencil sketch of the ruins of a medieval castle and, beneath it, the words CHÂTEAU D'YÈVRE-LE-CHÂTEL. He looked at it, but it didn't ring any bells.

There was a glass of water on the bedside table, and he managed to sit up a little and take a sip. He felt lethargic. His face was burning and his heart was pounding. When he went to wipe the sweat from his forehead, his fingers encountered cotton. Someone had bandaged his forehead.

He blinked in the daylight that streamed through a crack in the wooden shutters. He could feel that the fresh air was doing him some good, and that reminded him of the toxic gases in the underground sewer where he'd nearly lost his life.

He heard voices approaching on the other side of the door. Where was his gun? He looked around and saw no sign of his backpack.

He closed his eyes.

The door opened.

"He's still asleep," said a woman's voice. "I thought for a while he wasn't going to make it."

It was the same voice he'd heard in the Catacombs as the footsteps were coming closer. That was just before he'd lost consciousness. He'd had enough time to see that the voice belonged to a Frenchwoman with sturdy calves and bright-pink socks. She was wearing a safety helmet and carrying a torch, which she'd shone right in his eyes. He remembered what he'd asked her as he'd held his gun behind his back and the promise he'd made her.

"Who are you?" she'd asked. "Êtes-vous aussi cataphile?"

"That doesn't matter," he'd answered in French. "There's ten thousand euros in my backpack. You can have it if you get me out of here without being seen."

Then he'd promised her and the man who'd appeared another ten thousand euros if they'd take him to a safe place outside Paris, where he could recover. Under no circumstances were they to inform the police.

"Bien sûr, nous n'aimons pas non plus les cataflics," she'd said.

He'd quickly hidden his gun in his backpack and he had no idea what had happened next.

He peered through his eyelashes at the couple standing by his bedside. Putting his life in the hands of someone who wore bright-pink socks was one of the biggest risks he'd ever dared to take. Somehow he felt he could trust the woman.

He was less certain about the man.

Fabienne followed on Claude's heels as they entered the room where the wounded man lay.

"Your grandfather would be spinning in his grave if he knew his house was being used to hide an injured bank robber," said Claude.

"Leave my dear departed grandfather out of this. Anyway, you don't know for certain that the guy's been up to no good."

"Someone who's carrying around two guns and thousands of euros in cash isn't just some random day-tripper, Fabienne."

She didn't reply.

"We don't even know his name," he continued. "There was nothing in his wallet that gave away anything about his identity. Which is suspicious in itself, don't you think?"

"Well, I don't regret calling in sick, Claude. Or do you miss standing there like a tree at that Louis Vuitton store for hours on end and being happy because no passing dogs have cocked their legs?"

"Don't talk to me like that."

She sighed.

"I thought you understood me, Claude. This makes me feel… alive. And that I'm not going to be drifting around some stupid village until I die, like my grandfather. This place doesn't even have a baker's shop."

"I get that, but hiding a wounded criminal from the police is a different thing entirely. Now we're accomplices after the fact, or whatever it's called."

"But we're getting twenty thousand euros for it. We can finally go on a trip around the world. We can go to India or even Africa."

"With dodgy money."

"Now you really do remind me of my mum and dad and all those teachers who kept constantly nagging away at me."

Fabienne walked away from Michael and stood, arms crossed, on the other side of the bed.

The man looked pale.

"You took good care of his wound," she said.

"I did my best."

Claude leant forward and touched the man's cheek.

"We've almost run out of pills to bring his fever down," he said.

"Then someone will have to go and buy some, won't they?"

"It's more than an hour to the nearest chemist's, there and back."

"So?"

"When we get back, he might have gone. That shutter won't even close properly. And then we can whistle for the rest of our money."

"This guy really doesn't look as if he's about to make a run for it. Hey, what did you do with the stuff in his backpack after you counted the money?"

"Hid it somewhere nice and safe, along with his two guns."

"Where?"

"I'll show you, Fabienne. I'd like to find out more about him, but his telephone and his laptop are locked."

"If you don't trust the situation here, I can drive to the chemist's while you stay behind," said Fabienne. "If you're feeling brave enough."

"Yeah, with two guns in the house, I feel pretty safe," Claude bit back at her.

Then they left the room.

Michael had been able to follow their entire conversation, but he'd been getting sleepier. The two of them seemed helpful, but also naive. They would never imagine that his wallet had a secret compartment that contained one of his fake passports. He could do without naivety right now. Yawning, he tried to collect his thoughts. There was something he urgently needed to tell them. What was it again?

His eyelids were getting heavy. His body was pleading with his mind to be allowed to sleep. He tried to resist. There was something he needed to warn them about. It had something to do with what the woman, Fabienne, had just said. About driving to the chemist's.

He remembered. He had to stop them from leaving the house, and if they did, they had to borrow one of the neighbours' cars so that their own registration number wouldn't be recorded by one of the security cameras at the shopping centre or along the motorway.

He knew what Dolores's bloodhounds were doing right now. They'd long since hacked all the security cameras in the area around the Catacombs and were analysing the most recent video images, tracing the number plates of the cars that were there, checking for any connections to people who were familiar with the tunnels, and searching police and press databases for the names of all the people who had ever been arrested for illegal activity in the underground labyrinth.

One stroke of luck could be enough to lead the bloodhounds here.

And if they found them, not one of the three would live to tell the tale.

That was his last thought before his exhausted body dragged him into a dreamless sleep.

27

"DID YOU SLEEP WELL last night?" asked Hanssen as he came into Gaelle's room on Wednesday morning.

"What do you think? My left hand is tied to the bed."

"I'm sorry, but it's necessary to avoid…"

"I still don't understand. Why won't anyone tell me what exactly happened and why Bernd and Ebba haven't come to visit me?"

She paused for a moment.

"Do you have any idea what that does to a person?" she asked.

He wrote something in his notebook without answering the question.

"Your husband brought in a suitcase of clothing this morning," he said.

"Bernd? Where is he now? Is he out in the corridor?"

Gaelle jerked upright, forgetting that her left hand was still shackled.

"Damn it," she said.

"I'll ask if the nurses can release you soon," said Hanssen. "And if they'll give you the suitcase, so you can get dressed for the conversation with the police this morning."

Gaelle fell back onto the pillow.

"Why can't Bernd see me?" she asked quietly.

Hanssen swallowed.

"I'm not allowed to tell you anything," he said. "You know that by now, but your conversation with the police should clarify a lot."

He looked at her with something like sympathy, which suddenly terrified Gaelle.

"I'll be present during that conversation," he continued. "Just in case it gets too much for you."

Now she was even more scared.

"I don't have a clue what's going on," Gaelle said quietly. "Sometimes it's as if I can hear a voice whispering to me that I've done something bad. As if there's something I should feel guilty about, but I have no idea what it could be."

Hanssen scribbled something in his notebook again.

"Has that often happened before?" he asked.

"What do you mean?"

"Hearing voices inside your head."

Gaelle narrowed her eyes.

"What do you think?" she said. "I'm not crazy."

An hour and a half later, Gaelle was sitting in one of the meeting rooms, feeling increasingly anxious as she waited for the police to arrive. She had showered, put on a pair of jeans and a black blouse from her suitcase, and she already felt a little more human. The room she was in had presumably been kept free of stimuli on purpose. The white walls were bare, and the only furniture was a small table with four chairs.

Hanssen was sitting on the chair next to her.

He glanced at his watch. There was a brief knock on the door before it opened. A robust man and a woman who was at least one metre eighty appeared in the doorway. They introduced themselves as police detectives and said their names, which Gaelle instantly forgot.

The two detectives sat down on the other side of the table, and the female detective's green eyes looked at her so piercingly that Gaelle felt they were drilling holes in her soul.

"What exactly happened yesterday?" asked Gaelle.

"We were hoping you could tell us," said the male detective.

"I can't remember much about it."

"Start with what you do remember," the woman said.

Gaelle stared at the empty wall.

"My name is Gaelle. I'm married to Bernd. We live in a house in Potsdam."

It's a big house, and my dream is to have it converted into a guesthouse.

That memory's new, thought Gaelle. *Maybe more things will be shaken loose.*

There was a silence.

"Do you know where you were yesterday afternoon?" asked the man.

"At home, I think," said Gaelle. "I don't know why, but I can suddenly see our kitchen."

And the knives in the wooden block.

The woman nodded encouragingly.

"Anything else?"

"Not immediately," said Gaelle.

"Can you remember if you're taking any particular medication?"

"If I have a bad headache, I sometimes take an aspirin. Why do you ask?"

"How about antidepressants?"

Gaelle didn't reply.

Her first reaction was to deny it, but the mention of anti-depressants had triggered a memory.

A crying baby in a crib.

The baby just kept on crying.

The crying became screaming.

And beside the baby sat a woman with dark thoughts.

"Do you take antidepressants?" repeated the female detective.

"Not anymore," said Gaelle.

Only during that period just after my son was born.

She gasped. In her mind, she was wandering around the big house in Potsdam, the house with all the rooms. In one of the rooms on the first floor was a duvet cover with a football print and Bayern München posters on the wall.

Lukas.

"I have a son," said Gaelle. "Where is he?"

The two researchers exchanged a glance. She felt Hanssen stiffen beside her.

"Where's Lukas?" asked Gaelle. She stood up so abruptly that her chair clattered to the floor.

The Charité, the university hospital, suddenly popped into her mind, but she didn't know why.

"Is he hurt? Is he sick? I want to know what's happened to him."

"We'll tell you," said the man. "It's better if you sit down first."

28

"**N**o!" SCREAMED GAELLE. She was still in the meeting room, with the two detectives restraining her, one on each side.

"Call the nurses," the woman said to Hanssen, who looked like he just wanted to get away as quickly as possible.

"Let go of me," said Gaelle.

She kicked the woman's shins, trying in vain to free herself from their grip.

"I want to see Lukas."

The woman now put Gaelle into a hold, with her arms pulled so far behind her back that it hurt. She pushed Gaelle onto the floor, with a knee in her back to keep her there.

"Try to stay calm," she heard the other detective saying. "You're only making things harder for yourself."

"I want to see Lukas. I want to see for myself how bad it is."

"Your son is in a coma," the man said. "His condition is currently stable, and your husband is trying to spend as much time with him as possible. There's no more news for now."

Gaelle felt the woman's weight pushing her down so hard onto the floor that she could hardly breathe.

"I swear I didn't hurt him," said Gaelle, and she started crying. "How could you think that?"

The door opened and two nurses came in.

"Let her get her breath back," the detective said.

The pressure of the knee in her back eased.

"Will you stand up calmly?" the woman asked.

Gaelle nodded and slowly got to her feet.

The two nurses went and stood beside Hanssen, presumably waiting for a signal from him to take her away.

"I think that's enough for now," Hanssen said to the detectives.

"We still have a number of questions that need to be answered," said the woman. "We need more information before deciding how to proceed."

"Are you okay?" Hanssen asked Gaelle.

She was sitting on her chair again now.

Her "yes" was almost inaudible.

"Then you can continue for a while," said Hanssen to the detectives. "Ten minutes, no longer."

The two nurses disappeared. The woman sat down opposite Gaelle again and stared at her.

"An anaesthetic was found in your son's blood. Someone injected him with the substance that put him in a coma. Yours were the only fingerprints found on the syringe that was used."

Gaelle groaned and dropped her head into her hands.

"You used to be a top athlete. Maybe you knew people back then who you could contact for performance enhancers. And perhaps now they've supplied you with… other substances."

Gaelle looked up.

"I never used any performance-enhancing drugs," she growled.

"But you have used antidepressants," said the female detective. "Your husband confirmed that."

"That was years ago," said Gaelle. "Just after my son was born."

"We found an open box of Seroxat in your kitchen. There were no traces of the antidepressant found in your blood, but maybe you were planning to take the pills."

Gaelle raised her hands in despair.

"I don't know how that could be possible. I don't remember anything about what happened yesterday," she said.

The detective cleared his throat.

"I'll be honest with you. Right from the outset, this case has raised a lot of questions. At first we thought you and your son had been the victims of a violent burglary or domestic violence. But there are no signs of forced entry, and your husband has an alibi: he was at work at the time of the incident. There are enough witnesses who can confirm this."

"Well, Bernd obviously has nothing to do with this," said Gaelle.

The detective continued.

"When the antidepressants were found and we discovered that your son had been injected with an anaesthetic, you were transferred from the university hospital to this secure psychiatric unit."

"I want to get out of here."

"As it stands, it doesn't look as if we'll be able to let you go. Quite the opposite, in fact. If you officially become a suspect for the attempted murder of your son, you'll be sent to the prison psychiatric unit."

"What? Everyone knows I'd never do anything to harm Lukas."

"We have a statement from someone who told us otherwise."

"What do you mean?"

"Did your son cry a lot as a baby?"

"Yes, he had a severe form of reflux, but what does that have to do with what happened yesterday?"

"Was the baby planned?"

"What kind of question is that?"

"You were only twenty-nine. Perhaps you were hoping to remain a top athlete for a while, join the professional circuit."

"I don't see the point of all these questions."

"According to the same witness, after Lukas was born you felt the urge to silence him with a pillow."

Gaelle had no words. There was only one person she'd ever confided in about that. Ebba had sworn to her seven years ago that she'd never tell anyone. Ebba had found her sobbing in the living room one day, and Gaelle had said she couldn't cope anymore, that she was at the end of her tether, that she was all on her own because Bernd was so absorbed by his work, and that the night before she'd stood by Lukas's cradle with a pillow in her hands, just wanting to make him shut up. She'd immediately thrown away the pillow and had seen that nightmarish moment as confirmation that she was a bad mother. She couldn't breastfeed or comfort a crying baby, something that every other young mother she knew managed to do. Ebba had been really sympathetic and insisted that she should seek immediate help from a psychiatrist. Thanks to the right medication and lots of talking, she'd climbed back out of her pit of despair. The moment she'd stood there with the pillow in her hands had since been banished to the deepest recesses of her memory.

But now that memory was being flung in her face with full force. Something had changed in Hanssen's probing expression.

"I never used that pillow, just like I haven't done anything to harm him now," said Gaelle.

Her whole body was shaking.

"Since the birth you haven't returned to work. You took care of your sick mother for a long time until she died last year," said the woman. "Did you feel isolated? Was it all too much for you?"

"No," said Gaelle.

"We found a piece of paper with SORRY written on it," said the man. "Your fingerprints were on it."

"Around the time of the crime, you sent a text message to your friend Ebba, saying, AT HOME. HELP."

"I don't remember that."

"Were you planning to kill your son and then commit suicide?" asked the woman.

"Please stop."

"That sort of thing often happens with depressed women who want to end their lives without abandoning their children. They see it as an act of motherly love," Hanssen said to the detectives.

"I am not depressed," said Gaelle, slamming the table.

"Seroxat is controversial, by the way. It can cause aggression in certain cases," Hanssen added.

The detective wrote something in his notebook.

"Did you suddenly regret having injected Lukas with the anaesthetic? Did you panic and decide to send your friend Ebba a text message asking for help?" the man asked. "And then, in your state of confusion, did you fall against the kitchen counter?"

"No!" screamed Gaelle. "Stop telling these lies!"

She jumped to her feet and, flailing blindly in her struggle to reach the door, she hit Hanssen.

Yanking the door open, she ran away.

Halfway down the corridor, she was stopped by the two nurses, who had stayed nearby the whole time. Hanssen came to join them, holding a blood-soaked handkerchief up to his nose. She was screaming so loudly that she could barely make out what he said: "Take her to the isolation room."

29

I N A CAR PARK on the Paris ring road, there was a white van with a plumber's logo on the side. The vehicle looked empty, but there were three people in the back. They were sitting in chairs in a specially designed room without windows, with high-tech equipment that was even more advanced than the French police used. If a thief was foolish enough to break in or to attempt to make off with this vehicle, it would be the last crime they ever committed. If the traffic police happened to stop them, all the documents would be in order, and all it would take was one press of a button to hide their equipment behind a fake wall full of plumbing tools.

They'd exchanged the gear they'd worn last night for plumbers' work clothes. In addition to their visible tools, such as screwdrivers, they were carrying deadlier weapons in the pockets of their overalls.

Ludka drummed her fingers on the table.

They were under pressure.

Dolores had not said a word when Ludka had informed her that they'd returned from the tunnels empty-handed, but that silence had said enough. After walking around, trying in vain to find the location of the explosion, they'd had to retrace their footsteps.

She had no doubt that they'd find him, Michael, the Chameleon, the man who had killed her only brother. And then they'd torture him until he begged to be allowed to die.

Ludka looked up when Zoltan spoke to her.

"I think I've found something."

She slid her chair closer to Zoltan's. They were already convinced that Michael had had help getting out of the Catacombs.

Not one single informer or camera had spotted a man emerging from a manhole or an old metro exit alone.

She looked at the screen, carefully studying the image. Two figures were walking along a street in the darkness. They were wearing the kind of equipment that cavers use and between them they were holding up a man who couldn't stand, as if he'd had too much to drink. Then they disappeared from view.

"This is all I have. After that, they were outside of camera range."

"Follow their trail. There must be other cameras in the area. I want to know where they went. Maybe their car was parked somewhere in the area. As soon as you've got the number plate, we can enter it into our systems."

Ludka stared into the middle distance.

"And then it's a matter of minutes before we find out the owner's address."

Fabienne sat on one of the wobbly chairs in the kitchen of her grandfather's old house, sipping rosehip tea. It was just about the only edible or drinkable thing she'd found in the house, which was rented out as a holiday home in the summer. The house in Yèvre-le-Châtel was still in good condition and was only a ninety-minute drive from Paris. Not that the bookings came flooding in, but as she'd recently said to her mother, that was hardly surprising in a village of barely 700 inhabitants, where there seemed to be more centenarians shuffling around than anywhere else in the world.

She was hungry. After they'd found the man – she was still giving him the benefit of the doubt and, unlike Claude, refused to call him a bank robber – and brought him back up to the surface, they'd followed his request not to go back to their own apartment, but had driven him directly here. And here they were. They'd long since finished the energy bars they always took with them on the underground trips, and the last bottle of water was nearly empty.

She looked at her watch.

It was almost five o'clock. If she delayed any longer, the nearest supermarket would be closed when she got there.

Claude came into the kitchen.

"I tried to get him to drink some water," he said.

"And?"

"He got some down, but he's still exhausted. And he's rambling – he could still have a fever."

"Rambling?"

"He kept talking about our car. And before he fell asleep again, he gripped my hand and gave it a hard squeeze. That was pretty unpleasant."

"Maybe he wanted you to stay with him."

"He doesn't seem like the hand-holding type."

Claude sat down on another creaky chair.

"What now?" he asked. "We're out of pills that might bring his fever down, and the antiseptic alcohol in the first-aid kit is all gone."

"I'm heading to the supermarket in town in a few minutes. I'll stop off at the chemist's."

Fabienne stood up and took her wallet from the counter.

"Be careful," said Claude.

"I always am," Fabienne replied.

"That was what the man was trying to say to me," said Claude. "But I couldn't make sense of it. He said we had to be careful with our car."

"I won't drive through red," Fabienne laughed. "And I'm not about to start bumper-pecking or hassling old ladies who can't park in reverse. I promise." She gave Claude a kiss and disappeared.

Inside the van, there had been a development.

"We've got the address," Jorge said to Ludka. "The owner of the car was fined last year for being present at an illegal party in the Catacombs."

"What are we waiting for?" said Zoltan.

"Hang on," said Ludka. "Just to be sure, enter that registration number into our system. If no one's home, we'll be able to use traffic cameras to track the car's current location."

Jorge followed her instructions. Then Zoltan pressed the button so that the wall closed behind them to show nothing but innocent pipes and other plumbing equipment that wouldn't lead anyone to suspect three contract killers were on their way to their targets.

30

G AELLE AWOKE IN A WHITE ROOM that immediately
made her think of a cell. There were no windows and
the door could only be opened from outside. There was a steel
unit with a toilet and a washbasin with a tap, and everything
was made in such a way that no parts could be broken off. She
lay in the middle of the room on a bed that was anchored to
the floor, wearing a long sleeveless shirt made of a tough, white,
tear-resistant cotton fabric. It was the sort of clothing they gave
to people who might want to rip it into strips and use them to
make a noose.

Slowly, she sat up. In the top-left corner of the room, there
was a camera and she assumed that someone, maybe Hanssen
himself, was watching all her movements right now.

"I'm not crazy," she whispered. "I didn't try to kill Lukas."

She knew she'd better stop thinking out loud or they'd think she
was hearing voices again. She felt an urge to yell at the camera,
to shout that she hadn't done anything.

Or had she?

Maybe she really wasn't able to make a clear assessment of
herself. What if she really were in a state of extreme confusion?
Hanssen would probably pick some psychiatric label out of a
hat for it: schizophrenia, psychosis, paranoid delusions... And
Gaelle would be trapped within her own thoughts and she could
yell out a thousand times that she was innocent, never realising
that she was in a no-man's-land and had long since crossed the
line of normality.

She lay down again, closed her eyes and thought about Ebba and Bernd, who at first weren't allowed to come and visit her, and now probably didn't want to. What Ebba had told the police about that time she'd stood with a pillow in her hands felt like a betrayal. She wondered if she'd have done the same if their positions had been reversed. But that was pointless thinking. Ebba didn't have any children – and now she didn't have a husband either.

She opened her eyes and stared at the white ceiling. It acted as a screen onto which she could project her new memories. First she saw the image of Ebba, completely distraught, mascara running, sobbing as she told her that Rolf had left her that morning. The whole scene unfolded before her eyes as if it were taking place here and now. She had comforted Ebba and pushed her own marital problems, with the rainy weekend in Altensteig as the low point, into the background. The conversation with Ebba must have taken place on Monday at around midday, because that was when Ebba had her lunchbreak. Then Ebba had left and the rest of the day had been like any other Monday. She'd done a couple of loads of laundry, gone shopping and cooked dinner in the evening: sausage, fried potatoes and beans. She'd put Bernd's portion in the fridge because his meeting had run over again. And then? What had happened the next day? The day when her life had been blown to pieces.

She blinked, frantically searching for new images, lost puzzle pieces that would tell her that she hadn't tried to kill her son, how the box of Seroxat had come to be in her house, why the anaesthetic was in Lukas's blood, and what the explanation was for her fingerprints being found on the supposed suicide note and the syringe.

There also had to be a plausible explanation for the carving knife that had been found on the floor – it was, after all, the biggest knife in the block, the one that was normally used to carve the Christmas turkey or a roast. Her fingerprints were the only ones that had been found on that too. What on earth was she doing with a carving knife on a weekday lunchtime when she and Lukas usually ate sandwiches or leftovers from the day before?

She stared at the ceiling.

Danger.

There was someone in the house who didn't belong there.

Silently, she spoke to herself. *Focus. Focus even harder.*

In her mind, she saw the terrifying image of two men suddenly appearing in the kitchen.

Gaelle looked straight into the lens of camera. The memories were spinning like a whirlwind through her head.

The knife wasn't meant for killing Lukas.

She had grabbed the knife to protect herself and her son from the two intruders. And there was something else she couldn't quite place, a feeling of guilt, an inner voice that accused her of having done something wrong, of misjudging the situation and making everything worse.

She started breathing so quickly that she was almost hyperventilating.

"I know someone can hear this," she said.

Her voice was trembling. She tried to keep her hands calmly next to her body, next to the shirt that she wouldn't rip into strips, partly because the fabric was so tough, but mainly because she wasn't mad.

"I want to speak to the police. Urgently."

3 1

F ABIENNE LOADED THE SHOPPING into their Volkswagen Polo, slammed the boot and returned the trolley. As she went back to the car, she looked at the receipt, which had worked out quite a bit more expensive than she'd estimated. It must have been because of the bottle of champagne she'd bought to toast their world tour tonight.

She crumpled up the piece of paper and threw it into a litter-bin. Then she unlocked the car and climbed in. The supermarket bill wasn't the only unpleasant financial surprise she'd had lately. There were still some unopened letters on the table back home in their apartment. They were reminders from the water and electricity companies and bills for instalments on the smart TV they couldn't really afford.

She put the key in the ignition without starting the car. The truth was that their modest salaries as a museum attendant and a shop doorman weren't sufficient for their living expenses, their adventurous plans and the rent on their apartment in the suburbs of Paris. She thought about the mysterious man they'd found almost unconscious in the Catacombs and the twenty thousand euros he'd promised them. It didn't really matter to her where the money had come from, as long as they got it. Claude was less convinced. She looked at the lucky mascot attached to the rear-view mirror and touched it briefly.

With a smile, she started the car.

The stranger was a gift from the gods.

*

"I'm receiving a signal from where the car is now," said Jorge.

He was sitting on the right, Zoltan was at the wheel, and Ludka sat in the middle with a laptop on her knees, studying the details on the screen.

"Aren't we going to check their home first?" asked Zoltan.

"There's always time for that later," said Ludka. "It's better if we track down that car. They could have taken Michael to a different address."

"Next right," she instructed Zoltan.

Moments later, the plumbers' van pulled off the motorway.

Claude paced the kitchen, holding his phone to his ear.

"Answer the phone," he said impatiently.

He hoped Fabienne hadn't turned hers off, as she often did when she was in the car, because the ringing disturbed her concentration. As soon as her phone rang, she always thought something bad had happened to someone she loved, and she wanted to pick up straightaway, even if she was on a hairpin bend or overtaking on the motorway. After witnessing at first hand a few situations where she'd risked death by insisting on answering her phone – and then found herself talking to someone selling hair products – Claude had thought it wise for her to turn off her phone when she was driving.

And now he regretted it.

Because something bad had happened. His boss had just phoned him and told him that if he didn't turn up for work tomorrow, his contract wouldn't be extended. He'd turn a blind eye to one day's sick leave, but not two. And Claude shouldn't start thinking he was indispensable. There were dozens of other young men lining up for a prestigious job like being the doorman at a Louis Vuitton store.

Claude had assured him he'd be there tomorrow.

But that wasn't what he'd promised Fabienne.

He stood in the middle of the kitchen, looking at the cupboard full of cooking equipment. Fabienne had laughed when he'd shown her. The two guns were hidden under the lid of the pressure cooker and he'd stashed the banknotes – twelve thousand five hundred and twenty-five euros, to be precise – in the metal biscuit tin.

He got her voicemail.

Cursing to himself, he left her a message to call him. There was something else he wanted to tell her in person so that she wouldn't panic. A few minutes ago, it had started to dawn on him what the injured man had actually meant when he'd said that they had to be careful with the car.

There might be bad guys coming after them. It was possible that the man had stolen from some underworld figure who wanted his money back at all costs – drenched in blood if necessary.

Fabienne should never have got in the car.

But it was too late now.

Claude put the mobile on the table and sat down.

He looked up. Was that a noise in the hallway?

Michael had managed to have a drink of water and put the glass back on the bedside table without spilling any. That was a good sign. His strength was returning. Although he still felt dizzy and weak, he realised he had no time to lose. It was some time now since he'd heard a car pull away while he was half asleep. The sound of the engine was the same as the vehicle that had brought him here.

He'd tried so hard to warn them not to use their car. That would only lead Dolores's contract killers here. He assumed that one of his two rescuers had remained in the house.

A little later, he had heard a man speaking in the kitchen, and it was loud enough for him to recognise Claude's voice. As there were gaps in the conversation and there was no other voice involved, Michael imagined that he was on the phone.

It had alarmed him. The male half of the couple seemed less determined to help him than his partner did. So he'd done everything he could not to fall asleep again. He'd taken the rest of the glass of water and splashed it on his face before struggling out of bed and crawling across the floor to the door.

Standing up had taken him three attempts, but he'd got there.

And now he was standing in the hallway, by the kitchen door.

Fabienne stopped at the red light and looked at the phone lying temptingly beside her on the passenger seat. She'd promised Claude she wouldn't turn the thing on while she was driving.

But Claude wasn't here. He was now in her grandfather's secluded house with a man who had more money in his backpack than they'd ever had in their savings account.

She thought about the guns in the pressure cooker.

They were loaded, Claude had said.

Maybe something bad really had happened this time. Fabienne picked up her phone, turned it on, and, as the light turned green, she listened to the message Claude had left on her voicemail. She could hear the worry in his voice. At the junction, she drove straight on, before parking up at the side of the road and calling him back.

"Finally," she heard him say.

"You know I normally turn off my phone when I'm driving."

"Everything okay?"

"Yes, why do you ask?"

"Where are you now?"

"About fifteen minutes from Yèvre-le-Châtel."

"Come back as quickly as you can, Fabienne. Don't stop on the way, not for anyone whose car has broken down or anything else like that. Lock the doors and make sure you're not being followed."

Fabienne looked back. Nothing to see.

Then she turned on the automatic locking. She was on a road in a wooded area where there was hardly any other traffic.

"You're scaring the hell out of me, Claude."

"Be careful, Fabienne. That was what he was trying to tell me. I should have listened."

"What do you mean?"

Fabienne heard the sound of a chair falling over. And then nothing.

She threw her mobile onto the passenger seat and headed full throttle towards Yèvre-le-Châtel.

32

T HE OCCUPANTS OF THE VAN were preparing to go into action at any minute. They'd checked that their guns, knives and stun guns were in the right places in the side pockets of their overalls and pulled their caps down further over their faces, so that any witnesses would remember only the striking logo of the fake plumbing company and not the plumbers themselves.

They'd managed to track down the car via traffic cameras and now they were so close that they had the vehicle in their sight.

They'd been following the car at a safe distance for a few minutes. As far as they could see, there were no passengers. When the driver turned down a one-way street, the van waited around the corner for a moment, so as not to arouse their future victim's suspicions.

"We can force the car off the road and throw the driver into the back of the van," said Zoltan in his deep, growling voice.

"Be patient," said Ludka. "It makes much more sense to work out where exactly that car is driving to and who we're going to find there."

"Too bad it's a surprise visit," said Jorge. "Or we could have taken flowers."

No one laughed.

Ludka cracked her fingers – it had become a habit when she was preparing for hard work. Last month, in the Kruger National Park in South Africa, she'd ripped open the belly of an interfering environmentalist with one slash of her hunting knife and left his body behind as food for the lions.

She gave Zoltan a quick nod and the van started driving again. Turning the corner, they were just in time to see the car they were following take a left.

Fabienne left the ruins of Château d'Yèvre-le-Châtel behind, driving along a narrow road with high green verges planted with trees. It felt as if they were enclosing her. In a few minutes' time, she'd be back at her grandfather's house. Her hands gripped the steering wheel and she looked at the phone on the passenger seat, which had been silent since her last contact with Claude. She'd tried to call him a few times as she was driving, but he didn't answer.

This isn't good, she thought, her heart racing. *This isn't good at all*.

Yet again, she checked that the doors were still locked. Driving through the centre of Yèvre-le-Châtel, with its rows of houses, flower boxes and old ivy-covered walls, she thought about her options. This village wasn't just lacking a baker's shop – it didn't have a police station either. The only person she could turn to for help was their eighty-five-year-old neighbour, who lived down the road. There was one other possibility. She could park the car at the side of the road and call the police. She slowed down. What could she tell them? That there was a wounded bank robber in the holiday house, who was armed and dangerous? How could she explain to the police that she and Claude had voluntarily taken care of the man all that time? And the most important question of all: what would happen to the promised twenty thousand euros?

As she drove into the street, she saw her grandfather's house up ahead, partially hidden behind the bushes in the front garden.

Maybe the battery in Claude's phone had run out. It had been almost dead yesterday and they didn't have a charger.

She decided not to call the police until she was sure that Claude was actually in danger. She would play it smart. Her presence had to go unnoticed. She wouldn't park the car in the driveway, but along the street. Then she'd sneak into the house by the back door, which opened directly into the kitchen. She'd have to be really careful because the door squeaked. She'd be able to see at a glance if Claude was okay. If he wasn't, she would run outside and call the police.

She parked the car far enough along the street that it was impossible to see from the house and got out. As she crossed the road, she couldn't shake off the feeling that someone was watching her movements.

Claude sat motionless on the kitchen chair and did as he was told by the wounded guest, who was pointing a gun at him. Claude hadn't answered his mobile when it had rung a few times, although he felt like bawling Fabienne out for the miserable situation they were in. It was her fault. She'd thought only about the money and not about the risks involved.

Carefully, without turning his head, he took in the man who was holding him at gunpoint. He still looked pale. He was wearing only a pair of black boxer shorts and the bandage around his head. Standing motionlessly beside the antique kitchen cabinet, the man had positioned himself so that he wouldn't be seen by anyone coming into the kitchen through the hallway or the back door.

Claude rubbed his painful neck. When the guy had just come bursting into the kitchen, he'd given Claude a whack that had left him unconscious for a while. When he came to, he found himself staring down the barrel of a gun. His first thought was that he'd never been good at hiding things, even as a child. The man had then forced him to show him where the banknotes were hidden too.

He'd made Claude return the money to the backpack.

Claude was no longer interested in the money. If he and Fabienne survived this, he'd go to work with a smile on his face every day and when customers treated him condescendingly, he'd be immune, because the thought of a loaded gun being held to your head was a thousand times worse.

Suddenly the man looked at the back door. Claude swallowed and watched the door handle slowly descend. He wanted to yell at Fabienne to get away as quickly as possible, but the man motioned for him to be silent, still pointing the gun at him.

The door opened with a squeak.

Fabienne put her head around the door.

"Everything okay, Claude?" she whispered.

He didn't move.

The man stepped out from behind the cabinet and in a split second was standing beside Fabienne. He told her to go and stand by Claude.

Claude took Fabienne in his arms and realised he'd been a coward not to shout.

Now the man had them both at gunpoint.

33

A FTER SEEING WHICH HOUSE their target entered, they'd driven on and parked their van around the corner, where they went over their plan. Jorge, in his plumber's clothes, would ring the bell, toolbox in hand, while Ludka and Zoltan would go around the back and enter the house. They would be on their guard for anyone who might be Michael wearing one of his many disguises and disable him with their stun guns. As soon as he came round, they'd see if they'd got the right person. In the toolbox, they had equipment for waterboarding and for electrocuting the most sensitive parts of the body.

Under such circumstances, even the Chameleon couldn't help but show his true face.

Jorge pulled on his gloves, picked up his toolbox and stepped out of the van. Zoltan and Ludka waited briefly before following him. The three of them walked along the pavement, faces hidden under their caps, towards the house.

Fabienne was the first to speak.

"What are you planning to do with us?" she asked the man holding her and Claude at gunpoint.

"If you're sensible, nothing's going to happen to you."

"We saved your life last night," said Fabienne. "Or have you forgotten that already?"

She ignored the nudge that Claude gave her in an attempt to silence her.

"I owe you one," said the man. "Even we have a code of honour."

"Who's *we*?" asked Fabienne.

"It's better for you if I don't answer that."

He lowered the gun and asked them to sit at the table.

"Where did you drive to?" he asked Fabienne.

"To the supermarket and then the chemist's."

"You shouldn't have done that."

"We needed food and we'd run out of medication."

"I asked you not to use your car," he said to Claude.

"I'm sorry. I didn't understand what you were trying to tell me."

"Were you followed?" he asked Fabienne.

She hesitated.

"I don't know," she admitted. "When I just got out of the car, I did have the feeling that someone was watching me."

The man was about to say something when the front doorbell rang.

Ludka and Zoltan entered the house from the rear. They found one terrified occupant, who was the man they'd followed, and upstairs there was a second person, sitting in a cluttered room at a desk covered in papers. Zoltan and Jorge blasted the two young men with their stun guns, undressed them and set up their electrocution equipment.

Ludka was worried. Neither of the two matched the physical characteristics of the people they were looking for. They were clearly too young, in their early twenties, and their height wasn't right either. Neither of them was taller than one eighty.

With a grim expression, Ludka gave the first man a blast of electricity to the chest, making his whole body jerk.

Fabienne opened the front door and saw Emile, their eighty-five-year-old neighbour, standing there.

"Hello, Fabienne," he said with a smile. "I didn't know you were here. You usually come round to say hello, don't you?"

"It wasn't a good time, Emile," said Fabienne, trying hard not to think about the man standing behind the door with his gun and listening to everything she said.

"I just wanted to say that your car's blocking my driveway," said Emile.

"Sorry, I thought you'd stopped driving a long time ago."

"Yes, my horse has been in the stable for a while," said Emile, "but the beast is still in fine fettle. It's just that my great-grandson is visiting today to show me his car. And I'd like him to be able to park in my driveway."

"No problem, Emile. I'll move ours right away."

"And will you pop in for a visit?" he asked hopefully.

"Better not," said Fabienne. She swallowed. "I've got a lot on my mind right now."

"Fine. Well, I'll see you at some point. Say hello to Claude from me."

"Will do. Bye, Emile."

She closed the door and felt her heart thumping.

"Well done," said the man.

"What now?" asked Fabienne in the kitchen.

The man tucked his gun into his waistband, took a stack of banknotes from his backpack and tossed them onto the table.

"This is for you," he said. "Ten thousand euros. As agreed. I'll get the rest to you later."

"What do you expect from us now?" asked Fabienne.

He looked closely at her and Claude.

"If you value your lives, you won't tell anyone you rescued me from the Catacombs."

144

"I'd be more than happy to wipe that from my memory," said Claude, rubbing his painful neck.

"Ask that friendly old neighbour of yours if you can borrow his car for a couple of days. Use some excuse, say yours has broken down or something. I need you to take me to a place just over the border between France and Belgium. I'll give you the exact location when we leave. Under no circumstances should you return to your own apartment. Book a city trip or something like that, at least two nights away, and leave today."

"I'll lose my job," said Claude.

"Is it worth more to you than your life or Fabienne's?"

"Of course not."

"You have no choice. By the time you come back, you'll be out of danger. Then you won't matter anymore to the people you should be fearing now."

"Okay," said Claude. "And then I'll look for a better job. It's about time, to be honest."

"Same here," said Fabienne. "I'll go and sort it out with Emile."

She got up and left the house, heading to their neighbour's place for a chat.

Ludka looked at the mutilated bodies of the two students. They hadn't revealed anything new, except for confirming that they'd followed the wrong person. The two of them belonged to a student club that organised the occasional subterranean party, as had been the case last night. The third student, who wasn't in the house, had been so drunk that they'd basically had to carry him when they climbed back up through the manhole.

Ludka and her companions had realised pretty quickly that the boys had nothing to do with their search for the Chameleon and had channelled their fury into bursts of rapid electric shocks, until the students eventually succumbed.

They'd put the bodies in the back of their van and waited until it was dark to dump them somewhere on the edge of a cornfield.

"It's not over yet," said Ludka as Zoltan threw the corpses into a ditch. "We're coming for you, Michael."

34

G AELLE HAD SPENT a sleepless night in the isolation room. Although she'd begged to speak to the detectives yesterday, Hanssen had ignored her request. He thought it was better for her to calm down first.

"There's not much point having a conversation when you're in such an agitated state," he'd said to her.

She'd tried to explain that her agitation was caused by the new memories she'd recovered and had told him about the two men who had appeared in the kitchen, but it was no good. As Hanssen hadn't responded, Gaelle figured that he thought it was all some kind of delusion or hallucination, further demonstrating that she'd lost touch with reality.

Half an hour later, when her dinner was brought to the isolation room, the nurse gave her a glass of water and two sedatives, which she had to take, on doctor's orders. If Gaelle didn't swallow the pills voluntarily, they'd have to forcibly inject the drug instead. She had no choice but to put the pills in her mouth and swallow. The nurse stood and waited for Gaelle to show her that her mouth was empty.

The same thing happened this morning, and now she felt quite groggy.

She'd been allowed to get dressed in her room and was waiting in one of the open sitting areas for the police to arrive. She had a view of the double doors, which were secured with a keypad and a number code. It was like being in a vacuum, surrounded by bare pastel-green walls. She could hear the sound of the television in the nearby common room. Now and then, a staff member walked past and Gaelle couldn't shake the impression that they were keeping an eye on her. It was as if they started walking more slowly as they went past, and their gaze drifted in her direction. In some eyes, she even read an accusation: *that's the disturbed mother who tried to kill her child.*

I am not crazy, Gaelle repeated to herself. I am not like *her*. She looked at the woman, who was shuffling up and down the corridor, staring ahead and muttering words that Gaelle couldn't make out. She estimated that the woman was in her fifties. She was wearing a green skirt and a polo neck and had long black hair that was grey at the temples.

Sometimes the woman froze in the middle of the corridor, with her face to the double doors. She didn't move a muscle when another patient or member of staff went by, not even when a woman in a white coat came rushing towards the doors, tapped in the code and disappeared. *Must be another emergency somewhere,* thought Gaelle. It wasn't the first time today. The doctor was in such a hurry that she hadn't shielded the display with her hand, as most of the staff did automatically.

Gaelle watched as the doors slowly closed, only reinforcing the feeling that she was trapped in here.

She jumped when the woman with the black hair suddenly appeared in front of her.

"Red, white, green, brown, yellow," she said in a monotone.

She was staring above Gaelle's head at something only she could see.

Gaelle shivered and was relieved when the woman turned and went back to walking slowly up and down the corridor, on her way to nowhere.

Before long, the double doors opened again. *Finally*, thought Gaelle, *the detectives are here*, and she stood up. But it was just the nurse she'd spoken to yesterday. He'd told her that she wouldn't be getting her phone back for the time being. It had been confiscated for the investigation, and phones weren't allowed in the secure unit anyway.

The man came towards her, holding something Gaelle recognised immediately. She struggled not to yell out.

It was the craft project she loved most of all. She'd hung it on the board in the kitchen so that she could always see it. Lukas had made it for Mother's Day when he was a toddler.

The detectives were the same ones as the day before, but it was a different room. It was slightly larger or maybe it just seemed that way, now that Hanssen wasn't around. There was a window through which Gaelle caught a glimpse of the car park outside the psychiatric hospital. Beyond it, she could see trees and roads with cars driving along them, people on their way to work, parents with their children in the back seat, on their way to school or to daycare.

She looked at the craft project and hugged it to her body like a precious object. It was a cardboard mirror made of silver foil, and the playgroup assistant had stuck a heart-shaped card to it with the words *Mirror, mirror, on the wall, who's the loveliest mum of all?* The back had been painted by an enthusiastic toddler's hand. The nurse who gave her Lukas's craft project told her that her husband had dropped it off at the reception. As it wasn't an object she could injure herself with, she was allowed to have it.

Was this a sign that Bernd was reaching out? Maybe, unlike the two people sitting in front of her, he believed in her innocence. She'd just told them the whole story as she remembered it. The detectives hadn't interrupted her, but their body language said it all. The man had snorted noisily a few times during Gaelle's statement and, by the end, his colleague was restlessly tapping her notebook with her pen.

"To summarise," the female detective said, in a tone that made her scepticism obvious, "you entered the kitchen that Tuesday afternoon after picking your son up from school on your bike, and you were surprised by two men who were waiting for you there."

"That's right."

"Can you give us a description of these two men?" asked the man.

He was doing a slightly better job of remaining neutral than his colleague was, but he didn't seem to set much store by her account either.

"They were both tall and well built. One had dark hair and the other was blond."

"And their faces?"

"Just neutral features. I don't remember any details."

The woman gave a sigh.

"So you claim that these men drugged you and your son by holding cloths soaked in ether over your faces."

"Yes, I still remember that, that pungent smell. I saw Lukas fall to the floor and then he just lay there."

"And you were drugged too?" asked the woman in a way that made it clear she wanted to wind up the conversation.

"As I said, I don't remember exactly what…"

Gaelle broke off her sentence. She stared into the silver foil of the cardboard mirror and saw vague images taking shape.

She started talking so quickly that she stumbled over her words. "I remember! I remember what happened."

"Just keep calm," the man said, glancing at the door, where

someone was presumably waiting to intervene if Gaelle became angry again.

She took a deep breath, but couldn't stop the new memories from gushing out, as if she were vomiting. In short, hurried sentences, she told them that the dark-haired man had whispered that she should lie on the floor and pretend to be unconscious, but that she'd ignored him and secretly sent a text message to Ebba instead. And that then everything had got out of hand. The blond man had injected Lukas with something and had got into a fight with the other intruder. And she'd tried to use the carving knife to take down the blond man.

The woman had stopped writing a while ago.

"That's quite a story," she said. "It's just a shame there's no evidence."

"But that's exactly what happened!"

"No one except you saw those men at your house," the man said, as if he were talking to a stubborn child. "There are no signs of forced entry. And your fingerprints were the only ones found on all those objects."

"There are gaps in your story too," his colleague said. "How do you explain the packet of Seroxat on the kitchen counter?"

"I don't know. I've already told you that I haven't taken antidepressants for years."

She could hear her voice sounding more and more desperate.

"And you don't know how the word SORRY appeared on that piece of paper, with only your fingerprints on it?" the man continued.

"No, I've no idea. Maybe it was all staged by those two men after I fell on the counter and knocked myself out."

"Right. The same men who, after that fight, have since vanished into thin air," said the woman.

She closed her notebook.

"We'll leave it there for now," she said.

Gaelle knew what the woman was thinking – that they now had enough information to make her an official suspect and it wouldn't be long before they transferred her to the psychiatric unit at the prison.

The man stood up.

Gaelle looked at the cardboard mirror on her knees, reading Lukas's words once again through her tears. *Mirror, mirror, on the wall, who's the loveliest mum of all?*

Not me, thought Gaelle. *As far as other people are concerned, that's not me anymore.*

35

I T WAS THREE O'CLOCK in the afternoon. After the conversation with the detectives, Gaelle had been allowed to return to her room. A nurse had brought her a cup of coffee and a cake, but she hadn't touched them. She wasn't hungry and the smell of the coffee made her feel sick, as it reminded her of fun days out shopping with Ebba and then catching their breath over a cappuccino.

It seemed like scenes from a different life.

She looked out of the window, which couldn't be opened and only had a view of the other part of the U-shaped grey building, a collection of windows behind which people like her were neatly labelled and pigeonholed. The grogginess from the sedatives she'd had to take that morning had already ebbed away a little.

In the corridor, she heard a trolley going past. Hanssen had been to see her and had suggested she should join a gentle activity programme while the police decided how to proceed. This afternoon there was creative therapy and this evening she would have a final consultation with him and he'd write up his assessment. She'd listened to him with a growing sense of alienation, as if he weren't talking about her, but about someone she would never want to be part of her life.

When she was about six, an old woman with long, yellowing nails had grabbed her by the arm in the park and whispered to her with foul breath that she was actually a flower fairy. Gaelle had cried and run to her mother. Her mum had tried to comfort her and told her not to be scared of the crazy lady. After that, she'd had nightmares for a long time about the woman with the wild eyes and the dirty nails.

Now she was here herself. Crazy Gaelle. Everyone seemed to be convinced that she was a disturbed individual who'd tried to kill her son while in a psychotic state, and that she kept ranting away about two criminals who existed only in her imagination.

And her mum wasn't there anymore to tell her not to be scared.

Her hands shook as she brushed her hair out of her eyes.

She was terrified. She'd never been so afraid. It was the thought that, hidden deep within her, there might be a woman she really didn't want to know.

The creative-therapy class was held in a room with big windows and lots of daylight streaming in. It was led by an enthusiastic thirty-something in an apron covered in splashes of paint. He began with an explanation of what they were going to do: they could paint whatever was on their minds. The paintings would be used later during their individual sessions with their therapists.

In total, there were six participants, two men and four women. One of them was the woman with long black hair whose presence in the corridor this morning had given Gaelle the shivers. And now the woman stared at her so long that it made Gaelle uncomfortable. The workshop leader invited them to sit at the big table and they were each given a big sheet of paper and painting equipment.

Gaelle stared at the empty sheet and the paintbrush beside it, thinking about all the drawings Lukas had done over the years. She'd hung some of them in the kitchen and kept the rest in a box in the attic. Last summer, she'd had a blazing row with Bernd when he put the whole lot with the recycling. But she'd stood her ground and the box went back up into the attic. Bernd didn't understand why she wanted to keep all those childish pictures. She hadn't attempted to explain to him that she found it touching to see how those first scribbles had developed over the years into smiley faces and then stick figures. It showed how time passed.

And how everything could fall apart in a single moment.

She picked up her brush, dipped it in the black paint and emphatically placed a big black dot on her sheet of paper.

The woman beside her looked at Gaelle's work. "Nine is red," she said in a strange voice. "And six is black."

"What?" said Gaelle.

"Angela sees numbers as colours," the workshop leader said with a smile.

He walked around the table and stood beside Angela.

"Let Gaelle do her painting, Angela," he said.

An hour later, Gaelle walked out of the room, followed by Angela. While Angela had spent the entire time filling her paper with coloured numbers, Gaelle had sat staring at that single black dot. *If Hanssen wants to find some special meaning behind it, then let him*, she'd thought. It was all so pointless: the creative therapy, the individual sessions. What good would it all do if her truth didn't match the truth of those around her, and the detectives and the doctors kept insisting that what she'd seen and heard wasn't really there?

There really had been two intruders in her house that Tuesday afternoon.

Full stop.

During the painting session, she'd racked her brains about their motives and intentions and why the two men had got into a fight. All she could imagine was that it had been a failed abduction attempt, but why would anyone go to the trouble of kidnapping her or Lukas? At the thought of ransom money, she'd remembered the amount that would soon be released from her mother's investment portfolio, her inheritance. But other than her friends and family no one knew about that and besides it felt unlikely that the sum of a hundred thousand euros would be enough to inspire anyone to come up with a kidnapping plan.

She walked down the corridor, her mind turning. Who *were* those men? What were they doing in her house and how had they managed to cover their tracks?

She reached the door to the secure unit and waited for the workshop leader to type in the code while he shielded the display with his other hand, which was spattered with paint. He opened the door and held it until they'd all gone through.

"See you next time," he said.

The door fell shut behind Gaelle. As the other patients walked off, she paused in the corridor. She looked back at the display panel on this side of the door and suddenly remembered what the man had said about Angela: *Angela sees numbers as colours.*

She hurried along the corridor and tapped Angela on the shoulder. Angela whipped around and stared at her.

"I want to ask you something, Angela."

No reaction. She just walked on.

Gaelle hurried after her, trying not to speak too loudly, because a few metres away someone was walking into the nurses' station, the room with glass walls, where the staff hung out day and night and kept an eye on the patients.

"This morning in the corridor, you said a list of colours. Are they the code for the door? Did you see them on the display when that doctor was in a hurry and forgot to shield the numbers?" Gaelle asked in a muted voice.

Angela was silent.

Gaelle took hold of Angela's shoulder and stopped her walking.

"Please, Angela. Will you just repeat the colour combination?" she whispered. "Then I'll leave you alone."

Angela pulled away.

"Red, white, green, brown, yellow," she said flatly.

Nine is red and six is black, flashed into Gaelle's mind, but which numbers did the other colours correspond to? It was all on the paper that Angela had been working away on for so long. She'd painted hundreds of minuscule numbers on it, each one in exactly the right colour. Gaelle cursed herself for not realising sooner how important the information was. Five was green, she remembered that much, but she couldn't remember the colours of the remaining seven digits.

"Would you show me what you painted today?" asked Gaelle, her voice as friendly as she could make it. She pointed at the rolled-up sheet of paper under Angela's arm.

Angela shook her head firmly, went into her room and closed the door behind her. Gaelle was about to follow her when a nurse stopped her.

"You're not to go into each other's rooms. You know the rules," he said.

He looked at her in such a way that she knew better than to try it again while he was around.

Gaelle slunk off to her own room, repeating the colour combination in her head like a mantra.

Red, white, green, brown, yellow.

The door to freedom had opened, just a crack.

36

MICHAEL WAS IN HIS RENTAL CAR on the way to Berlin. Although he was rattled by the thought of being late, he had enough self-discipline not to break any speed limits. He could do without being followed by a police van or losing time by getting a ticket.

After Claude and Fabienne had driven him in their neighbour's car to the location just over French-Belgian border yesterday evening, he'd rented a room in a nightclub where a security guard on the door was also included in the price. The man, who looked like an ex-boxer who'd been punched a few too many times, wouldn't be up to dealing with Dolores's contract killers on his own. But if they showed up, he would be quick enough to press the button to alert Michael so that he could leave the building through a hidden door. The security guard was there to make sure Michael could do what his body needed to do: sleep.

As soon as he'd entered his room, he'd fallen onto the waterbed and thrown the heart-shaped red velvet cushions onto the floor. He ignored the tired-looking man in the big mirror on the ceiling and, gun in hand, he fell fast asleep. At midnight, he was startled awake by some noise out on the street. He'd gone to the window with his gun and seen that it was a drunken customer being thrown out of the club. He could tell right away that the couple of hours of sleep had done him some good. He was less dizzy, and he finally felt hungry. He'd ordered a large meal from room service, which was deposited at his door on a silver tray. Michael had worked his way through it in no time. Then he'd fallen asleep again and didn't wake until about eight.

He had got up straightaway. The wound on his head wasn't as bad as he'd initially thought. He'd taken off the bandage and estimated that he was at about ninety per cent of his usual physical strength. That was the minimum for what he had in mind. Before he checked out, he'd given the guard a generous tip and then gone in search of a new rental car.

The wipers swished across the windscreen, and a truck in front of him sent water splashing up from the road surface. He thought about Fabienne and Claude, who had sworn to him that they would drive straight to a hotel on the Belgian coast. When he got out, Fabienne had thanked him in advance for the package of cash that they'd find in their letterbox when they got home. Claude had looked convinced that they could whistle for the second instalment of their twenty thousand euros, but Michael knew better. The courier service he'd used always delivered his packages without any problems and without even thinking of opening them or helping themselves. With a client base consisting mainly of arms dealers and drug suppliers, that could be a very bad idea.

In a few hours, he'd be in Berlin. For the first time, he wondered if trying to regain his strength before heading there had been the right decision. That had given Dolores's people a day's head start. He thought about Lukas and Gaelle and assumed Dolores would leave them alive for the time being. She would probably follow the same logic as three years ago when he'd been given the job of liquidating an Albanian mafia boss. The man had proved tricky to get. He was as slippery as an eel. But he had one weak spot, Dolores had told Michael. He had a fifteen-year-old son with terminal bone cancer, who was staying at a private clinic in Switzerland. After months in the area on the lookout, Michael's patience finally paid off. On a dark winter's day, a visitor turned up at the Swiss clinic asking about the boy. That same day, the father's car was riddled with bullets as his chauffeur drove it through a tunnel in the mountains.

Dolores had known the father would show his face sooner or later.

Sometimes you just need to have patience, she'd said.

He looked at himself in the rear-view mirror.

He saw a forty-six-year-old man with brown hair, bright-blue eyes and a worried expression. The clothes he was wearing were casual: beige trousers and a long-sleeved green shirt.

Dolores's killers knew where he would be going. Once again, he checked that he wasn't being followed. It was a bizarre thought that, for the first time in his life, he was both hunter and prey.

37

Poland, February 1982

*A*fter a month at the detention centre, Michael dared to start counting down the days to the end of his sentence, eleven months later, hoping he would make it that far without being beaten up or worse by the older boys. Commandant Kaminski hadn't been lying when he said he was strict but fair. The day when it had frozen so hard that they couldn't even get the door of the dormitory open at first, he'd had extra blankets delivered and after their drill exercises in the freezing cold, they'd been given bowls of steaming soup. But he hadn't lied about his firm hand either. In the morning they had lessons: complex subjects like algebra, grammar and the military history of Poland. The teacher was a former soldier who rapped their fingers with a metal ruler when they didn't know the answer – not that it was much of a problem for Michael, but most of the boys weren't as bright as him.

Like Kaz.

At eleven sharp, the classroom door opened and it was time for Commandant Kaminski to find out what they'd learnt that morning. He always did it in the same way: he picked up the sheet of paper with five multiple-choice questions that the teacher had prepared. Then he summoned a boy to the front of the classroom to answer the questions. If you didn't get every answer right, you had to copy out the answers a hundred times, which meant missing lunch, the only hot meal of the day.

Michael, Janek and Kaz had never had to miss a meal. They'd worked out a system that allowed Michael to pass on the right answers to the other two without anyone in the classroom noticing: a code that consisted of subtle movements of the head, frowns and blinks. Kaz, who was always hungry, showed his gratitude by staying nearby whenever Janek and Michael were in the shower. He'd already saved them from the clutches of a couple of fourteen-year-olds who clearly weren't looking for the soap.

I'm going to make it, *thought Michael, as February was coming to an end. He was lined up with Janek and five other boys by the gate, waiting for Sergeant Nowak. A few times a week, they went into the forest, under his guard, to gather wood or cut down trees. But Nowak hadn't shown up yet today.*

The gate opened and Commandant Kaminski came marching in with four soldiers.

"What are you boys doing here?" he barked at them.

None of the boys said a word. He turned to Janek.

"I asked you a question."

"We're waiting for Sergeant Nowak so we can go into the forest, Commandant." Janek hesitated. "We've been here more than an hour."

The commandant ordered the other soldiers to find out where Nowak had got to. A few minutes later, the sergeant showed up. He looked a bit dishevelled and smelt of alcohol.

"According to this boy," said the commandant, with a slight nod in Janek's direction, "you should have left an hour ago."

"He's talking nonsense, Commandant," Nowak hastened to say. "Janek has the brains of a shrimp. It's not the first time he's misunderstood what I said."

The commandant stared at Nowak.

"Then I shall count on you to make yourself perfectly clear in the future, Sergeant Nowak, so that there are no more misunderstandings."

"Yes, Commandant."

When Nowak saluted, a muscle at the corner of his mouth twitched.

*

When they were in the forest, Nowak quietly separated Janek and Michael from the rest of the group. "Stop now. You've come far enough," Michael suddenly heard him say.

Michael looked back, his hands full of firewood, which Nowak had told him and Janek to collect. It was only now that it dawned on him that all the other boys had gone off with another soldier to chop wood. Nowak sat down on a fallen tree, laid his rifle across his knees and lit a cigarette.

"Come and stand by me," he said to Michael.

Michael didn't move. Nowak's free hand slid over his rifle.

"A shooting accident can happen just like that," he said. "You know we're allowed to fire if one of you makes a run for it."

"I'm not trying to escape, Sergeant."

"There's no one to confirm that," said Nowak. "Except this untrustworthy little shrimp."

Cigarette dangling from the corner of his mouth, he picked up his rifle and aimed it at Janek.

"And I'm going to teach you what it means to be on time, so you never need to remind me again, and certainly not when the commandant's there, got it?"

Michael saw Janek turn white.

"Remember that dead oak tree we passed a while back?" asked Nowak. "I think I dropped my pack of cigarettes around there somewhere."

"What do you want me to do?" whispered Janek.

"Run there as fast as your crooked legs will carry you and make sure you're back here before this goes out."

He held his cigarette between his fingers and took a long drag.

"Or I'll stub out my next cigarette on your friend's arm."

Janek turned and ran, disappearing into the undergrowth.

Michael was still standing beside Nowak and didn't move when the sergeant blew the smoke into his face.

Half a cigarette to go.

Maybe Janek won't come back, *Michael thought.*

This was the perfect opportunity to escape.

Beside him, Nowak tapped the ash from his cigarette.

Another few drags to go.

Nowak's cigarette was almost out when the undergrowth moved and Janek came racing out, panting and sweating, with a pack of cigarettes in his shaking hands.

"Just in time," said Nowak. He tossed his smouldering cigarette onto the ground and stamped it out with the heel of his boot. "Maybe next time we should reverse the roles."

As Michael looked into Nowak's grinning face, he realised it was going to be eleven long months.

38

A T HALF PAST SIX in the evening, Gaelle was in the common room, which consisted of a small kitchen, a dining room and a sitting area with a TV. She was sitting at the table with the nine other residents of the unit and their nurse. Gaelle offered the cheese to Angela, who was sitting opposite her, but she just turned away and slurped her coffee. Gaelle put the plate back down and took a slice of cheese to put on her bread. When they'd sat down to eat, Gaelle had made an attempt to question Angela about the colours that went with the numbers, but Angela had started rocking in her seat and the nurse had told Gaelle to leave her alone.

When anyone spoke at the table, it was about something trivial, like the weather – shame it was so cloudy today, but it'd be better tomorrow. Or the bread – a bit stale. Or which programmes they'd watch on TV tonight. That resulted in a discussion, which the nurse tried to steer in the right direction.

Gaelle drank her coffee without taking her eyes off Angela, who still had three quarters of her sandwich to go and seemed to have forgotten that she was supposed to be eating it. Gaelle weighed up her chances. Right now, everyone was at the table, and then they would clear away and wash the dishes together, which would be the perfect moment to slip into Angela's room and memorise the colours she'd painted in her picture.

Red, white, green, brown, yellow.

"I need to go to the loo," Gaelle said. "I'll help with the washing-up when I get back."

The nurse nodded and Gaelle pushed back her chair.

"Can you hurry up, Angela?" she heard the nurse say. "You have an appointment with your therapist at seven."

Gaelle looked at the clock. Ten to seven. She hurried out of the common room. Angela's room was next to the toilets. Gaelle took a quick glance around as she stood outside Angela's room, before slipping inside and closing the door. Angela's room was the mirror image of her own: a simple space with, on one wall, a bed, a washbasin and a bedside table and, on the opposite wall, a wardrobe. She walked around the room, looking for the sheet of paper with the numbers.

It was nowhere to be seen.

From the common room, she heard the sound of laughter and of chairs being moved. Where was that damned picture? Tearing the wardrobe open, she saw part of the paper sticking out from under the blankets on the bottom shelf. She pulled out the sheet of paper and tried to focus on the colours and the numbers. The paper shook in her hands. The exhaustion and tension of the past few days made the figures dance before her eyes.

Out in the corridor, she could hear voices, people who had stopped to talk just outside Angela's door. As quick as a flash, she slid the picture back under the blankets, closed the wardrobe, and, just before the door opened, she dived under the bed. Her heart was pounding in her chest as she recognised Angela's slippers coming into the room. Her fellow patient left the door open and headed straight for the wardrobe. From under the bed, Gaelle heard the wardrobe opening, followed by the sound of the sheet of paper being pulled out from under the blankets. Turning her head, she saw a pair of shoes under the bed and hoped desperately that Angela would keep her slippers on for her appointment with the therapist. The woman's slippers were so close now that she could touch them. She held her breath and waited for Angela to bend down to pick up her shoes – and then start screaming.

But Angela left the room and turned off the light.

Gaelle waited a moment before coming out from under the bed. Then she opened the door a crack and peeped into the corridor. Empty. She darted out, closing the door behind her, and dashed to the common room, trying to convert the colours that Angela had listed into numbers. It would have to be tonight – when the morning shift came, they keyed in a new code for the day. She'd heard a nurse tell a trainee about it. He'd added with a smile that she should keep on her toes. You could make one mistake, but not two. Two mistakes and the alarm would go off.

92508.

She froze as she took hold of the tea towel the nurse handed her.

"What's wrong, Gaelle? Would you rather wash than dry?" the nurse asked.

Gaelle shook her head and took a wet coffee cup from the counter. Her hands were shaking as she dried the cup and returned it to the cupboard.

She should have been concentrating harder.

Suddenly she was no longer certain of the last digit of the code. She wasn't sure if it was an eight or a three that Angela had painted in yellow.

When the washing-up was done, she went to the sitting area in the corridor, beside the locked door, took a magazine from the rack and pretended to read.

About three quarters of an hour later, someone opened the door and Angela came through. Gaelle stood up. When she realised that Angela had left her painting with the therapist, it felt like falling into an abyss.

Wearing a white coat and carrying a clipboard, Michael headed into the Intensive Care unit at the Charité, Berlin's university hospital. His hair was grey, as were his goatee and his trousers. He had a fake badge, made from a real one he'd stolen from the staff changing room earlier that day.

Head bowed, he walked straight towards his goal: the room where Lukas was. According to his information, it was the fourth room on the right. The rooms all looked identical, with large windows that made it possible to observe the patients from the corridor. Each room contained a lot of equipment, connected to the person in the bed by wires and tubes.

Michael looked at his watch. He had just a few minutes before some staff member would spot him, look at his badge and ask him what a radiologist was doing in this unit. He'd planned his visit at this time of day for a reason. Visiting hours were from eight to half past eight in the evening, and the doctor on duty was in one of the rooms he'd just passed, deep in conversation with a woman who was holding the hand of a patient seemingly in a coma. No visitors were allowed in some of the rooms, and relatives had to remain in the corridor.

He didn't slow down until he came to Lukas's room. He stopped at the window and looked at the little boy, who appeared to be sleeping. His mouth was half open and he was receiving oxygen through his nose. The sheets were folded back, and a number of tubes were attached to his exposed chest. On his arm was a tube connected to a drip.

Michael swallowed. He took out his phone and held his clipboard in such a way that no one would notice he was taking a photo.

The scene before him was the result of Vasili's work. An anonymous client had been willing to spend a lot of money in order to destroy this young life. He looked at the motionless child, who would normally be complaining at this hour because he didn't want to go to bed and then secretly playing with his game console under the duvet.

Lukas might never be able to move as much as his little finger again.

"What do you think? Is he going to be okay?" Michael heard someone ask.

He was startled out of his thoughts but managed to regain his composure when he recognised the man who had come to stand beside him. Bernd was unshaven and looked tired.

"Let's hope so," said Michael. "With coma patients, it's very difficult to predict how their condition will develop. Most people who end up in a coma wake up after a few hours or days, but there are those who take much longer and sadly some who don't make it."

"That's what they told me yesterday," said Bernd. "And they said we have to bear in mind that there are some things he won't be able to do, or at least not when he regains consciousness."

Out of the corner of his eye, Michael saw a door opening. It was the room where the doctor was.

"I need to get going," Michael said to Bernd. "I hope it turns out well."

He headed down the corridor to the exit, seemingly studying the details on his clipboard. He passed the doctor, who was approached by a worried-looking man who had been waiting for him in the corridor.

Michael walked out of the unit, turned the corner and headed to the end of the corridor, where there were two lifts. He pressed the button to go down and waited. Meanwhile the door of the other lift opened, and a woman in a white coat stepped out of it and gave him a searching look. Her eyes moved to his badge.

He nodded at her without saying anything, before stepping into the lift and waiting for the doors to close.

As the woman went on staring at him, his hand slid to the inside pocket of his doctor's coat, where there was a gun with a silencer.

The lift doors closed. Michael still had his hand in his pocket when he stepped out on the ground floor. Cautiously, he looked around before leaving the lobby in search of a taxi. To throw any pursuers off his trail, he didn't give the taxi driver the address where he was staying.

During the ride, he constantly checked that he wasn't being followed. In the back seat, he took off his doctor's coat, turning it inside out so that the brown lining would transform it into a normal overcoat, and thought about what he'd learnt during his visit to the Charité.

Firstly: Lukas was in a bad way.

Secondly: the boy would be even worse off if Dolores got her hands on him.

Thirdly: the security in the building would be no challenge at all to Scorpio's people.

He thought about the woman in the white coat who had come out of the lift. He had been about to shoot her. Not because she seemed to doubt that he was who he was pretending to be, but because she could have been one of them.

39

I T WAS HALF PAST MIDNIGHT and Gaelle was waiting behind the door in the darkness of her room. She was fully dressed and listening to the sounds in the corridor. Someone had a coughing fit and then everything was silent again. Half an hour ago, when she was lying in bed and pretending to be asleep, she'd heard the door of her room quietly opening and the emergency lighting in the hallway had revealed the silhouette of one of the two night nurses. Then the door had closed again. She'd climbed out of bed and piled a few pieces of clothing and a couple of blankets under the covers in the hope that her absence would remain unnoticed when they came to check on her again.

It had been quiet for half an hour now. The nurses' station was in the left section of the corridor; the entrance door with the code was on the right. She'd have to be quick. She knew she had only two chances to tap in the right number – and then the alarm would go off.

All her muscles were tense and she was conscious of her rapid breathing and heartbeat, caused by the adrenaline rushing through her body. It had been years since she'd felt anything like this. It reminded her of the state her body was in just before a race: feet in the starting blocks, hands on the ground and one hundred per cent focus, so as not to lose even a nanosecond as soon as the starting shot sounded.

This time she'd have to fire the starting shot herself. She grabbed hold of the handle, pushed it down and gently opened the door.

On the other side of the corridor was a green light showing the way to the emergency exit.

It was an ironic image, she thought, in a unit where no one was supposed to get out. She felt her heartbeat speed up even more and tried to control her breath as she always had during running sessions. *Breathe with your stomach.*

Her hand slipped under her T-shirt to Lukas's craft project, which she'd tucked into the waistband of her jeans. The thought of Lukas and what had happened to him made the adrenaline pump even faster through her body. She felt a mixture of disbelief, fury and sadness.

Breathe deeply through your nose so you feel your lungs expand. Do it six to ten times a minute.

If she wanted to get out of here to find out exactly what had happened, she'd have to keep her emotions under control. She wouldn't be able to do that if her body wasn't prepared for what might be the most important sprint of her life.

After a couple of minutes, her breathing and her heartbeat had slowed sufficiently for her to focus on the next step: opening the door without setting off the alarm.

She had slipped silently along the corridor and now stood at the door with the code. As her fingers touched the display, doubt set in. She was already uncertain about the last digit, and maybe there were other numbers that were wrong or perhaps Angela hadn't seen all the numbers properly. Or worse than that: maybe Angela hadn't seen the code at all, and her list of colours was just one of the many confused thoughts whirling around inside her head.

Muted voices came from the nurses' station.

Gaelle looked over her shoulder. For now the corridor was empty, but the longer she waited the less chance she had of escaping.

She keyed in the first four digits of the code and paused before pressing the last one. Should she go for eight or three?

Her father had always advised her to go with her first instinct when it came to multiple-choice questions. But that instinct had failed him when he'd made an error of judgement when overtaking on the motorway. Alone in the car, he had died instantly.

She had been about the age Lukas was now.

Did Lukas realise what had happened to him? Did he know his mother could never have done what she'd been accused of doing to him, which people were presumably busily discussing around his bed, falling for the common assumption that coma patients couldn't hear anything?

Her fingers were trembling. She heard the rain tapping against the windows in the corridor and that brought her back to the here and now.

She had to get out of here as quickly as possible.

She pressed the eight. No green light.

One more chance. The last one.

She keyed in the same code, but this time with three as the final digit. At the thought of the alarm going off, her heart thumped so fast she thought she was going to hyperventilate.

Breathe deeply and let the breath escape slowly.

Her breath caught in her throat as the light turned green. Without hesitating, she opened the door, checked that the corridor was empty and made straight for the stairs. She didn't wait for the heavy door to close behind her, but headed down the stairs to the basement, three floors below.

Soon she was opening the steel door to the basement. The space was dimly lit. She could see a dark corridor with lots of pipes on the ceiling. As the door closed behind her, she walked down the

173

corridor towards a set of double doors with a monotonous hum coming from behind them, presumably a room of industrial washing machines for the hospital laundry. There was a good chance that someone was around to operate the machines.

She decided not to go through the double doors but first to check for an escape route via any of the other rooms in this part of the corridor. She could see five side doors. The first two were locked. The third door, though, opened. It was pitch dark in the room. She felt around for the light switch and turned it on. The small space apparently served as some kind of broom cupboard. There were cleaning materials and a small table with a chair, which had a man's black jacket hanging on it. On the table, she saw a lunchbox, a big bottle of fizzy pop, half empty, and a few chocolate bar wrappers. A dark-blue hoodie hung on a hook, a hideous piece of clothing that was way too big for her, but this wasn't the time to be thinking about fashion. She grabbed the hoodie, wrinkled her nose at the blast of body odour and put it on. She pulled the hood up over her head. It was the ideal garment for someone who wanted to hide their face.

She cast a quick glance around the windowless room. There was no way out. She walked over to the jacket hanging from the chair and searched the pockets. It yielded a few euros. Seven in total, but that was still more than she had herself: not a single cent. She put the coins in her pocket.

Another two rooms to go.

She was about to leave the room when she heard the double doors in the corridor opening. Looking around in panic, she saw she had nowhere to hide. She turned off the light. Her only hope was that whoever was coming out of the room wasn't hungry or thirsty.

The footsteps came closer.

She waited for the door to open. But it didn't happen. Another door opened and then she heard a toilet flush.

The footsteps moved away.

A couple of minutes later, she dared to open the door. In the dim light of the corridor, there was no sign of movement. She slipped outside and walked to the first of the two rooms she hadn't checked yet.

The first one was the toilet that had just been used. The water in the toilet bowl was still running. The next one was some sort of dusty filing room with metal cabinets and shelves full of folders.

At the top was a small window. She climbed onto a filing cabinet and was at eye level with the window. It opened onto the back of the hospital, a grassy area bordered by bushes and the kind of fencing she'd easily clambered over in her teens when she wanted to sneak off to parties.

She looked for something to break the window with.

40

IT HAD STOPPED RAINING. Gaelle stood in the wet grass by the basement window, which she'd just climbed through after smashing the glass. In the distance, a church clock struck one, and then it was silent except for the barking of a dog and the sound of a car driving past.

She slipped her hand under her T-shirt to check that she hadn't lost Lukas's mirror and then ripped a strip off her T-shirt to bandage her left hand. When she'd squeezed through the smashed window, a shard of glass left in the frame had cut deep into her palm. She'd had to hold back a scream as she pulled it out of her hand and then continued climbing through the opening. By the light of a lamppost, she looked at her bandaged hand. The blood had already seeped into the fabric and the excruciating, throbbing pain made her want to vomit.

She needed antiseptic to stop the wound from getting infected. Maybe there was a night pharmacy somewhere near the hospital. She immediately rejected that thought though. She might have been able to do that a few days ago, when she was still a normal woman with a normal life, the kind of woman who wouldn't make a pharmacist consider raising the alarm when she rang the bell at night because she urgently required medication. She looked at her blood-soaked hand. Now she was an injured woman with barely seven euros to her name, without a passport or a telephone. With her exhausted face half hidden in the oversized hoodie, she probably looked like a drug addict.

There was nowhere she could go.

Suddenly she heard rustling in one of the bushes. She ran from the light of the lamppost and ducked behind a wall by some bins. She waited. It was probably just some nocturnal animal in the undergrowth who was more scared of her than the other way around.

From behind the wall, she looked at the fence. She was still in good condition – before she'd ended up in that wretched psychiatric hospital, she went running three times a week – and even with an injured hand, it would still be possible to climb over it.

She heard more rustling.

Emerging from behind the wall, she walked to the fence and found places to put her hands and the tips of her shoes. Like someone climbing a rock face, looking for handholds and footholds, she slowly hoisted herself up. Just as she came to the top, a flash of pain shot through her injured hand, making her let go for a moment. But she quickly recovered.

She climbed over the top of the fence and dropped onto the other side. She looked around. She was in a street of medium-sized detached houses, part of the residential area that backed onto the hospital. At this time of night, there was no sign of movement, the cars were probably neatly parked inside their garages and the residents long in bed, getting a good night's sleep before waking their children the next morning and heading to work after breakfast.

She felt like an outsider, running in the darkness through the silent streets, past the trees, the houses, generally safe cocoons where parents and children were living their ordinary lives. She would do anything to turn back the clock and get back to the daily routine that had seemed such a drag the week before. And every ten minutes she would grab Lukas and give him a hug, on guard against the dangers that could be lurking behind every tree and every door.

In the middle of the pavement, she stopped. She heard the quiet throbbing of an engine somewhere nearby, but she couldn't see any signs of the vehicle's headlights. With a weary gesture, she pulled the hood all the way over her head, as if trying to make herself invisible, and continued down the street.

The more she thought about what had happened on Tuesday afternoon, the more convinced she became that it wasn't a botched kidnap attempt. It felt as if something dark were hanging over her, a danger that she couldn't grasp, one that was far from over.

As she passed a house with a wrought-iron gate, an automatic security light went on, illuminating the whole street. She quickened her pace. Turning the corner, she glanced back. She froze. Just before the security light went out, she'd glimpsed a car with dimmed lights on the other side of the street. Someone was behind the wheel. She thought about the quiet throbbing of the engine she'd heard before. That car hadn't been there when she'd gone past, which meant that the driver was slowly following her. She started going faster, her footsteps hitting the pavement to the beat of a frightened heart. Without looking back, she carried on down the street, which came out onto a main road that the busy city traffic raced along during the daytime, but which was now deserted.

She stopped, looked around and then recognised the neighbourhood: Charlottenburg, in the west of Berlin. She and Ebba had been here last year on a bargain hunt. To get to the centre, she had to turn right, then cross the road, and she'd be in an illuminated shopping street that was inaccessible for cars.

She stepped onto the bike path and starting running. Her pace was no longer that of an athlete testing her own limits, but a woman on the run.

A car was coming towards her along the main road. She considered waiting at the crossing until the driver was close enough for her to stop him and ask for help.

But that would only be a waste of time. As if any sensible driver would see a woman who looked like a junkie and was raving about someone following her and invite her into his car. She looked at her left hand, where the bandage she'd made from her T-shirt was coming undone. The wound was still really painful, and a few drops of blood dripped onto the pavement. She looked up, at the street she'd just left. She didn't see any movement or hear any sound. Was her pursuer waiting to see what she'd do before suddenly going into action?

When the light turned green, she headed over the zebra crossing and straight on towards the big shopping street. The car she'd seen coming along the main road had already disappeared in the other direction. Without slowing down, she looked back and saw a dark-grey Mercedes with tinted windows approaching. It could be the car with the dimmed lights that she'd seen in the residential area.

She'd almost reached the shopping street. The dummies in the illuminated shop windows looked terrifyingly real, as if their eyes were following her. *I'm not crazy*, she thought to herself, trying to calm her runaway mind. She walked into the shopping street and, panting, went and stood behind the concrete flower boxes that closed the street to traffic. The car with the tinted windows slowed down before continuing along the road. She didn't like the look of it. Maybe the driver was looking for a place to park so he could continue the pursuit on foot. Or maybe he was looking for a side street that would take him as close as possible to the shopping street.

She couldn't allow herself the time to catch her breath.

If the driver, or whoever else was in the car, got out now, they could be here in a couple of minutes. She walked down the shopping street, turned the corner and walked on towards a square with some restaurants and bars. There were still lights on in some of the pubs. In the distance, she could see a police van approaching. Her first reaction was relief. But then she realised who she was now: a woman suspected of attempted murder who had just escaped from a psychiatric unit. Instead of running out into the street to attract the police's attention by waving her arms, she darted into a dark doorway, where she waited until the police had driven by. The throbbing in her hand was making her dizzy. She didn't step out of the doorway until she was sure the police had disappeared.

She calculated that she was about three hours' walk from her house in Potsdam. She touched Lukas's cardboard mirror, which was still tucked into the waistband of her trousers as a talisman. Bernd had thought to bring it to her in the hospital, so he must still care about her.

Home was the only place she could go now.

As long as no one caught up with her.

Zoltan turned the key in the ignition and the engine of the dark-grey Mercedes started with a quiet hum.

"Shall we grab her now?" he asked. "She's about to pass a deserted industrial estate."

Ludka slowly shook her head.

"Not yet," she said. "It's too soon. Looks like Michael hasn't located her yet."

"You'd expect someone of his calibre to be faster," muttered Jorge.

"Seems he's not as fast as her," said Zoltan. "Who'd have thought she'd escape from the secure unit?"

"Let her run as much as she likes," said Ludka. "It's like hunting. The more you chase the prey, the more exhausted it becomes."

She tapped the screen, where a moving red dot on a map showed Gaelle's position.

"And for now we know exactly where our prey is."

41

A T AROUND FOUR O'CLOCK in the morning, Gaelle reached the street where she lived. It was as if she'd run a double marathon. Exhausted, she leant against one of the birch trees that lined the avenue and listened. She hadn't heard the sound of the car that had followed her by the hospital for a long time. At this hour, the silence of the night held sway, but it wouldn't be long before the birds would announce the sunrise, and then the first of the curtains would open and people would hit the road.

And it probably wouldn't be long before the people at the hospital noticed her disappearance and informed the police. Maybe that had already happened.

She walked along the pavement towards her house, trying to avoid the light of the lampposts.

Slaloming from one patch of darkness to the next, she felt like a stranger in her own street, someone who had no business being there. She was close to her driveway now, the nearest lamppost was a few metres away and her house was cloaked in darkness. Before she stepped onto the driveway, she turned and looked at the house of the man across the street. Something was moving by the front door and for a moment she was worried that someone would appear on the doorstep.

It was just a cat, which darted into the bushes.

Her exhaustion was playing tricks on her and she felt the urge to burst into hysterical laughter. She managed to control herself; she turned around, walked up the driveway and stood hesitantly at the front door.

How could she be certain that Bernd would let her in? Could she be sure that he wouldn't call the police?

She took a few steps back and then walked around to the left of the house, where the adjoining double garage was. She stood on tiptoe to look through the window. In the semi-darkness, she could just see her Opel Corsa. Bernd's company car wasn't there. His Audi wasn't on the driveway either or parked out on the street. She wondered if that meant he wasn't at home. He never drove the Corsa, which she'd chosen. He didn't think the car's size matched his status.

Thoughts were racing through her head. Either Bernd was at home and his car was somewhere else – which didn't seem likely – or he wasn't at home right now. But where could he be?

As she walked to the back of the house – towards the summerhouse, where the spare key was hidden in a box – she suddenly realised where he most likely was. It was the only place any parent of a sick child would want to be: at their child's bedside. There were probably rooms at the hospital where family members could stay during those first few rough days, so they could be near their child.

At the Charité.

Once again, the name of Berlin's university hospital drifted through her mind, like stubbornly lingering mist, although she couldn't remember anyone having mentioned it to her.

The door of the summerhouse made a squeaking sound as she headed inside. She looked for the light switch but thought better of it. A light might alert observant neighbours. She felt around for the wooden wine box on the shelf, opened the lid and, to her relief, felt the cold metal of the spare key. She closed the box, picked up the torch that was always on the top shelf and slipped back outside, carefully closing the door behind her.

Walking across the grass, she heard the first of the birds. Routinely, she put the key in the lock of the back door and went inside. She switched on the torch and shivered as the light passed over the kitchen, the place where her nightmare had begun. Standing here, it felt like she was reliving everything. The way she'd cheerfully come into the kitchen that afternoon, before she and Lukas were overpowered by two men with ether-soaked cloths. Lukas had immediately lost consciousness, but the man who'd grabbed her – the one with the dark hair – hadn't pressed the cloth to her mouth but whispered that she should pretend to be unconscious. The torch shook in her hand as she walked to the spot where she'd lain as she sent the text message to Ebba, after which the situation had got out of hand. The blond man had spotted what she was up to and, with a quick movement, he'd done something to Lukas that she'd been unable to see properly, and the two men had started fighting. None of it made sense to her. If the two of them had different plans, why did they come here together?

She walked to the counter and saw that the wooden block of knives was missing. It had presumably been taken as evidence.

She turned off the torch and used the darkness to gather her thoughts. She had two options. The first one was more appealing: she could go and lie in her familiar bed, fall asleep and wait until she was woken by Bernd coming home from the hospital. Then she'd have to see how he'd react. Either he'd believe her and try to help her or he'd stare at her as if she were some escaped lunatic and call the police. The second, less attractive option was, if she couldn't assume Bernd would support her, to act like a burglar and, as quickly as possible, to find money, food and the things she'd need to help her disappear, for as long as necessary, hoping that a day would come when someone would expose the truth and believe her story.

She walked to the fridge, took out a bottle of water and raised it to her lips. The water poured down her chin and onto the floor. The pain in her left hand was getting worse and she realised she should take care of the wound before she did anything else. She put the bottle back in the fridge and walked out of the kitchen and into the hallway before climbing the stairs to the first floor.

The stairs creaked with every step. When she reached the top, she turned on her torch and lit up the hallway. The bedroom door was slightly ajar. Although Bernd continued to deny it, he snored or at least breathed with loud snorts, which meant she couldn't sleep. She couldn't hear anything. Slowly she crept along the hallway. At the bedroom door, she paused. Taking a deep breath, she pushed the door open.

The bed was empty.

She walked on. Before she reached the bathroom, she passed the closed door of Lukas's bedroom. Gently, she opened it and when she saw the empty room, the duvet cover with the football print, the poster of his favourite team on the wall, she could no longer hold back her tears. She stroked his pillow and held it to her, trying to feel a sense of closeness through his scent.

Somewhere in the street, a car door slammed.

She put the pillow down, brushed away her tears and walked to the bathroom. Soon her hand was disinfected and bandaged.

It was as if all the effort of the past few hours had sucked her body dry. All she wanted to do was sleep.

She walked back to their bedroom and went inside.

The shutters were down, so it was safe enough to turn on the light.

I want to close my eyes, she thought, and when I wake up someone will tell me it was all a bad dream. She lay down on her usual side of the bed. Her head touched her pillow, and she knew she would fall asleep as soon as she turned off the light. She sat up and reached for the switch on the wall, just above their bed.

Her hand hovered in the air when she spotted a sheet of paper on Bernd's bedside table. She leant across the bed and picked it up. It was a printout of a bank statement, showing a transfer of thirty thousand euros. From Bernd to E. Steinsfeld.

Ebba.

She sat up with a jerk. As she looked at the number of the bank account the money had been transferred from, it dawned on her that it wasn't their usual joint account. This was an account she didn't recognise.

What was Ebba's name doing on that statement? Why had Bernd transferred such a large amount without ever having mentioned it? Why had he opened a bank account behind her back? And where did that money come from?

She did most of the banking herself, online, so she was sure nothing odd had happened with their current or savings accounts over the past few months.

She looked at the clock radio.

Not long before the neighbourhood would start waking up.

Suddenly she remembered the papers Bernd had shoved under her nose about six weeks ago when she'd been watching her favourite thriller series. He'd told her they were documents she had to sign in connection with the investments her mother had left her. He'd given her some sort of complicated explanation involving terms such as "optimal tax scenario" and "inheritance tax", but she'd barely been listening. As an investment advisor at the bank, he would know what measures to take to pay as little tax as possible on her inheritance, she'd thought. Besides, it was an exciting scene, with the female detective coming face to face with a murderer.

She cursed herself for not looking at the documents more closely. Maybe he'd chosen his moment deliberately.

She couldn't do anything about it now. At least now she knew for certain that she couldn't trust him. It had been careless of him to leave that statement lying around, she thought, but then he'd never have expected her to turn up here.

She stood up, walked to her wardrobe, grabbed her gym bag, unzipped it and threw in some clothes that she quickly grabbed from her drawers and shelves: socks, underwear, T-shirts and her trusty trainers. Anything that would be comfortable for a woman on the run.

But on the run to where?

She'd have to decide that on the way. There was no time now. She walked to the bathroom, opened the medicine cabinet and tossed in whatever came to hand: antiseptic, painkillers, sterile bandages. With her torch in her good hand and her gym bag over her other shoulder, she headed back downstairs.

She searched the kitchen and living room for her phone before realising that it had probably been confiscated as evidence. The keys to her Corsa were nowhere to be found either.

Then she would walk.

Before leaving, she mentally ran through which rooms she'd been in. She'd closed all the cupboards and wardrobes. She assumed he'd never notice that her gym bag and some clothes were missing. He didn't even notice when she'd been to the hairdresser and on a number of occasions he'd complimented her on a "new" dress that had been in her wardrobe for three years.

If he didn't think she'd been here, he'd be less wary about what she'd found out.

She grabbed a few more coins from a kitchen drawer full of rubber bands, toothpicks and other stuff, then locked the back door and walked to the summerhouse. She thought about taking off the sweaty hoodie and leaving it there, but that might also give her away. As soon as she saw a rubbish bin a few streets away, she'd dump the thing and put on a clean T-shirt.

She paused on the street for a moment and looked at the house where she had lived. Then she turned and disappeared, like a thief in the night.

42

MICHAEL SAT IN HIS RENTED MOTORBOAT, moored at Kastanienallee, part of Potsdam Marina, and watched the morning coming to life around him.

He thought he was dreaming when he saw a woman walking along the dock, slim, elegant and with her head slightly tilted, the way Bellefleur had always done whenever he taught her a few sentences of Italian. Sometimes he thought she wasn't even listening because her eyes were closed, and one time he had asked her if she'd fallen asleep, but she'd replied with a smile – and in Italian – that that wasn't the case. When the woman stopped at a luxury motor yacht and walked across the gangplank and on board, he was catapulted back into harsh reality.

Bellefleur was dead.

And now they were after him.

Michael picked up his binoculars and scanned the area. There was nothing that concerned him at first glance. He put down his binoculars and went out onto the deck through the sliding doors. A sports boat went by, splashing water against the jetty. When Michael had got here, he'd decided it would be safer to rent a boat than a room. There were plenty of waterways for him to move around on, he could moor wherever he wanted, and with a boat he'd rarely be picked up by the traffic and security cameras in and around Berlin. He was sure they'd long since been hacked by Scorpio's contract killers, looking for any suspicious person circling around their two targets.

He was tired. Some drunk guy staggering past his boat last

night, the drumming of the rain on the roof and his memories of Bellefleur had kept him awake for the past few hours. He'd got up, made some coffee and then started his laptop to go through all the points of his plan for getting Gaelle and Lukas to safety. It was going to be an expensive and risky venture, and he couldn't possibly carry it out all on his own. He'd made arrangements with people who, like him, were invisible and who had assured him that not only could they be trusted one hundred per cent, but they were also the best of their kind, something for which they were generously rewarded. He'd made the agreements with a certain reluctance. Not because money was an issue, but because he'd been forced to depend on other people in order to achieve his goal.

Turning around, he looked through the open sliding doors at the table with his laptop on it. An icon was flickering on the bar at the bottom of the screen. It was from a special computer program he'd instructed to scan police reports for Gaelle's name. Looked like there was a hit.

He hurried inside and sat down at the table, almost knocking over a coffee mug when he read that Gaelle had escaped from the secure psychiatric unit last night.

That blew his entire plan to pieces.

Gaelle was walking along Brandenburger Strasse, the main shopping street in the old centre of Potsdam. Ahead of her she could see the tower of the Church of Saints Peter and Paul on the edge of the Dutch Quarter. It was nine in the morning, and the first shops were opening. She walked past the café where, only last week, she and Ebba had sat gossiping about a colleague of Ebba's who was having an affair with a man young enough to be her son.

If they'd both known what was in store for them, they wouldn't have found it so amusing.

She looked at her reflection in the window and saw a woman in her mid-thirties who at first glance looked lean and athletic, with her tracksuit and her running shoes and her hair up in a ponytail. Someone who was ready to shoot out of the starting blocks and hit the day running, after a morning of sport.

But her face told a completely different story.

She walked into the café and looked around. The place had an air of luxury and exclusivity with its deep-red velvet upholstery, mirrors, antique walnut tables and crystal chandeliers. A few tables were occupied by well-dressed ladies and people who looked as if they had nothing to do but drink coffee and read the newspaper. She walked straight behind a waiter and on to the toilets. After using the toilet, she splashed her face with water from the tap. She tried to avoid her reflection in the mirror, the scared expression of a stranger, with the unhealthy glow of sweat mixed with dust on her skin. She felt like taking a shower, and the thought that she had no home hit her like a sledgehammer.

What if she'd judged too quickly? Maybe there was some sensible explanation for why Bernd had transferred that considerable sum. Maybe Ebba had got into debt and was ashamed to ask her friend for money.

She hadn't even given Ebba the chance to explain.

Gaelle glanced at her reflection. The face in the mirror still looked tired. She stooped, picked up her gym bag and left the toilet. If she wanted to call Ebba, she'd need a phone. Halfway to the door, she stopped, with her hands in the pockets of her tracksuit, where the coins jingled. Not enough to buy a phone with a prepaid card, but she did have enough for a strong coffee near a couple of ladies of around forty, one of whom had carelessly deposited her expensive handbag under her chair.

She sat down at the next table and put her gym bag right next to the handbag of the woman, who was waving her hands around dramatically as she expressed her displeasure at the below-par service at a five-star hotel in Cannes. She was talking about lazy idiots who were always scavenging for tips. All the more reason to steal her handbag, thought Gaelle.

She ordered a coffee. In a corner of the café, there was a TV and she pretended to be glued to what was happening on the screen. An ad break from the local broadcaster recommended first a delicatessen and then a women's clothes shop.

After she'd paid, she pretended that she wanted to get something out of her gym bag and, as she did so, she brushed her hand against the woman's handbag. At the next table, there was a heated discussion about which face cream was the best and neither of the two women had so much as glanced at her as she bent down.

Gaelle sat back up, having left her gym bag open so that she could put the handbag inside it with one movement before leaving.

She finished her coffee.

Her cup landed on the table next to the saucer when she saw what was on the TV screen. The newsreader announced that the police were on the lookout for someone – and then Gaelle's passport photo appeared on screen above the telephone number people could call to reach the police.

Her mouth went dry. It was as if every sound had faded away, except for the voice of the newsreader saying her name and informing the public that she required urgent medical assistance and could be dangerous.

As her stunned deafness slowly lifted, she heard the tinkling of cups and glasses behind the bar, the hubbub in the room, the man rustling his newspaper, the laughter and high voices of the women at the table next to hers.

No one was looking at the TV.

She stopped, grabbed the black leather handbag, shoved it into her open gym bag and zipped the gym bag shut. Then she stood up and left the café without saying goodbye to the waiter.

As soon as she was out of sight of the café, she started running.

43

G AELLE WALKED THROUGH the Dutch Quarter, past the red-brick houses with their step gables and the little boutiques. The sun was shining, there wasn't much wind and she couldn't see anyone else walking around hunched over with a hood up like she was. Maybe it would attract unwanted attention, but as she'd been perfectly recognisable on the TV news, she had no choice for now. She was on her way to a chemist's shop to buy what she needed to change her hair.

As she walked past one of the bistros that advertised Dutch poffertjes and pancakes, a young waitress in a white apron stepped outside. The woman stood in the doorway as Gaelle walked past. Their eyes met and the woman frowned.

Gaelle walked on quickly and turned into the next side street, away from the bustle, the tourists and any attentive waitresses who might have been watching the regional news. Halfway down the street, she stopped between two parked cars, put her gym bag on the ground and crouched down. She was out of sight now of any passers-by and people who might happen to look out of the window. She opened her gym bag and searched through the contents of the stolen handbag without taking it out. A packet of paper tissues, a bag of make-up, a comb, a mobile phone – half charged and not locked – and a red patent-leather designer wallet. The contents were somewhat disappointing: a fifty-euro note and a few coins, an ID card, a bunch of keys, a driving licence and bankcards that were no good to her without the PIN codes.

In one of the side pockets was a memorial card. The sight of it made her feel queasier than she already was. The photo showed the smiling face of a girl with Down's syndrome, who, according to the dates of birth and death, had barely made it to the age of eleven. Underneath the photo was printed: OUR BELOVED DAUGHTER, ELSIE.

Gaelle was startled when a bearded man with a dog stopped on the pavement.

"Lost your keys?" he asked.

"Found them!" Gaelle replied, jangling the woman's keyring. *The woman she'd stolen them from had lost her handicapped daughter last year.*

She thought about Lukas's craft project for Mother's Day, which she'd put in the bottom of her gym bag. *Your mother is a thief, Lukas. She's doing things now that she's always taught you you're not allowed to do.*

"Seek and ye shall find," said the man, continuing on his way after imparting this piece of wisdom.

Gaelle grabbed the money, the comb, the telephone and the make-up bag, stuffed them into the side compartment of her gym bag and crossed the street, avoiding the man, who had stopped to let his dog pee on a lamppost. Rounding the corner, she saw a bin and looked around before shoving the handbag into it, still visible enough that some honest soul might spot it and hand it in to the police.

A few streets on, there was a chemist's shop. She walked in, turning her face away from the security camera just a little too late. Without wasting any time comparing prices, she searched the shelves for a pair of scissors, flashy earrings, a baseball cap and a box of black hair dye. She calculated that she'd have barely five euros left of the stolen fifty euros. A skinny cashier with a bored look on his face took her money, and then some more people came in, and all Gaelle could think about was getting away as soon as possible. She took her things from the conveyor belt and was just walking away as the cashier called her back.

She stopped and wondered if the chemist's also had TVs showing the regional news.

Slowly she turned around.

"Your change," he said tonelessly.

Gaelle took the coins and left.

Some time later, she emerged from the bushes in Babelsberg Park, where she'd retreated to a secluded corner to apply the dye. As per the instructions on the box, she'd squeezed out the contents of the tube, given the mixture a good shake and then took a deep breath before distributing the disgusting colour evenly over her head. Then she waited in the bushes for half an hour to let it soak in. Inside the stolen make-up bag was a powder compact with a small mirror. A brief look was enough to confirm that casual acquaintances and people who had seen the news would walk past her on the street without recognising her as the wanted woman who had been on the TV. To fool the police and people who knew her better, she'd have to go a step further.

She inserted a fifty-cent coin in the slot of the self-cleaning public toilet, and the automatic metal door slid open. No one was waiting behind her. That was just as well, she thought, because she was going to need all the time she had. She had a maximum of seventeen minutes – the system worked by detecting body weight on the floor. There was just a weak flow of water from the sink, but it would have to do. She put her head under the tap and used the special shampoo from the box to rinse her hair. The sink – and her fingers – turned black. She looked in the mirror and used paper towels from the box beside it to pat her face dry. It looked as if black tears were rolling down her face.

She was startled when there was a knock on the metal door. The display said she still had nine minutes left. Quickly, she took the scissors from her gym bag and without hesitating she cut the first chunk of her shoulder-length hair and she went on cutting until she had a short cut that wouldn't stand out in a crowd. She put on her earrings – the big silver rings would draw attention away from the features she couldn't easily change, like her jawline and the shape of her nose – and then she put her cap on and used a red lipstick to make her lips look a little fuller than they actually were.

She cast a glance in the mirror. The old Gaelle was gone, but the determination with which she'd once won her medals had remained intact. Before her stood a woman who had overcome many hurdles and knew that bigger obstacles lay ahead.

Once again, there was a knock on the door and she heard a high-pitched voice shouting something. She fished the tufts of hair out of the sink, put them in the bin, wiped the sink and the floor as clean as she could with toilet paper, threw it into the toilet and flushed. Then she picked up her gym bag, checked to see if she'd forgotten anything and headed outside.

There was no one by the cubicle. In the nearby bushes she saw a woman leaning forward to hold a toddler who was going to the toilet. She ignored whatever the woman was yelling at her.

She walked through the park until she found a bench that looked onto the water of the Tiefer See, where she sat down and took out the phone. It was getting on for midday. She keyed in Ebba's number and waited.

It wasn't long before someone picked up. She heard Ebba's voice asking who was calling. That threw Gaelle for a moment.

Of course, Ebba normally saw her name on the screen when she called, so she didn't need to ask, but now she was using the woman's phone. Correction: the woman's *stolen* phone.

"It's me, Ebba. Gaelle."

There was silence on the other end and then, "Where are you, Gaelle? The police called me this morning. They're looking for you."

Gaelle heard women's voices chattering away in the background.

"Are you alone, Ebba? Can you find a place where your colleagues can't hear our conversation?"

When she answered, Ebba's voice sounded hoarse, and she seemed to be struggling to form a sentence.

"I… I'm not at work. I'm at home on sick leave, because of the whole business with Rolf and what happened with you and Lukas."

Silence. Then Ebba saying something, but not to her.

"For God's sake, Gaelle, why… Where are you now?"

"Who's with you?"

"Mum and Lore."

Like a couple of meddlesome hens, thought Gaelle. They'd obviously descended after Rolf had fled the coop and were now cackling away and pecking his reputation to pieces. She certainly couldn't expect any support from that quarter. They were the last people she wanted around now that she needed to ask for Ebba's help.

"I don't have much time, Ebba. Just listen to me."

In a few sentences, she summarised the situation and told her what had happened on Tuesday, exactly as she remembered it.

"I don't know who those two men were, Ebba. No one believes my story, but they really were there."

"What do you want me to do?"

"I urgently need money, clean clothes and a car."

"Do you want to come here?" asked Ebba.

Gaelle thought that would be just about the dumbest thing she could do now, with those two busybodies there.

"I want to meet up with you, Ebba, just you. Don't go telling Bernd, your mother, your sister, the police or anyone else."

"Okay," whispered Ebba.

Gaelle had always been able to tell from Ebba's body language if she was lying. She'd be able to test that out later when she brought up the subject of the thirty thousand euros.

"Tonight at eight at the Brandenburger Tor in Potsdam," said Gaelle.

"In Potsdam?"

Ebba was apparently checking that she didn't mean the famous gate of the same name in Berlin.

"You heard me right, Ebba. Potsdam. By the pedestrian passageway, on the left-hand side, looking from Luisenplatz. And remember what I said."

She ended the conversation and looked out at the Tiefer See, where a motorboat was sailing in the distance.

44

THE SETTING SUN turned the sky above the Brandenburger Tor red, as if the sky were on fire. Gaelle was tucked away in one of the doorways on Luisenplatz, watching the people near the gate. She'd got changed in a public toilet and was wearing jeans, sneakers and a dark-blue cotton sweater. Her cap was in her gym bag. She wondered if Ebba would recognise her with that short black hair, flashy earrings and way-too-heavy make-up.

If Ebba turned up.

From where she stood, she could see the clock tower of the Church of Saints Peter and Paul. Ten to eight. A few tourists with cameras were walking around the Brandenburger Tor.

Two men had stopped to study the menu at the restaurant where Gaelle was standing. She didn't look up but acted like she was busy texting, with the disgruntled expression of someone who'd arranged to meet a person who hadn't shown up. In reality, she'd turned off the stolen phone after calling Ebba this afternoon, so that the police couldn't trace her. As the men walked away, Gaelle thought about how lonely she'd felt the past few hours, wandering around town. She'd considered buying a train ticket to Berlin with the rest of her money and going to look for Lukas at the Charité. She would have given anything to see him close up, to touch him and to keep herself strong as she whispered encouraging words to him, even though his body might be lying there like a broken doll.

But even with her altered appearance, that would be foolish. A woman without ID wouldn't be allowed into the secure ward where the coma patients were. Besides, the police were bound to have informed the hospital about her escape and they'd be extra vigilant.

She looked again at the passage through the Brandenburger Tor. It was five to eight now. Still no sign of Ebba.

The 4x4 was parked near the Brandenburger Tor. Ludka was behind the wheel. She picked up her phone and looked at her two companions walking across Luisenplatz in the distance as she called a number.

She heard the voice of Zoltan, who, as agreed, answered in German. He and Jorge were pretending to be two acquaintances looking for a decent restaurant.

"I thought she was more attractive with her old hairdo," said Zoltan. "Now she looks a bit like a whore."

"Keep your mind on the job."

Her threatening tone had an immediate effect.

"It's as if she's waiting for someone," he said, sounding more professional now. "She's watching the west side of the gate."

"It's not like Michael to arrange to meet her there. Far too risky."

"I don't think he's the one she's waiting for."

"Then who is it?"

"Other than her husband, she doesn't have any immediate family, and she's a stay-at-home mother, so she doesn't have any work colleagues. Maybe she's called a friend."

"If she gets someone else involved, it makes things even more complicated. Do your job. I'm on my way."

"Wait!"

"Why?"

"Something's wrong. Stay in the car."

*

Michael walked towards Luisenplatz, bundled up in a coat and scarf, looking like a middle-aged man who was afraid that a cool breeze might grab him by the scruff of the neck. Under his coat he was wearing a bulletproof vest, and there was a gun with a silencer in his inside pocket. It had taken him considerable time and a few thousand euros to track down Gaelle. He'd assumed she'd stayed in the Berlin area. It was common knowledge that people on the run generally went to places they knew. Besides, she didn't have the money or the necessary documents to go abroad.

One of the specialist hackers he'd contacted had screened the traffic and security cameras for someone who matched Gaelle's physical characteristics and way of moving, which, thanks to her sporting career, could be found on YouTube. He'd forwarded some pictures from a security camera over the course of the afternoon, showing Gaelle paying for something at a chemist's shop in Potsdam's Dutch Quarter. The timer on the camera showed that it had been at around ten in the morning. Michael had zoomed in on the products she'd bought and deduced that she was planning to change her appearance. On the basis of that, he'd sent a new description to the network of local informants. He'd asked them to look out for a woman in her mid-thirties, athletic physique, one metre seventy-four, with short dyed-black hair, possibly wearing a cap, large hoop earrings and striking make-up.

A quarter of an hour ago, he'd received word that someone matching that description had been spotted near the Brandenburger Tor.

At the end of the street that led to Luisenplatz, Michael stopped. He took a handkerchief out of his pocket, pretended to blow his nose and ran his eyes over the square. He saw her standing across the square in a doorway next to a restaurant. There was a sports bag at her feet, and she was staring at the Brandenburger Tor.

As he put his handkerchief away, he felt the hard shape of his gun. There was something about this situation that he didn't like, something fake, as if he were watching an advert in which perfect-looking people just happened to be walking by.

At the edge of the square were two men, one of them talking on a mobile phone. They didn't look like a couple of friends on a fun night out. They seemed more like tense professionals waiting for the signal to spring into action. It was also strange that the one man stood with his back towards his companion, looking in Gaelle's direction, while the man on the phone was keeping an eye on the west side gate. Both of the men were wearing sports shoes and large coats that might be concealing all manner of things.

Practical training course, tip 43: always wear comfortable clothing during fieldwork operations, to enable an easy getaway or a pursuit.

Michael slowly unzipped his coat. His right hand slipped inside, and his fingers touched the butt of his gun.

45

A S THE CLOCK STRUCK EIGHT, Gaelle saw Ebba's familiar figure appear from the pedestrian passage on the left of the Brandenburger Tor. Ebba was wearing black trousers and a coat with a high collar. She looked nervous and kept fiddling with her left earlobe as she stood looking around. Gaelle held her breath when Ebba looked in her direction. For a moment, she thought her friend would see straight through her disguise and call out her name, but Ebba's gaze moved over the spot where Gaelle was standing and across the square.

She's here, thought Gaelle. Ebba hadn't abandoned her.

She waited a few seconds to make sure no one else had come with Ebba. At first glance, it appeared that she hadn't let Bernd know and had left Lore and her mother at home.

Gaelle picked up her gym bag and walked slowly towards the Brandenburger Tor. She was still some way from where Ebba was standing when she noticed something strange. Ebba had tilted her head and her lips were moving, as if she were talking to someone invisible in the collar of her coat.

At the same moment, Gaelle noticed that one of the backpackers who had spent the entire time walking around the gate, as if he couldn't get enough of it, had raised his hand to his ear and was talking to no one in particular.

Gaelle turned and changed direction as inconspicuously as possible, walking away from the Brandenburger Tor and away from Ebba, who had clearly betrayed her and contacted the police.

*

"What's wrong?" asked Ludka on the telephone. "Why do I have to stay in the car?"

Zoltan had abruptly broken the connection shortly before, and Ludka had called him back.

"At least two undercover cops by the gate. Target is leaving the area. She may have noticed something too."

Ludka cursed.

"Should we follow her?" asked Zoltan.

Ludka thought about it. She looked at the screen of the laptop, where a red dot was moving across Luisenplatz.

"We'd better do that from a distance, on the screen. It's way too risky now, with those undercover police around. Abort the operation immediately."

"Will do."

"And if those undercover cops turn up again later, it'll be dark enough in a few hours to take out anyone who gets in our way."

Babelsberg Park looked very different in the dark, thought Gaelle. It had started raining and she'd found a place to shelter under a canopy, where there was a wooden picnic table. During the daytime, it was presumably a place where families with children would pause for a snack and a drink.

At night, it was a place that offered protection from the rain, but that was about all that could be said for it. This shelter without walls offered no protection from the cold, the insects or the drunken tramps, like the one who'd been hassling her an hour ago.

The park was dimly lit, and one of the lampposts shone on the surrounding trees and bushes. She hoped that the rustling of the leaves was just the wind and not the man with the dirty clothes and the wild eyes who had grabbed her in an unguarded moment when she was sitting on a bench near the water. It had been after nine, and the families had left the park some time before to make way for the denizens of the night: runaways, men out cruising, drug users and drunken tramps.

The tramp had appeared just after she'd fished a big ball of aluminium foil out of a bin, taken a look at the contents and wondered if she was hungry enough to eat the remains of someone else's lunch. Suddenly the man had sat down beside her on the bench, a grimy type, around fifty with a grey beard and a fug of alcohol around him. At first she'd thought he was after her pathetic meal, but then his hand slid eagerly over her leg and she'd jumped up, grabbed her gym bag and run. She'd managed to shake him off and since then she hadn't seen him. But every time she heard a sound from the trees, she thought he was coming.

Like now.

She looked up. Quickly, she screwed the cap back onto her last bottle of water and threw it into her gym bag. The car park was some distance away. There were no cars here, no houses where there might be people who could help her.

Spending the night in this park was as dangerous as wandering around town by herself. There she ran the risk of a police patrol stopping her and asking for her ID. Here she had to be on her guard against other dangers.

A twig snapped somewhere nearby.

Her decision was quickly made. She wouldn't be able to sleep a wink here anyway. She took the scissors from her gym bag and left the shelter, holding the scissors as a weapon in her hand.

Then she walked along the gravel path around the lake, the moonlight casting a silvery glow on the dark surface of the Tiefer See.

Hearing footsteps behind her, she turned around.

No sign of anyone.

She started walking faster, straight through the puddles on the path.

In a couple of minutes, she'd be out of the park and would leave the creepy noises behind her. Just one more curve in the path to go.

The figure emerged from the bushes. Before she knew what was happening, someone had grabbed hold of her. She was thrown to the ground in the middle of a muddy puddle. The scissors were yanked from her hand. Tape was stuck over her mouth to prevent her from screaming. Her attacker held her down with his body, and her clothes were soaked through with rain and mud.

But the worst of it was his hands.

They were everywhere.

46

S HE COULDN'T CRY OUT and she couldn't move. She could only imagine that the tramp had got her. His body was still pressing her to the ground, his hands slipping under her sweater, under her bra, touching her skin and crawling over her body like insects she couldn't swat away.

Her attacker had dragged her into the bushes, away from the gravel path and out of the light coming from the car park. In the semi-darkness, she could see the scissors lying at the foot of a tree beside her gym bag, which he'd thrown down there. She struggled to get closer to the scissors, but her arms were nailed to the ground by the force of his knees.

His hands were no longer on her skin. They were searching her pockets, then moving to her head, running through her hair, touching her ears, and finally her neck, as if he were planning to strangle her.

She struggled to breathe.

I'm never going to see Lukas again, she thought. I'm never going to find out who did all of this to us.

Then it stopped.

The pressure of his hands around her throat was gone. Without taking his body off hers, he leant towards her bag and pulled it closer. Her initial panic gave way to confusion: this man was bigger and more sturdily built than the tramp and he didn't smell of alcohol.

He'd touched her all over without tearing off her clothes. If her attacker wasn't the tramp, then who was he? And what the hell was planning to do with her?

Now he'd turned on some kind of torch that cast a bluish light and was lighting up the contents of her gym bag. She still couldn't see his face clearly, but she could see what he was doing. Quickly and systematically, he was taking all her things out of the bag, and he'd placed the torch on the ground to give him some light. He seemed to be looking for something and was going through the contents of her bag with the same thoroughness he'd used when searching her body. After carefully examining each object or piece of clothing, he placed it next to the bag. She watched every movement he made. Maybe he was after her money or thought she was carrying jewellery or even drugs. That would explain why he'd found it necessary to rip the lining of her bag to pieces. She felt a spark of hope. Maybe the attacker would just run off after establishing that she had nothing of value.

She heard footsteps coming closer on the gravel path, followed by a phlegmy cough. Whipping around, the man who was sitting on her turned away from the bag. Before he switched off his torch, she saw him pull a gun from his inside pocket.

It's over, she thought.

As the footsteps came closer, he slowly leant forward and put his lips to her ear.

"If you try to make any sound through that tape, I'll have to kill him," he whispered.

To kill *him*, not her.

"I touched you because I'm looking for something," he said almost unintelligibly. "The tape's to keep you quiet. Or we've both had it."

She swallowed.

"Believe me, Gaelle. Some of the people out there don't have your best interests in mind like I do."

He knew her name.

"I know what happened to you and Lukas and I'm the only one who can help you now."

She had only a few seconds to decide. If she shouted really loudly, she might make enough noise through the tape to alert the passer-by. But that throaty cough made her think of the tramp and, besides the fact that he'd be no match for this armed man who was asking her to trust him, she also doubted the tramp's heroic nature.

The footsteps were now close to the bushes where she was lying. She didn't make any attempts to call out and, after a while, she heard the footsteps moving away.

The blue light went back on. This time, the man placed it so that she could see his face. She estimated that he was in his mid-forties, but the stubble made him look a little older. As far as she could remember, she'd never seen him before.

He got off her body, put his gun away and leant towards the gym bag. There was one object in there that he'd not examined.

"We don't have much time," he whispered. "That tramp who just went by isn't the one we need to worry about."

Now that her hands were free, she tore the tape from her mouth and was finally able to breathe freely again. But her breath caught in her throat when she saw that he was pointing the scissors straight at her face.

"Stay where you are," he said quietly. "And take a look at how they were able to trace you. Maybe then you'll believe that you shouldn't underestimate the people who are after you."

His torch was in the breast pocket of his leather jacket and lighting up Lukas's cardboard mirror, which Bernd had delivered to the hospital and she'd kept with her ever since.

He looked at the side with the silver foil and read the words out loud: "Mirror, mirror, on the wall, who's the loveliest mum of all?"

He paused.

"They clearly know your weak spot," he said, running his fingers over the mirror. With the tip of the scissors, he removed the silver foil and showed her what was behind it. There was a flat black disc about the size of a drawing pin attached to the cardboard.

"That's how they're tracking you," he said.

"What on earth is it?" asked Gaelle.

"An advanced tracking device."

He raised his head and listened. Except for the rustling of the leaves, Gaelle couldn't hear a sound. His right hand slipped into the inside pocket of his jacket – and to his gun.

He dropped the cardboard mirror.

Gaelle went to pick it up.

"Leave it," he said. "Your bag too."

He grabbed her arm.

"I know you can run," he said. "You're going to have to."

By around midnight, they were fairly certain that Gaelle and Michael were no longer in Babelsberg Park. They'd combed the entire area for the two of them. They'd found no one except for a drunken tramp and two men nervously emerging from the bushes and heading to the car park while doing up their flies.

The tramp had caused trouble.

Ludka kicked the foot of the dead man lying on the ground in front of her, worried about the call she was going to have to make.

"What are we going to do with the body?" asked Jorge.

"Dump him in the lake," she said. "Drunk people often end up in the water."

"What about his head injury?"

"Walked into a tree. How should I know what they'll make of it? He's not our problem anymore."

She looked at the tramp's body. His head had fallen to one side, and there was blood trickling from his mouth. When they were hiding in the bushes at the edge of the park, the tramp had spotted them and asked them what they were up to. Instead of clearing off, as they'd told him to, he kept following them and asking for money.

He shouldn't have done that. One whack with a thick branch had been enough to silence him forever. But it had distracted them from their goal. The red dot of the tracking system hadn't moved for a while now and they'd been on their way to check if Gaelle was hiding somewhere to rest, as she'd done under that wooden canopy, or if there was something else going on.

In the bushes beside the gravel path, they'd found her bag and the mirror with the silver foil torn off. That was when they'd realised they'd blown their chance.

Michael had been here. He'd found her and they'd run off together.

And now Ludka was going to have to tell Dolores.

She picked up her phone, heard the splash of the body being dumped in the water behind her and made the call.

She gave Dolores a brief summary of what had happened. For the first time in her career, Ludka received an ultimatum. Dolores would allow them three more days.

Then Dolores gave her an extra assignment.

"Get the boy out of that hospital as soon as possible."

47

G AELLE SAT ON THE WHITE leather corner sofa in the motorboat, which was quietly puttering across the Tiefer See in the darkness. The man at the helm had introduced himself as Michael and then had largely kept silent. Gaelle was shivering. The mud caked onto her skin had mixed with sweat and she felt like an intruder in this immaculate space. There was a glass of water on the table in front of her, and on the opposite wall was a kitchenette with a refrigerator, a two-burner hob and a sink. To her left was the utility block with a toilet and a shower cubicle. The ceiling had built-in spotlights, only two of which were on, creating an intimate atmosphere which seemed inappropriate in the circumstances. Michael had closed all the curtains except at the front, so that people on any passing boats wouldn't be able to see in. Not that they would meet many other boats, he'd said – it was unusual for anyone to be sailing after midnight.

She wrapped herself in the blanket that was on the sofa and took in Michael's profile. Short-shaven brown hair, a few days' stubble, unfathomable blue eyes, an athletic body and a voice that conveyed no emotion, not even just a little while ago in the park, when he'd urged her to run as fast as she could.

"We'll be mooring up in about ten minutes," he said without turning his head to look at her. "If you like, you can use the shower. There are clean clothes in one of those cupboards, maybe not entirely to your taste, but you're not about to hit the catwalk, are you?"

She put the blanket down beside her.

"Who are you?" she asked. "Why are you doing all this?"

"It's better if I tell you as little as possible," he said.

"You just threw me to the ground, felt me up, threatened me with a gun, fished some kind of tracking device out of my belongings, and then told me to run for my life. There's no way you can expect me not to ask questions."

He was silent for a moment. "I'll explain later."

With a bath towel around her wet hair, Gaelle stepped out of the shower cubicle. She put on the clean clothes, which she'd laid out ready on the stool: a decent brand of sports underwear, slim-fit jeans, a grey T-shirt, a sweater and running shoes.

Everything fitted like a glove. It couldn't be a coincidence. Not only did the mysterious man know her name, he also knew her clothes sizes perfectly. Something that most women would appreciate in their partners only made her all the more anxious in this situation. Who was this Michael, who claimed he wanted to help her, and how did he know there was a tracking device among her belongings?

She opened the bathroom door and stepped into the cabin. The boat had moored on a jetty at Kastanienallee, a marina she knew from the past, as her dad had often taken her sailing when she was a child.

Michael was standing over the hob. A delicious smell rose from the pans. Gaelle went and stood closer: omelette with rings of onion in one pan, fried potatoes in the other. The curtains at the front were now closed too.

She sat down at the table.

"Are we safe here?"

"For now," he said. "But we can't stay here too long. I'm planning to leave tomorrow."

He took two plates from a cupboard and placed them on the table with two mats and the cutlery. Then he put down the steaming pans and waited for Gaelle to fill her plate before helping himself.

Gaelle didn't start eating.

"Do you know who you've brought on board?" she said. "I'm currently wanted by the police. I escaped from the secure unit of a psychiatric hospital last night."

"I know."

"The police suspect me of attempting to murder my son. His name's Lukas. But I was only trying to protect him from two intruders who were lying in wait for us at home on Tuesday afternoon. One of them injected Lukas with something and pushed me over. I fell against the counter and passed out. Then the two men vanished without a trace and now no one believes my story."

"I know you're telling the truth."

Gaelle felt the hairs on her arms stand up.

"Why are you so sure?"

He put down his knife and fork.

"Because I was there," he said.

She managed to listen to Michael's story without interrupting him even once. The relief she'd felt at someone finally believing her hadn't lasted long when she realised exactly what it was that she'd escaped from. Someone had called in the services of Scorpio, a syndicate of contract killers, to eliminate her and Lukas. The client was known only to Dolores, the woman at the head of the organisation. And right now she was sitting at a table with a man who was calmly telling her that his career had reached a turning point when he was ordered to kill a child.

He looked at Gaelle.

"I planned to do it at first, but then I couldn't," he said.

She swallowed.

"I was there too, that weekend in Altensteig," he said, "preparing for the hit. I was watching both of you. I saw Lukas having an asthma attack and gasping for breath on that path in the forest."

Gaelle stared at him speechlessly.

"I was there the entire time," he continued. "That afternoon I sat at the next table on the terrace of your hotel, and I was there again the next day. I saw you standing under an awning in the rain on the Sunday afternoon, when you left that packed bistro to go and call someone."

"But your face doesn't look at all familiar," said Gaelle, "and you don't look like either of those two attackers who were waiting for us at home."

"They call me the Chameleon," he said. "I'm exceptionally good at changing my appearance to suit the circumstances."

All that time she still hadn't touched her food.

"Who are you now, Michael?" she asked.

"A man who wants you and your son to survive."

48

I T WAS LONG AFTER MIDNIGHT, many questions were still unanswered and lots of new ones had taken their place. The table had been cleared and Gaelle was warming her hands on her teacup. Michael had told her that he was the dark-haired man who'd been waiting for her at home, while the blond man had been Vasili. She had learnt that Michael had had to make a last-minute change of plan.

"It's my fault it went wrong," she said. "After you asked me to pretend to be unconscious, I sent Ebba a text message. And when Vasili saw that, he got mad and injected the drug into Lukas's arm, and then you started fighting and I don't remember anything about what happened afterwards."

"Well, Vasili won't be telling any tales. That's for sure," said Michael.

Gaelle briefly shut her eyes.

"In my dreams I blamed myself for something bad happening to Lukas. Now I know why," she said.

"What happened to Lukas isn't your fault. And neither is what happened to Bellefleur."

She had shivered when Michael told her, with carefully considered words, that Scorpio had taken the only person who mattered to him.

Gaelle looked at him.

"But you didn't have to do any of that, did you?" she asked.

"What do you mean?"

"You could have just passed on the contract for the double

killing to someone else, as you'd been planning to do, without bothering about Lukas and me, couldn't you?"

"Yes, I could have done that. Then Bellefleur might still be alive and Dolores wouldn't have sent her bloodhounds after me."

He'd taken his phone out of his pocket and shown Gaelle the photos he'd taken of Lukas at the hospital.

"But if I hadn't done anything to save him, I wouldn't have been able to live with myself a day longer."

Gaelle heard the water lapping gently against the hull of the motorboat. A while ago, Michael had turned out the light and said that, in spite of everything, she should try to sleep. She'd taken a blanket and a pillow and installed herself on the corner sofa, which also served as a bed. Michael was sitting in a chair, which creaked every now and then. He claimed he could sleep anywhere, even in the top of a tree. But he probably wasn't doing much sleeping now. She imagined he was constantly on his guard against strange noises. He'd said that Scorpio's contract killers weren't far away.

The way he spoke about the organisation, it seemed as if he was no longer part of it.

"Michael?"

No answer. She heard his breathing and the creaking of his chair.

"Who's behind this?"

"I told you. I don't know. Only Dolores knows the client's identity."

"But why on earth would anyone want to murder Lukas and me?"

"There can be many motives for a contract killing: jealousy, greed, revenge, maybe you saw something you shouldn't have, or maybe someone's got a grudge against you. But thinking about whoever's behind it isn't going to get us one step further right now."

She told Michael about the bank statement she'd seen on Bernd's bedside table.

"Why would Bernd have transferred thirty thousand euros to Ebba's account without either of them telling me about it?" she asked.

"No idea."

"I thought I could trust Ebba, but she told the police that we were meeting at the Brandenburger Tor, as you saw for yourself."

"You might have done the same in her position. Don't forget that, as far as the outside world's concerned, you tried to kill your own child and you're wanted as a dangerous fugitive."

"Ebba's my friend."

"Right now you can't trust anyone, not even your husband."

"I can't believe Bernd would want to harm his own flesh and blood."

"There are plenty of people who have thought the same thing and ended up in an early grave, thanks to some beloved family member."

Gaelle shivered and pulled the blanket up to her chin.

"Bernd was actually the one who delivered that cardboard mirror with the transmitter in it to the hospital," she said.

"That's what they told you at the hospital. But it could just as easily have been someone from Scorpio who broke into your house without leaving a trace, took the mirror from the board in your kitchen, hid the tracking device in it and handed it over at the reception, pretending to be your husband."

He paused.

"Whoever the client is, it's not our concern right now, Gaelle."

Maybe not for you, but it is for me, she thought.

"What matters is staying out of Scorpio's clutches: you, Lukas and me."

She sat up with a jerk.

"What if Lukas isn't as safe at the Charité as you claim?"

"Go to sleep, Gaelle. We need our rest. In a few hours, I have to leave to take care of a couple of things."

"I don't want to stay here alone."

"There's no other way. Don't go up on deck, keep all the curtains closed, lock the door behind me and don't open up until you hear the agreed knocking signal."

She heard something being placed on the table.

"I showed you how the gun works. If you need to use it, don't hesitate for a second."

Michael thought Gaelle had finally fallen asleep, but then another question came in the darkness. "How can you just kill a person like that?"

He was silent.

"I think it's awful," said Gaelle.

Silence.

"The worst thing I ever did was think about letting go of Lukas when I was giving him a bath as a baby," she said. "I don't know why I'm telling you this. I've never told anyone before."

He didn't reply.

"I was disgusted with myself afterwards," she said. "I still am now, when I think back to it."

Her very last question was one that would keep him awake for the rest of the night.

"How old were you when you first killed someone?"

He stayed silent. She wouldn't understand anyway.

He'd been barely fourteen years old.

49

Poland, 1983

*M*ichael knew that, sooner or later, something was going to happen. It was inevitable. Over the past year he'd spent at the detention centre, things had only become worse. There'd been times when the world around him had collapsed and he'd just hoped he'd crumble with it, so he'd be relieved of his misery. One of those moments had been when Sergeant Nowak had come to tell him – two months before his sentence was supposed to end – that his stay at the detention centre was going to be extended.

That day, Michael was in the carpentry workshop, where the boys had been given the job of sanding down and varnishing old furniture, one of the skills they were taught in their practical classes. Michael suspected that the money from the sale of the refurbished furniture disappeared straight into Commandant Kaminski's pockets. But he didn't actually care what happened to the chairs and tables. In these bleak surroundings, where lunch was the highlight of the day, using his own two hands to give new life to a discarded piece of furniture offered a form of hope.

And it was still better than cleaning the latrines, as Janek had been doing for months now. Nowak seemed to have found a new pastime in tormenting the shrimp, as he continued to call Janek. Nowak was also cunning enough to do his bullying out of Kaminski's sight.

With the same taunting attitude, Nowak came to the carpentry workshop to tell Michael that he'd never see his mother again.

"I don't understand," Michael said. "I can go home in two months, can't I?"

Nowak laughed out loud, as if someone in the canteen had just told a good joke.

"There is no home."

"What?"

"Your mother's dead. Died of TB."

The steel brush fell from Michael's hands. He stared at the rifle dangling from Nowak's shoulder, and all he could think about was grabbing the gun and killing Nowak and all the others who had taken him away from his mother so that he couldn't take care of her, until she'd got sicker and sicker and died of exhaustion.

"Pick up that brush and keep working," ordered Nowak. "Now you've got nowhere to go, you'll have to stick it out here for a bit longer, the commandant says."

"Please let me go home in two months. I can look after myself."

Nowak just sneered.

"You're nothing more than a thief, an enemy of the state. We're not going to send the likes of you back out onto the streets."

"Then at least let me ask Commandant Kaminski."

The other boys had stopped working and turned their heads to watch. Their teacher, a stocky man who always wore a dustcoat, disappeared nervously into the equipment room next door.

Michael bent down and picked up the steel brush.

Nowak came a few steps closer.

"Still got a big mouth, eh? You and that scrawny friend of yours."

Michael said nothing.

"As of tomorrow you can start helping him to clean the latrines. And if you don't do it properly, I'll shove your head in," said Nowak.

Michael held the steel brush behind his back and stroked the sharp points with his fingers. In his mind, he could see himself using it to lash out at Nowak and slice his face open.

Maybe that's what would have happened if Nowak had said one more word. But the sergeant spat on the floor and left the room.

The inevitable took place one cold spring night during Michael's second year at the detention centre. Because of the political unrest, Commandant Kaminski had to go to an important meeting in Warsaw for a few days, leaving Nowak temporarily in charge.

The first day, the sergeant had been quiet. But the next night, he called Michael and Janek from the dormitory and ordered them to follow him, threatening them with his gun. Michael just had time to grab the plank with the nail that Janek had taken from the truck when they arrived. He'd kept it hidden under his mattress all that time.

Nowak took them outside, through the gate and towards the forest. Michael noticed that there was no one on guard in the lookout post. Nowak had probably lied to the guard and said he'd take over.

The full moon gave the forest an eerie glow. Nowak took them to a clearing surrounded by old oak trees.

There was a noose hanging from one of the branches. Beneath it, someone had placed a big tree trunk.

Nowak grinned.

"It's time you two learnt who's in charge."

He ordered Janek to stand on the trunk and when the boy didn't move at once, he dragged him over to it. Nowak pulled a length of rope from his pocket and tied Janek's hands behind his back. Then he picked Janek up, stood him on the tree trunk and put the noose around his neck. Janek had to stand on tiptoe to avoid being hanged. The tree trunk moved under his feet, as if it might roll away at any moment.

"It's a bit short," said Nowak. "Seems you're even smaller than I thought."

He turned to Michael.

"Time for a little game," he said. "I owe you one."

He explained the rules to Michael in the tone of a child who knows it's doing something forbidden behind its parents' backs.

"It's chilly for the time of year," he said. "Don't you think?"

Michael didn't reply.

"So you'd better go and fetch my fur hat. It's hanging on a hook near the gate."

Nowak prodded Janek's stomach with the barrel of his rifle.

"The sooner you're back, the better it will be for your little friend. Then we can end this little excursion and go back to bed."

Michael saw that Janek was struggling to keep his balance.

"Please let him go," Michael pleaded. "Let me stand there. I'm taller."

Nowak took a bottle from his inside pocket and raised it to his lips.

"Tick, tick, tick, tick," the sergeant said. "Do you hear that? All those precious seconds ticking away, while you waste time."

Michael turned and started running towards the gate. Branches whipped his face, he fell, scrambled to his feet and finally reached the gate. He had to look for the hat, and as soon as he saw it, he grabbed it and clutched onto it, together with the spiked plank.

I'm coming, he thought, as a branch cut his face open. Don't give up, Janek.

His throat was dry and he was covered in sweat when he got back to the clearing. His first thought was that it was much too quiet.

Nowak was gone.

Janek's body was dangling from the branch. His legs were hanging in the air, not far from the tree trunk, which had rolled away.

Suddenly there was a rustling sound from the bushes and Nowak appeared, buttoning up his trousers.

When he saw Michael, he stopped. The cigarette he'd lit fell from his mouth.

"He's dead," whispered Michael.

Nowak cursed and muttered something about just going for a piss. And how it wasn't his fault that the shrimp couldn't stand on his own two legs.

Nowak walked over to Janek's body and tried to lift it out of the noose. He turned to Michael.

"Don't just stand there staring, Help me, for God's sake."

Michael's fingers slid over the plank and the nail, which he was holding behind his back. At fourteen, he was almost as tall as Sergeant Nowak. He attacked the sergeant from behind and they both rolled over the ground. He didn't give Nowak a chance to shoot. Slashing Nowak's throat with the nail, he snatched his rifle.

And there, in that godforsaken place, he committed his first murder.

50

THE DAY DAWNED cold and drizzly. A mist rose from the water, and Gaelle zipped her fleece up all the way. She stood at the door of the cabin without going on deck, as instructed by Michael. A little earlier, she'd woken to the smell of fresh coffee. She wondered why she hadn't heard the coffee machine, and then saw that he was making coffee the old-fashioned way, by pouring hot water through a filter. It was completely in keeping with who he was, she thought, someone who passed through the world silently and unobtrusively and wanted to keep control of as much as possible himself.

If he hadn't explained to her before why his nickname was the Chameleon, she'd probably have screamed when she saw the stranger in the cabin. With his thin black moustache, short goatee and office attire, Michael looked completely different from the night before.

He seemed tense as he stood there on the deck and asked her again if everything was clear.

"I'll stay here in the boat with the curtains closed, the door locked and wait for the agreed knock before I open the door," said Gaelle.

"With the gun always nearby."

"Just looking at the thing scares me."

Michael ran his fingers over his chin. It looked like the habitual gesture of someone who'd had a goatee for years.

"I still don't think you realise what they're capable of," he said.

"You don't need to say that to someone who's just escaped death by the skin of their teeth."

"I need to get going," he said after a quick look at the jetties. "I'll be gone at least a couple of hours. How do you warn me if you sense danger?"

"Hang the flag at half-mast." She paused. "It's kind of frustrating that I don't have a mobile."

"You don't need one."

"Can't you spare yours? Then I can look at the photos of Lukas for as long as I want."

He shook his head.

"Don't you trust me?" she asked.

"The last thing you should be doing now is phoning people you know. You might as well put out signposts for Dolores's bloodhounds."

He turned around.

"Lock the door," he said before he disappeared.

Gaelle turned the key in the lock and slid the bolts. She walked over to the table, poured a cup of coffee and sat down, trying to ignore the gun on the table beside her.

She aimlessly turned the mug in circles on the tabletop, thinking about Lukas. His pale face in the hospital bed, his closed eyes, deceptively endearing, as if he were asleep – if only that were true! – tubes connecting his little body to devices, a doctor in a white coat standing over the bed...

Was it a real doctor though? If those Scorpio people were so cunning that they could pass themselves off as Bernd at the hospital reception, if they were so brutal that they'd murdered Michael's girlfriend – he hadn't even wanted to tell her exactly how it had happened – if they wouldn't rest until the double murder was carried out, if, as Michael feared, they turned their attention to Lukas now instead of her, then he was in serious danger.

And she was supposed to sit here and wait.

Half an hour later, the coffee was cold, but she had made a decision. She walked to the door, unlocked it and opened it. It was eight in the morning. It was still quiet around the marina, but she could hear the traffic in the distance.

Just as she was about to leave, she thought of something. She walked into the cabin, picked up the gun from the table and put it inside a small backpack that was empty except for a few coins.

She closed the door behind her, locked it and hurried along the jetty.

The first two people she spoke to just walked on without responding. They probably thought she was one of those beggars who come up with excuses for getting money out of people. *Do you have a phone, sir? I urgently need to call someone and mine's been stolen.* She didn't get the chance to add that it was just a short local call and she could pay for it.

When the third and fourth passers-by didn't reply to her question, she decided to try a different approach. On the corner, she saw a petrol station with a small shop section. She walked over to it and stopped in front of the glass door. Behind the counter, an older man stood looking rather glumly in the direction of a gum-chewing teenage girl, the only customer in the shop. Next to the cash register was a telephone in a holder.

She pushed the door open and stepped inside. According to Michael, for now only Scorpio knew that she'd changed her appearance. The police were still circulating her original description. She walked straight up to the manager. The teenage girl didn't look up and was apparently having difficulty choosing which flavour of crisps to have for breakfast.

"Could I ask you something?" said Gaelle.

"You just did," he replied.

Gaelle pointed at the phone on the counter in front of him.

"I urgently need to call the hospital. A family member's been admitted in a critical condition, and my phone's at home."

"I'm a small business owner, not a charity."

Gaelle dug the euros out of her backpack and put them on the counter.

"Not for free. It'll seriously take just a couple of minutes. I just want to know if he's okay."

He looked at the coins, almost six euros, as if calculating what was in it for him.

"Okay," he said, handing the phone to Gaelle with a weary sigh.

"Will you look up a number for me?" she asked. "The Charité, the university hospital in Berlin."

51

THE MANAGER LOOKED UP the hospital's number on his computer and scribbled it on a piece of paper, which he slid across the counter to Gaelle. She put her backpack on the floor, picked up the phone and keyed in the number. The man made no moves to step aside discreetly, so Gaelle moved away and stood with her back to him. She saw that the teenager had finally chosen a big packet of crisps and was sauntering towards the counter. The girl paused again in front of the fridge of soft drinks.

As the phone rang, Gaelle looked outside. There were no cars at the petrol station and except for a ladies' bike in the rack, the shop's car park was empty.

"Charité, reception desk," said a friendly woman's voice on the other end of the line. "How can I help you?"

"Could you please connect me to the head of the unit where Lukas Römer is currently a patient?"

She heard fingers tapping on a keyboard.

"Are you close family?"

"Lukas is my godson. His condition is critical and I'd urgently like to speak to the doctor who's treating him. I have medical information that could be vitally important."

A silence followed. Then the sound of a keyboard again.

"I'm afraid I can't help you. Lukas Römer is no longer a patient here."

It was as if the ground had opened up beneath Gaelle's feet. "What?"

"He was transferred by ambulance to another hospital early this morning."

"Where? And why?"

Her words were so loud that the girl turned her head. Gaelle could hear muffled voices on the other end of the line, as if the receptionist were arguing with someone. Then the woman's voice again, but not as friendly as before, more cautious.

"What was your name again?" she asked.

Gaelle hung up. Still with her back to the manager, she quickly keyed in the number of Ebba's mobile.

After a few seconds, it was answered, and she heard Ebba's sleepy voice.

"It's Gaelle, and I don't have much time. I want you to be honest with me."

"Where are you? You didn't turn up at the Brandenburger Tor."

"I was there, Ebba. And I saw that you weren't alone."

There was a silence.

"I just found out that Lukas was transferred to another hospital this morning," Gaelle continued. "I don't know where it is or who gave instructions for the transfer."

"That's strange. Bernd didn't mention it last night."

"Don't lie, Ebba."

"I'm not lying."

"Then tell me why Bernd transferred thirty thousand euros to your bank account."

"What kind of nonsense of this?"

"I saw the statement with my own eyes."

"You're talking gibberish, Gaelle. You urgently need to be admitted. And that was why I let the police know: to help you."

Behind her, Gaelle heard the manager coughing, apparently as a signal that the telephone call had lasted long enough now.

"I'm not done with you," Gaelle said before hanging up.

With the telephone in her hand, she walked back to the counter. The girl hurried to get to the till before Gaelle and, as she did so, her foot brushed the backpack that Gaelle had dropped there. Gaelle had apparently forgotten to zip it up. The gun slipped halfway out of the backpack. The girl saw it too. She stopped chewing, and her jaw dropped. Her eyes moved from the backpack to Gaelle, to the unsuspecting manager, and then back to Gaelle.

Before the girl could do anything, Gaelle stooped, dropped the phone, grabbed the gun from the backpack and stood back up.

Staring at her with a look of utter amazement, the manager slowly put his hands in the air. The teenager did the same, with a bottle of Coke in one hand and an XL packet of crisps in the other.

"Come out from behind the counter," Gaelle said to the manager.

He did as he was told and went to stand beside the girl. With an unsteady hand, Gaelle pointed the gun at both of them. She heard the sound of a car driving past. The manager glanced at the exit.

"Don't move," said Gaelle.

She hoped neither of them could hear the trembling in her voice.

She took a few steps backwards until she was near the door. Without taking the gun off them, she quickly turned the OPEN sign to CLOSED. The manager lowered his hands a little, but within a couple of seconds, she was back at the counter.

"Don't do anything stupid," she said.

He put his hands high in the air.

Behind the counter, she saw two doors: one of them had a sign saying PRIVATE and the other had a key in the lock.

"What's behind the door on the right?"

"A storeroom."

"Walk to it," said Gaelle. "Slowly and with your hands in the air."

"What are you planning to do to us?" asked the manager.

"If you do as I say, nothing's going to happen to you."

The man swallowed.

"Open that door," Gaelle said to him. "And switch the light on."

The storeroom turned out to be a small space with no side doors or windows.

"Go inside," said Gaelle.

Then she told them both to empty their pockets and put the contents on the floor. The manager didn't have a phone, but the girl did. Still holding them at gunpoint, she slowly knelt down and took the girl's phone.

"I only just got it," said the girl, ready to burst into tears.

"I'll leave your phone on the counter," said Gaelle. "And I won't touch the till either."

"What exactly are you hoping to achieve?" asked the manager.

I just want to buy time, thought Gaelle.

She closed the door, turned the key, walked to the counter and left the mobile there. Then she put the gun in her backpack and left the shop.

Outside, she passed the rack with the solitary bike. It wasn't locked up. The girl would have to do without her bike for a while, unlike her phone.

Gaelle jumped on the bike and raced down the street. At this speed, she'd be at Ebba's in just over quarter of an hour.

52

GAELLE PEDALLED AS HARD as she could, glancing back now and then to make sure she wasn't being followed. A black Volvo had been driving behind her for a while, and when both she and the car had to stop for a red light, she took a quick glance inside. The only occupant was a woman of about seventy who was staring at the traffic light, her hands gripping the wheel.

The light turned green. Gaelle turned right along the bike path and the Volvo crossed the junction. Without slowing, she cycled on along the street as the houses and trees flashed past, as impossible to grasp as her thoughts.

What if Lukas hadn't been taken to another hospital at all but had fallen into Scorpio's clutches? According to Michael, the organisation had the right resources and connections to arrange something like that. Using false documents, accomplices and a fake ambulance, they could fool the hospital staff, and they wouldn't hesitate to dispose of anyone who got in their way. She rode over a bump and the backpack bounced, as if someone were tapping her on the shoulder to remind her of its contents.

She glimpsed her reflection in the window of a house. A woman with a gun on her way to see another woman, desperately looking for answers.

She turned down the dirt road that led to the renovated farmhouse where Ebba lived. Just as well Rolf was in the south of France now. She remembered how happy Ebba had been when they'd signed the contract more than fifteen years ago. It had been the height of summer, and Ebba and Rolf had invited them to celebrate the purchase with a barbecue in the garden of their new house, which was still uninhabitable. Bernd had got so drunk that he'd fallen asleep in one of the garden chairs and no one could get him to budge. Ebba had just put a blanket over him, and they'd left him to sleep it off. After Rolf had headed back to the place they were renting, because he had to work the next day, she and Ebba had gone on talking all through the night, until Bernd had woken up the next morning with a raging hangover.

There was no bike path along the narrow road and when she heard a tractor approaching from behind, she stopped and stood on a driveway. She tried to figure out exactly what she wanted to know, questions Ebba would answer only with a gun pointing at her. As her hand slid over the backpack and she felt the hardness of the weapon, she thought about how smoothly it had gone at the petrol station. Her fear of the gun and what she could do with it had pretty quickly given way to a different feeling: power. The power to make other people do what she wanted. If this gun could get Lukas back to her unharmed, put an end to this nightmare, help her to prove her innocence and make sure that whoever was behind all this would get what they deserved, she wouldn't hesitate to use it.

The tractor went by, sending dust into the air. Gaelle rubbed her eyes. The man at the wheel, with his powerful neck and sturdy physique, made her think of Bernd for a moment. As the tractor drove off, Gaelle pondered the considerable sum of money that Bernd had transferred to Ebba's account without either of them telling her about it. What if the shares in the investment portfolio she'd inherited from her mother had been released earlier than Bernd claimed? What if that was where the money had come from?

She wondered if she'd ignored anything else in recent years that should have been a warning.

Bernd coming back from an evening at the gym in the same clothes he'd supposedly worn to go straight from the office to the gym. But the sports clothes in his bag weren't sweaty. And the towel was unused.

Her suspicion hadn't lasted long. He always had an explanation.

"I didn't go, had to finish something at the office."

"Went for a drink with a colleague. I'll do fitness for two next time."

"The place was shut. A death in the family, apparently. So I went to play snooker with an old schoolmate I bumped into."

She'd fallen for all of it. She simply hadn't wanted to see it. It was because of the mist inside her head, the dark thoughts that had risen up after the birth of Lukas and had stayed there during her mother's sickness and death.

The cloud of dust on the track had settled by now. She jumped onto the bike and rode on, wondering if she was strong enough to face whatever was hiding behind those mists.

The names raced through her head with every rotation of the pedals.

Bernd and Ebba. Ebba and Bernd.

Lukas.

Lukas. Lukas.

He could hear strange voices in a language he didn't recognise. The men who were speaking were in the room with him, but they couldn't see him. Or at least they were pretending they couldn't. He didn't know if they were doctors – neither of them was wearing a white coat – but the bigger one was carrying one of those machines doctors use to check people's heart rates.

Looking down, he saw that he was lying in a bed, wearing a disgusting pair of purple pyjamas he'd never have chosen himself – and neither would his mum.

Where was she?

Where were his mum and dad?

He tried to turn his head, but it felt like his body was being held in some kind of clamp. He couldn't move his arms and legs. On the ceiling directly above him, a bluebottle was crawling slowly along. *Any minute now it's going to fly down and sit on my face*, he thought.

He tried to say something to the men who were in the room. He wanted to ask them to swat the fly, but no sound came from his mouth.

Worse than that, there was a sort of tube in his throat, so he couldn't even close his mouth.

If that fly falls, it'll go into my mouth and I might choke on it.

Where's Mum?

Why isn't she coming?

He started crying.

There was no one to answer him.

53

E BBA'S FARMHOUSE was along a private road. If Gaelle turned down the driveway now, everyone inside the house would see her coming. It would better to put her bike down somewhere and enter the garden through the cornfield at the side. She could easily push her way through the surrounding line of spruce trees.

Somewhere nearby, she heard the sound of a tractor again. Maybe he'd gone the other way at the fork, but she didn't want to risk the driver seeing her here. She jumped off her bike and walked it into the cornfield until she couldn't be seen from the road. She put the bike down. She could just see over the top of the maize. Orienting herself by Ebba's tiled roof, she headed in the right direction. She came to the edge of the field and pushed the stalks apart. The restored house was built of red bricks with white woodwork and had a carport with space for two vehicles. Peering through the spruces, she could see that there were no cars parked on the driveway or in the double carport. Perhaps Ebba wasn't at home.

This would be the ideal moment to break the window of the pantry at the back of house, and then to climb in and search the house for anything that might shed some light on the affair. A suspicious document, a bank statement, an email on Ebba's laptop, anything that might be evidence she could take to the police.

She stood in the cornfield and looked back, wondering if she was just imagining it or the corncobs in the middle of the field were moving a little.

As if someone's making their way through the field.

She shivered. She thought about Michael, how he'd warned her about Scorpio's assassins and insisted she shouldn't leave the boat. She could imagine his anger when he found her gone.

But it wasn't his child who was in danger.

She took a few steps forward, squeezed her way through the spruces and into the garden and went round to the back of the house. The garden, so neglected when Ebba and Rolf had bought the house, had since been transformed into an elegant space with a swimming pool, a wooden deck, a lawn without a trace of weeds and a pool house. There was wicker furniture on the deck, in more or less the same spot where Bernd had fallen asleep that first night and Ebba had tucked him in with a blanket.

Maybe a little too lovingly.

There was a rake against the wall of the pool house. She grabbed it and headed straight for the pantry window. Using the handle, she smashed the window, removed the shattered glass as well as she could, and climbed inside.

The glass cracked under her shoes.

She stopped to listen for any indication that someone was in the house.

Nothing.

In the corner of the room she saw the light of the security system. She walked through the house to the enclosed porch and tapped in the code, which Ebba had never bothered to shield from her.

But maybe Ebba had changed the code now that she had a friend who was on the run from the police.

Heart pounding, she waited.

The display signalled that the alarm was off.

239

She left the porch and stood in the hallway. The door on the right led into Rolf's office, where he stayed in touch with clients in the evenings. Ebba never went in there.

Gaelle pushed open the door and looked inside. It looked like Rolf was already preparing for his move. The filing cabinet was open and empty, except for a few binders. There were no files on his desk, just a few cardboard boxes against the wall. She went over and took a quick look. Nothing out of the ordinary. Brochures for houses, model contracts, documents related to an estate agent's work.

She left the office and paused in the hallway.

There was a sound coming from upstairs. A sort of rapid tapping sound. She grabbed the gun from her backpack and slowly headed upstairs, weapon at the ready. Ebba and Rolf's bedroom was on the first floor. Next to it was the guestroom, which doubled as Ebba's hobby room. Gaelle had always thought it was a bit cluttered, with a single bed in there, an exercise bike, a television and a desk where Ebba kept her laptop. If there was anything to be found in the house, it would probably be there.

When she got to the top of the stairs, she stopped on the landing. There was that rapid tapping again. It was coming from the bathroom. The door was ajar, and she went in.

Someone hadn't turned off the tap in the shower properly. As soon as she turned it all the way, the dripping stopped.

She walked from the bathroom to the guestroom and pushed the door open. No sign of a laptop on the desk. The bed was neatly made, with folded pyjamas beside the pillow and a few items on the bedside table, which suggested someone had recently slept there. A half-full glass of water, a tissue and what looked like a romance novel.

Maybe Ebba had been sleeping there because the scent of Rolf lingering in their former bedroom was a constant reminder of the impending divorce. Gaelle placed her gun on the bedside table and began searching the drawers, but she didn't find anything that warranted extra attention.

She looked at the clock.

She wondered if anyone had found the girl and the manager of the petrol station yet and how quickly the police would be on her trail. As if that were the worst danger. The warning Michael had given her was worse: *The last thing you should be doing now is phoning people you know. You might as well put out signposts for Dolores's bloodhounds.* She remembered the unseen presence she'd felt out in the field.

Imagination – it was just the imagination of a woman under extreme stress. Now she just had to try to focus and search the house for any clues that might help.

She bent down to look under the bed. All she saw was a week-end bag that, at first sight, appeared to be empty. She reached out and pulled the bag towards her. On the bottom was a neatly folded blue Armani shirt. It looked exactly like the one she'd found for Bernd last year during the summer sales. She'd told him she thought it might be suitable for an evening walk on the beach, followed by a candlelit dinner.

He'd worn the shirt only once, on a walk that had ended in an argument because she thought he never listened when she wanted to talk about her dead mother. Lukas had been staying at a friend's. Having abandoned the walk, they'd come home. Bernd had said that he'd go out and find some fun for himself. Then he'd climbed into his car and raced off. He hadn't come home until the small hours. She'd heard him clattering about in the living room, where she'd found him snoring on the sofa the next morning.

The shirt had never made its way into the laundry and she'd never found it in the house. She'd assumed he'd thrown it away after the argument. So as not to fan the flames, she'd never asked him about it directly.

But now she'd found the same shirt, in a weekend bag that belonged to Ebba. Hands shaking, she picked it up.

There was no doubt about it. She could smell the faint traces of his aftershave.

She tried to remember if she'd really missed that many signals: eyes intimately meeting, a hand that rested on an arm too long, exaggerated laughter after jokes or telephone conversations that abruptly ended.

Then she gasped.

She could hear a car pulling up on the other side of the house. And then the sound of the front door.

54

THE GUESTROOM DOOR was slightly open. Gaelle walked over to it and stood out of sight, listening. Downstairs, doors opened and closed. She heard heels on the wooden floor.

Ebba had come home. Gaelle wasn't worried that she'd see the alarm wasn't on. Ebba was so laid-back that she often forgot to switch on the alarm when she left the house – much to Rolf's annoyance. Presumably she'd just think she'd forgotten again.

She didn't hear any voices, which suggested Ebba was alone. That would make it easier to surprise her, but it wasn't going to be a pleasant visit. She looked at the gun in her hand. For a moment, she considered giving Ebba the chance to confess everything honestly, without using the weapon, but that would just be a waste of time.

Lukas's life was on the line.

She walked out of the guestroom, across the hallway and slowly down the dark wooden stairs, her footsteps muffled by the carpet. Her blood was rushing in her ears and every fibre of her body was tense. She barely looked at the framed etchings on the walls. They were all drawings of a female nude, seen from behind, and Ebba had always been cagey about whether or not she had been the model.

It seemed there were other things she didn't know about Ebba. Her grip on the gun tightened as she reached the last step and set her foot on the black tiled floor. It was time. In a few minutes, she'd know the truth.

Just three steps, and she was at the door to the living room. Resting her hand on the door handle, she listened.

She heard a man's voice.

Followed by music.

The radio, she thought. Ebba's turned on the radio in the living room. *Or has she?*

Her fingers trembled on the door handle. These were the last few metres, the crucial moment during a race when everything was still open and you had to judge your opponent's strength without overestimating your own reserves before you started the final sprint.

It was a question of timing – not a second too soon and not a second too late.

And sometimes you just had to go for it.

She pushed the door open and aimed her gun at the figure sitting on the sofa by the open fireplace, back towards her.

When the woman turned around, all kinds of thoughts went through Gaelle's mind. *Unexpected things happen in races too: false starts, an opponent getting in your way by veering from her track, your shoe suddenly coming loose.*

That was what she was thinking as Lore jumped up from the sofa and dropped her wine glass on the floor.

Ebba's younger sister looked at her with a mixture of surprise, horror and desperate fear. She had her blond hair in a bun – something Gaelle should have noticed immediately, as Ebba never wore it that way. She was wearing a black dress and had swapped her heels for slippers, as if she were in her own home.

The silence seemed to last forever. Lore stood up, just few metres away from her, close to the open fireplace, which was not lit.

Shivering, Gaelle realised that there was a chill throughout the whole house. She was the first to speak.

"Where's Ebba?"

"Out shopping."

Gaelle heard a trace of anger in Lore's next question.

"What are you doing here?"

"I'm waiting for your sister. She was the one I wanted to see. Not you."

Gaelle's gaze slid out through the window, where a rundown Mazda was standing in the driveway. If the guestroom hadn't been at the back of the house, she'd have seen whose car it was and she wouldn't have been taken by surprise.

"What do you need Ebba for? You've completely lost it, Gaelle. Only the doctors can help you now."

"I'll decide that for myself."

"You're scaring me to death with that gun."

"When's Ebba coming home?"

"I don't know."

Lore looked at her phone, which was on the glass coffee table.

"Want me to call her?"

"Don't you dare," said Gaelle.

Lore's eyes moved restlessly around the room. She glanced through the windows that looked out onto the driveway.

"What is it?" asked Gaelle. "Are you expecting Ebba back any minute? Is your mother coming?"

Lore shook her head and took one step to the side, closer to the coffee table. Gaelle saw that she was wearing Ebba's suede slippers.

"Stay there," she said, looking down. "Seems you feel quite at home here now that Rolf's not planning to come back, don't you? Got a bit cramped lived in your council flat above the chip shop, did it?"

Lore pursed her lips.

"Mum and I are here because Ebba needs us. The two of you know each other inside out. You should know what a state she's in because of the whole thing with Rolf and…" – she paused for a moment – "she was the one who found you and Lukas, after you…"

"After I *what*, Lore?" asked Gaelle. "Feeling brave enough to say what you and the rest of the world suspect me of?"

Lore didn't reply.

Gaelle took a step closer. "I'll tell you what's been going on. It'll change the image you have of Ebba – your dear sister and my so-called best friend – for ever."

"How do you mean?"

Gaelle swallowed.

"Bernd and Ebba are having an affair. No idea how long it's been going on. He recently transferred thirty thousand euros into her bank account. I don't know what stories she's been telling him, but it looks like she used the money to send a bunch of contract killers after me and Lukas."

"That's bullshit. You really are out of your mind."

Just as Gaelle was about to reply, she heard the crunch of the gravel outside. Then an engine stopped. Even before she saw the driver get out of the car, she knew who it was.

She'd recognise the sound of that diesel engine anywhere.

Through the net curtains, she saw Bernd closing the car door and, head bowed, walking to the house.

55

G AELLE LEANT ON THE WALL in the living room, waiting for the doorbell to ring. There was a tension between her and Lore that she couldn't quite grasp. Even though she was being held at gunpoint, there was something defiant about Lore's attitude. And it had something to do with Ebba's slippers.

I'm missing something, thought Gaelle. She quickly took stock, snapping out of it when the doorbell rang.

"Walk slowly into the hallway," said Gaelle. "Leave the door to the living room slightly ajar and open the front door. Let Bernd in without doing anything stupid. Don't forget I'm holding a gun."

Lore didn't move at first. She didn't start walking slowly towards the door until Gaelle waved the gun at her. Gaelle stayed about a metre away from her and followed her, watching out for unexpected movements.

What the hell am I missing here?

Ebba's slippers were a couple of sizes too big for Lore. Why would someone walk around in her sister's slippers?

Because they're more comfortable than high heels. Because she's not planning to leave any time soon.

Because she's staying here.

Lore was now standing by the door into the hallway.

"Stop there," said Gaelle. "Turn around."

"You told me to open the door."

"Look at me," said Gaelle. "I want to see your face."

Slowly, Lore turned around.

"You're the one who's using the guestroom, aren't you?" said Gaelle.

Lore didn't reply.

"Ebba doesn't read crappy novels – and you do," Gaelle continued.

"What does it matter what I read?"

"That weekend bag under the bed is yours, not Ebba's." *With Bernd's shirt in it.*

The bell rang again. Twice this time.

"I was wrong," said Gaelle. "Bernd and Ebba never had an affair."

"So you finally realise the stupid ideas you've got into your head?"

Gaelle's voice was hoarse when she continued.

"It's not about your sister. It's about you, isn't it, *Eleonore*?"

Lore. That was what everyone called her. It sounded better than her official name, Eleonore, Ebba had once said – so long ago that Gaelle had almost forgotten.

E. Steinsfeld. That was what the bank statement had said. It wasn't Ebba who had sent Scorpio's killers after her. It was Eleonore.

There was a knock on the window. Gaelle saw Bernd peering through the net curtains without seeing her.

Had he known what Lore was going to use that thirty thousand euros for? That thought was too awful for words.

Out of the corner of her eye, she suddenly saw a dark shadow diving at her. Nails dug deep into her right arm.

Gaelle screamed and lashed out at Lore.

The gun fell from her hands. She saw Lore duck, grab the gun off the floor and aim it at her. She sprinted towards the kitchen, heading for the back door.

A shot rang out.

The doctors who stood beside his bed and regularly checked the machines were talking in a language he didn't understand. They definitely weren't German doctors, but they also weren't British or American, because even though he was only seven, he already understood a few English words. A boy from Afghanistan had joined his class this year and he could speak English as well as his mother tongue. His new friend had taught him a few sentences, like *How are you?* and *My name is Lukas.*

No one here asked him how he was.

"How are you?" he'd whispered to the doctor who removed the tube from his throat.

It had hurt a bit, but he'd mainly been glad because now he could close his mouth and the bluebottle, which was still in the room, wouldn't fall into it.

The doctor, a man with glasses, didn't reply. He studied the machine with all the dials and buttons and said something in that strange language of his to the female doctor with the short grey hair who came to join him. They were apparently arguing about something and after a while the female doctor nodded at the male doctor.

Then she turned to Lukas. She had cool blue eyes.

"My name is Lukas," he said in a hoarse voice.

"We've removed the feeding tube," she said. Much to his surprise, she spoke fluent German. "You must eat something this afternoon."

It was an order. She didn't even ask what he liked to eat.

"I'm not hungry."

"You must eat to get stronger," said the woman.

It didn't sound friendly, but it wasn't unfriendly either. Maybe she had a face that wasn't made for smiling, thought Lukas. That was what his mum sometimes said when they met sour-faced people.

The doctors left the room. Lukas looked around. There were no windows. He was still tied to that horrible bed with a tube connected to one of the machines. His brain was working a bit slowly, as if he'd slept in and his brain hadn't quite woken up yet. He remembered a few things: who his mum and dad were and what they looked like, that his mum stayed at home and his dad worked at a bank, that they lived in a big house in Potsdam, that his classmate from Afghanistan was called Mo and that, like Mo, he loved football. He remembered all of that.

So what was he doing here? Why wasn't he playing football with Mo in the school playground or sitting at the table at home? Something bad must have happened.

Maybe a car had run him over on the way to school and he'd banged his head, so he didn't even remember that he'd been in an accident.

That would explain a lot.

But not everything.

If he'd ended up under a car and then in the children's ward at a hospital, where were his mum and dad? And why weren't there any other children here? And why weren't the doctors speaking German to each other, when they clearly could?

All these questions were making him really tired.

His eyes fell shut.

A while later, he awoke with a start. He'd had a really scary dream and there was no one to comfort him.

He'd dreamt he wasn't in a hospital room, but in a cell.

56

From behind the three-seater sofa, Gaelle saw that the bullet had drilled a hole in the wall, around five centimetres from a painting Ebba had said cost a few months' salary. She quickly crawled on all fours behind the sofa, peeped around it and saw Lore approaching with a look of determination on her face – and the gun in her hands. Apparently Lore's marksmanship was about the same level as her own and she couldn't hit a target from a distance, but if she just stayed here and waited, Lore would be standing next to her in a few seconds and would shoot her at point-blank range.

She heard the sound of breaking glass from the kitchen next door – Bernd, who in his haste probably hadn't noticed that there was already a broken window and had now shattered the glass of the back door to get in. He shouted to ask if everything was okay.

For a moment, Lore was distracted. Gaelle reached out, grabbed a vase of flowers off the table beside the sofa and threw it in Lore's direction. She didn't wait to see if she'd hit her assailant. Hearing a scream and then the sound of the vase smashing on the floor, she leapt up and ran across the living room and through the open door into the kitchen.

Just around the corner, she bumped into Bernd. He seemed worn out in his creased shirt, with dark circles under his eyes. Her husband looked at her in surprise and grabbed her by the shoulders, the panic audible in his voice when he asked her what she was doing here.

"I thought it was burglars," he said.

"Let go of me!" Gaelle screamed. "She's trying to kill me!"

"Who?"

Lore appeared behind Gaelle.

"Her! Your mistress," said Gaelle. "She hired contract killers to get me and Lukas out of the way."

"What?"

"She used that thirty thousand euros you gave her. I saw the bank statement on your bedside table. But her plan failed, and Lukas and I survived. And that's what happened in the house on Tuesday."

Lore was coming closer.

"She's insane, Bernd," she said. "She came bursting in here like a madwoman, and this gun is hers too. She's the one who was trying to kill *me*."

Bernd loosened his grip on Gaelle's shoulders and in a single movement he pulled her behind his back so that his body formed a shield. He held out his hand in a defensive gesture and told Lore not to come any closer.

Lore stayed where she was.

"Give me that gun before any accidents happen, Lore."

She held the weapon firmly in her hands.

"Step aside, Bernd."

"That thirty thousand euros was a loan, meant for you to buy a car for your new job as a sales rep," he said slowly. "You were going to pay me back in monthly instalments. I had to bend over backwards to keep it hidden from Gaelle. You knew that the money came from the investment portfolio she'd inherited from her mother."

Lore just looked at him.

"But it seems you're still driving around in that old Mazda. So what happened to the money, Lore?"

"The new car's on order. Now get out of my way."

He slowly shook his head.

"That loan was kind of a goodbye present," he said. "Whatever happened between us... you knew it was over and that I'd chosen my family."

A look of grim determination passed over Lore's face.

"After a year and a half together, you wanted to dump me," she whispered. "Put me out with the rubbish, to go back to your wife and child for good. I couldn't just let that happen, could I?"

Bernd was still holding his left arm protectively behind him, around Gaelle's body, hugging her tightly to him.

"What was the plan, Lore?" he asked. "To comfort the poor widower after his wife had killed their child and then herself in a fit of madness?"

Bernd's hands became fists.

"To clear the way for you to move in with me and live off the inheritance from Gaelle's mother? Was that the plan?"

"Stop it, Bernd."

"Crazy bitch. Tell me where the hell my son is, our Lukas. The police say he was abducted from the hospital this morning by people with fake documents. They've lost all trace of him. Where did those people take him?"

"I don't know, Bernd," said Lore. "Honestly. You have to believe me."

"Call them. Tell them not to hurt Lukas. That the whole thing's called off. Tell them I'll pay twice what you paid as long as they leave Gaelle and Lukas alone."

"I don't have a telephone number for them."

"If you ever cared about me, Lore, then do as I ask."

She didn't react.

"Get out of the way, Bernd. It's the last time I'll ask."

Gaelle felt Bernd's body tense as if he were preparing to jump.

What came next happened so quickly that there was nothing she could do. Bernd pushed her away, yelled at her to lie on the floor and, in a couple of steps, was beside Lore. He tried to pull the gun from her hands, but Lore didn't let go and, in the ensuing struggle, a shot was fired.

A bloodstain appeared on Bernd's creased shirt. He staggered, looked at Gaelle and grabbed his chest. Then he crashed to the floor and lay there, motionless.

Lore shrieked like a creature in agony. Then she came for Gaelle. The look on her face said she had nothing left to lose.

57

"I'M GOING TO DESTROY YOU, Gaelle," she said. "I'm going to shoot you, and then I'm going to watch as you slowly bleed to death."

She raised her gun.

"Wait," said Gaelle. "Bernd's still breathing. Call an ambulance. You can still stop this before it's too late."

"It's already too late. For you, for me. And I've lost Bernd anyway, whether he survives or not."

Gaelle was beside the kitchen table, struggling to get to her feet, but Lore kicked her in the head and she fell again, dizzy, and stayed on the ground. Lore had lowered the gun a little. It looked like she was getting tired and her attention was drifting.

"Where did they take Lukas?" asked Gaelle. "Is he still alive?"

"No idea and, to tell the truth, I couldn't care less what happens to the little brat."

"Don't talk like that about my son."

"He was in the way, just like you."

Bernd tried to say something, but his words were unintelligible.

"Please, Lore," said Gaelle. "Call an ambulance."

"I'm planning to." She smiled unpleasantly before continuing. "After shooting you dead here in the kitchen and when I'm sure Bernd can't tell any tales, I'm going to call the emergency services to tell them that something terrible just happened here."

Gaelle looked at Bernd through a haze of tears. He was lying so still on the kitchen floor, as if already dead, but she could still see his chest rising and falling irregularly.

"I'll tell the police that you broke in here, with that gun of yours – which is true – and that you threatened me like a crazy person and then shot Bernd because he tried to protect me. I'll also explain to them that I managed to grab the gun and had no choice but to shoot you in self-defence. I'll use your dead fingers to fire at Bernd again, so the gunpowder traces on your hands will confirm my story."

"You're good at making up stories, aren't you, Lore?" said Gaelle. "Do you get your inspiration from your trashy little novels? Do you fill your own empty life by invading other people's lives? You've always been a parasite."

"Shut your mouth," said Lore. "I'd better just end this now, so I don't have to listen to you anymore. You always have to be so condescending, don't you? About me, and my benefits, and my council flat. Well, look where it's got you."

She spat on the floor next to Gaelle's feet.

Gaelle's right hand slowly slid backwards to clutch the nearest chair leg.

Lore's voice was shrill when she started talking about her sister.

"Good old Ebba. Why did she have to be the one to intervene when you and Lukas were supposed to die? I don't know what went wrong that day or how you managed to send a message to warn her. Those guys aren't worth the damn money. You shouldn't have survived."

"Sometimes things happen that you don't expect," said Gaelle. "Or help comes from an unlikely quarter."

She had a firm hold of the chair leg now and was ready to scramble to her feet and strike.

*

From the living room came the sound of Lore's ringtone, a cheery film tune that cut through the silence. Automatically, Lore looked in that direction.

Gaelle leapt up, dragging the chair with her, raised it in the air and smashed it onto Lore's head. Lore blocked the move too late and couldn't help dropping the gun on the floor.

Gaelle let go of the chair and dived for the gun. Clutching it tightly, she aimed it at Lore, who was holding on to the counter after the blow to her head. Her left eye was closed, and her bottom lip was bleeding.

"Where's Lukas?" said Gaelle.

Lore's face creased into a ghastly, bloody smile.

"Even if I knew, I'd never tell you."

She stepped towards Gaelle.

"Stop there," said Gaelle.

Lore lunged at her and, before Gaelle realised what she was doing, she pulled the trigger. Two, three times. Lore collapsed on the floor. Gaelle turned around, put down the gun and crouched down beside Bernd.

"Hang on. I'll call an ambulance before I go."

The front of his shirt was soaked with blood.

Slowly, he opened his eyes and looked at her.

"I'm sorry," he whispered.

Gaelle was about to go and use Lore's phone to call an ambulance, but Bernd grabbed her wrist. His eyes were closing, but he was trying to say something else.

"Lukas."

She leant towards him and held her ear above his lips so that she could make out what Bernd was whispering to her.

"Find him, Gaelle."

Then she felt his grip around his wrist loosen. For what felt like minutes, she tried in vain to find a pulse.

Then she headed outside with the gun in one hand and the keys to Bernd's car in the other.

She started the engine, but she broke down when she saw, on the passenger seat, his favourite jacket, which he'd never wear again.

58

HALF AN HOUR LATER, Gaelle parked Bernd's car in a dead end near Kastanienallee, where Michael's boat was moored. She'd driven on automatic pilot and it was only when she turned off the engine that she realised where she was. Her hands were trembling and covered with splashes of dried blood. She looked at them as if they weren't her own hands, but those of a person she would never have wanted to become: a murderer.

The thoughts shooting through her head made her feel like she was losing her mind.

Was it Bernd's blood on her hands or Lore's?

What do you call a child who's lost his father?

How do you tell your son that someone took a hit out on him?

There was a loud knock on the driver's side window.

Startled, she looked up. There was a woman on the pavement in a baggy tracksuit and with a broom in her hands. Gaelle tried to look as neutral as possible as she pressed the button to lower the window.

"Your car's in front of my garage," the woman said in an unfriendly voice.

Gaelle looked at the woman's garage door and saw that the bumper of Bernd's company car was about ten centimetres onto the woman's territory. Unless she drove a limo, getting out of the garage wouldn't be a problem. But this was not the time to argue. She mustn't attract any attention. Although she'd taken the gun, it wouldn't be hard for the police to find out that she'd

259

been at the crime scene. Her fingerprints were everywhere, and she'd also trodden in a pool of blood as she'd walked out of the kitchen past Lore's body.

She shivered.

"Well, are you going to move?" the woman asked, chin in the air, ready for battle.

"I'll be gone in a minute," Gaelle said, keeping her blood-stained hands hidden from the woman. "I just had to make a quick phone call."

The woman glared at her.

Gaelle forced a smile and even managed to wish a her a nice day. She started the engine. In her rear-view mirror, she saw the woman watching as she drove out of the street. A few streets on, close to the water, she found a free parking space. She took the keys from the ignition, got out of the car and locked it.

She stared at the boats by the jetty up ahead. Although there were only a few clouds in the sky, it seemed as if a veil of grey were covering the whole area.

Bernd was gone. And if she didn't find Lukas in time, she'd not only be a widow, but also a mother without a child.

It was almost midday. A few hours had passed since she'd left the boat and returned here. In that time, a lot could have happened. She had to go on hoping that Michael had found a way to get Lukas back.

If he was still alive.

As she did up her zip, she felt the bulge of the gun in her pocket. With her hands in her pockets and her gaze fixed on the ground, so there was no chance of eye contact with passers-by, she strolled towards Michael's boat. She tried to imagine how he would react when she told him what had happened. Presumably he'd be furious because she'd ignored his advice and left the boat, which had only complicated the situation. Maybe he'd refuse to work with her and disappear for good.

The best-case scenario would be a cold silence.

She saw the boat, in the same spot, with the curtains still closed. And yet something had changed.

She stopped in the middle of the path to the jetty.

The significance of the flag at half-mast slowly dawned on her.

Michael was on the boat. He opened a closet and took out his wetsuit. He'd made the necessary arrangements with the representative from the rental company about what would happen with the boat. He'd leave the keys in the ignition, and the tip was in an envelope next to the wheel.

Quickly, he took off his clothes and changed into the wetsuit. If he chose the right moment, he'd manage to lower himself off the back of the boat and swim away.

He'd never expected Gaelle to make a run for it. He'd waited a while for her to return, but he couldn't stay here any longer. Two suspicious-looking men had been hanging around for a while. Maybe a third was on the lookout somewhere. He'd seen the two of them inspecting parked cars, watching the boats and using hand signals to communicate with each other at a distance. As soon as it got dark, they might well come and check out the interiors of the boats too.

He'd hung the flag at half-mast and hoped that Gaelle wouldn't make another foolish mistake by ignoring the signal.

He looked outside, slipped out onto the deck and sank into the water at the back of the boat.

*

Lukas thought the vanilla custard his mum made at home was way better than this stuff out of a pot. After one mouthful, he'd made up his mind, but there was no one in the room he could tell about his mum's vanilla custard. Or about how much he missed her. He forced himself to eat it all, so the doctor wouldn't have any reason to nag at him that he really needed to eat something, as he'd done before he left the room. If the doctor didn't have to complain about his food or about Lukas drinking enough water, then he'd have more time to answer his questions. Because the doctor had said he was far too busy for that.

Lukas scraped the pot empty and put it down on his bedside table with the spoon, next to his glasses. Although he was both hungry and queasy, he felt better than before. The woman doctor had disconnected all his tubes and taken him to the toilet. The bathroom was through a side door. He didn't even need to go out into the corridor. That was too bad, because then at least he could have seen more of this children's ward, he thought. And no one had answered when he'd asked if he was in a hospital near Potsdam or if he'd been run over on his bike.

Like his room, the bathroom had no windows. When he was standing in front of the toilet bowl, he'd asked the woman to leave the room, because he couldn't pee if anyone was watching. She'd done as he'd asked, but she'd left the door open a bit. He'd taken his time to pee and then wash his hands, hoping he might spot something that would tell him something about where he was. But he couldn't find a single clue. The towels didn't have a logo like the ones in the hotel in Altensteig where they'd stayed and there weren't any funny posters like the ones in the school toilets that said that clever children always wash their hands.

When he left the bathroom, he'd staggered and had to hold on to the door handle so that he didn't fall. The woman had hurried over and grabbed him rather roughly. He'd had no choice but to accept her help to get back to bed. All that time she said nothing.

He looked at the door into the corridor. Would he be strong enough to stand up by himself, to open the door and take a look out there? If he saw other sick children or their parents, he'd feel less alone. And then he could speak to a visitor and ask where his mum and dad were and what the hospital was called.

He picked up his glasses, put them on and pulled the sheets aside. He was still wearing the disgusting purple pyjamas. It was high time his mum came to visit.

As his feet touched the ground, it felt like he was on a boat. His legs were so wobbly that the whole room seemed to be swaying.

But it wasn't far to the door, and he'd come second in a race at school not long ago. And he'd just had some vanilla custard. It had to work.

It seemed to take an eternity to reach the door. He took hold of the door handle. At first, he thought his arms were too weak to open the door. But after four attempts, he realised the door was locked.

For hours, Gaelle had been wandering around a neighbourhood a couple of kilometres from Kastanienallee, like a tramp looking for a safe place to shelter. She'd hidden in doorways and in an underground garage. She'd gone to a park, where she'd washed the blood off her hands in a pond and then sat on a bench for a while, hidden from view by the trees. She'd wondered if she should return to Bernd's car and drive away.

But she hadn't dared. Scorpio's killers or the police might already have found the car and they could be waiting there for her. She kept seeing the image of Michael's boat, with the flag at half-mast. He must have gone back and seen something that had made him use the agreed signal to warn her to keep away. No matter how desperate she was, how exhausted, hungry and disgusted by the dirty clothes she was walking around in – with a dried bloodstain at the bottom of one leg of her jeans – she also saw Michael's attempt to warn her as a positive sign. It was a sign that he hadn't abandoned her.

Her feet hurt. She looked around. It was just before eight in the evening and the streets were quiet. She walked past terraced houses and saw the light of TV screens through the windows. Sometimes she could look inside at the children and adults sitting together on sofas in front of their televisions.

There was no way to make this right.

That thought hurt more than any physical injury ever could.

She stopped on a street corner and stared at the gaudy neon sign of a kebab shop across the road.

Maybe she'd have been better off dead. She took a step back as a man passed by with a boy in football kit, who was a little older than Lukas.

Lukas still had his entire future ahead of him.

Although Lore had set something in motion, maybe it could still be stopped. Michael had said it would be very difficult to find Lukas, but that they should at least try.

She turned around and walked down the street, heading towards Kastanienallee. The twilight gave her a false sense of security. The closer she came to the jetty where Michael's boat was moored, the faster she began to run.

She was out of breath when she reached the water.

Someone had once told her that a good athlete knew whether they'd lost the race even before they crossed the finish line.

She stared at the empty spot on the jetty, where Michael's boat was no longer moored.

59

THERE HAD BEEN TIMES in her life when she'd felt lonely, like the summer camp when she was nine and she'd lain in bed at night, counting down the days until she was allowed to go home, scared of spiders and of her mean fellow campers who teased children who were homesick. She'd felt even lonelier as a new mother when she couldn't comfort her crying baby, and people like Ebba had only made it worse with their well-meaning advice: "It's good for his lungs." Or as a cousin of Bernd's had said on her first and last visit: "At least he's healthy." It was only later that Gaelle had found out she had a child with a serious disability, who was in an institution and, according to the doctors, would never have a mental age of more than two. Bernd's absence after the birth – *Yes, these meetings really are necessary if I want to get promoted, Gaelle* – had only made the loneliness worse.

As she walked the dark streets of Potsdam, she watched the shadows cast by lamplight flickering in the doorways. Every time a car drove past, the shadows seemed to leap out at her, whispering what she already knew: it was over. She'd lost.

Under the awning of a bakery, she stopped. The police station was a few streets away. Although it was already nine in the evening, there must still be someone there who would talk to her. She could beg them to use all their resources to rescue Lukas from the hands of the contract killers. Without any evidence – Lore's death certainly wouldn't work in her favour – and having been labelled as a dangerous psychiatric patient, it seemed like a kamikaze mission.

A light went on in a nearby house, making her visible to the entire street. She forced herself to keep walking. Having no home to go to was so exhausting. When her mother had died, she thought she'd reached the depths of loneliness. She'd just become an orphan and she had no brothers or sisters to share her grief. But now she knew that loneliness in its pure unadulterated version was a thousand times worse. Real loneliness descended upon you out of nowhere, dark and heavy, impossible to shake off as it dug its claws into your shoulders. It was present night and day, making you feel smaller with every step you took, weakening your body and sucking you dry until you were just a shell. When you'd given up everything and weren't even capable of bearing the loneliness any longer, that was when it would finally disappear.

But by that time it was far too late.

She heard a dog barking.

Turning the corner, she saw the illuminated sign of the police station. And she knew that if she went inside, she would lose her freedom for a long time.

She stood across the street, directly opposite the entrance. In the distance, she heard a motorbike approaching. The loneliness hit her harder than ever, trying to push her towards the door of the police station, where she could see the glow of an intercom system.

She fought the urge to cross the road and ring the bell. First she'd let the motorbike go past, she decided, clinging to the pathetic magical thinking that reminded her of her childhood.

If the driver's wearing a red helmet, everything will be okay.

As soon as the motorbike had gone past, she would cross the street, turn herself in at the police station and place her last bit of hope in their hands.

The motorbike drove along the street.

The light of the lamppost reflected off his black helmet. She should have known, she thought. Luck had been absent for a while, visiting other places.

She tried to cross the road in front of the motorcyclist anyway but had only reached halfway when he screeched to a stop, blocking her path. He raised his visor. He was wearing a leather suit, had brown eyes and a dark complexion.

"Jump on the back," he said.

He took a second helmet from a pannier and shoved it into her hands. Automatically, she took the helmet and looked despondently at the entrance to the police station.

"Quick, before someone comes out," he said.

There was nothing familiar about the way the motorcyclist spoke or about his posture or the glimpse she caught of his face. It was what he'd whispered to her that had made her put on the helmet and get on the bike behind him. She wrapped her arms around his waist and they raced away.

There was only one person who knew that after Lukas's birth, she'd reached the bottom of her black thoughts and had briefly considered letting go of him when she was giving him a bath.

60

DOLORES BARTOSZ cracked her fingers, one by one, as she looked through the window of her safe house at the rosebush on her lawn. In spite of the late hour, the blood-red flowers were clearly visible in the spotlight that was aimed at them. She'd taken a big risk last year when she'd told Vasili to bring Paul de Groot here, a world-famous Dutch rose grower. De Groot had agreed to the conditions: the rosebush would be transported in a small truck, which the client would send, along with a driver. De Groot himself would have to remain in the back of the truck with the rosebush. He would not be permitted to leave the vehicle until they reached their destination, where he would explore the site and identify the most suitable spot for planting the rosebush, which would take place under the supervision of the driver and the client's butler. Under no circumstances was he to ask questions about the location or the client's identity. And he wasn't allowed to question whether the blind butler would be capable of carrying out his pruning and maintenance tips to the letter. After the rosebush had been planted, he would be returned home under the same conditions – in the windowless back of the truck – and once he was home he had to keep quiet about the special delivery and remain available for any questions about how to care for the rosebush, such as spring and winter pruning and fertilisation. The generous payment – even the business of a grower who had won many international awards for his luxury varieties of roses felt the competition from the imported flowers from Africa – and Vasili's hint that they knew where his twin sons went to school had ensured the man's sworn secrecy. De Groot had assured her, via Cédric, that the *Semper Dolor*, the name his anonymous client had given to the rose, would remain the only one of its kind in the world.

There was a knock on the door: Cédric's quiet, polite signal, which was never obtrusive, not even in troubled times.

"Enter."

He pushed in a trolley with a dish of homemade pastries and a porcelain pot of her favourite tea, made from fresh lime blossom. The scent of flowers as Cédric poured out the tea reminded her of the rose grower.

Maybe in hindsight she shouldn't have left the man alive, but the grower had explained to Cédric that the genetically manipulated rosebush that had cost her a fortune was more vulnerable than common varieties. She thanked Cédric for the tea, and he nodded and left as discreetly as he'd come. With a steaming cup in her hand, she walked to the control panel, took one last look at the rosebush that had been cultivated especially for her and turned off the outside light. Then she looked at the screen beneath the panel, which showed images from the security cameras around the safe house, but she saw nothing suspicious. The motion sensors on the wall around the site showed nothing alarming either.

She had asked Cédric to be even more alert than usual today, to take every auditory signal picked up by the sensors seriously and not to dismiss it as a temporary glitch or some animal wandering too close to the exterior wall. She'd added that he should be ready to give any unwanted visitors an appropriate reception. Cédric had spent all day checking the security systems.

She knew that in Michael she'd found an opponent who was her equal. She'd gone through the Chameleon's file again the previous day and realised that they had a lot in common, more than he would ever want to admit.

Dolores pressed the button for a full lockdown and heard the heavy panels sliding shut. In combination with the lime blossom tea, that should have had a calming effect on her. But she wasn't enjoying the tea and the built-in blood-pressure monitor in her watch indicated an alarming rise. She slammed the mug down on her desk and picked up her phone.

It was time to put things in order.

The water lapped against the jetties at Kastanienallee, making waves in the spot where Michael's boat had been. Three figures stood in the dim light of a closed bar and, although the blossoms and trees all around were heralding the sweet scent of summer, the tension in the air could have been cut with a knife.

"So it was all wasted effort," Zoltan said to Ludka.

"He's outsmarted us," said Jorge, kicking a stone into the water. "I don't know how he spotted us or how he managed to get away."

"He asked someone from the boat-hire company to take his place at the wheel. Sadly that man can't give us any more details, and his customer seems to have disappeared off the face of the earth."

"Yeah, so when the boat left, we were following the wrong guy," said Zoltan.

"And it's not just Michael we've lost," said Ludka. "We've still found no trace of the woman."

She stared into the dark water.

"We've already missed Dolores's deadline by a few hours," she said.

"We were so close," said Jorge. "She knows we'll get it right next time."

Ludka's telephone buzzed and she took it out of her pocket to read the message. In one smooth movement, she slipped the phone back into her pocket, pulled out her gun with a silencer and aimed it at Jorge.

"There won't be a next time," she said.

The bullet made a perfectly symmetrical hole in his forehead and penetrated his brain. Out of the corner of her eye, she saw him fall, and she was just fast enough to shoot Zoltan before he could turn on her.

Two dull bangs, a steady hand and a little precision. That was all it took to get rid of people who didn't keep their promises, as Dolores had instructed her to do in the message. She kicked the bodies, one at a time, along the dock, until they landed in the water.

Before she put her gun away, she scanned the area, looking for any inconvenient witnesses. But there were no boats moored near the pub, and the terrace chairs were stacked in such a way that they formed a wall for anyone who might happen to look their way. It had all happened in barely a couple of minutes.

Quickly, she walked down the jetty, her mind already on the next task Dolores had given her.

THE MOTORCYCLIST STOPPED near a level crossing at a detached building that looked like a squat. The beam of the headlight revealed smashed windows, graffiti on the walls and a broken padlock and chain lying on the ground by the front door. Gaelle made no attempt to get off the bike until the driver, who had still not made his identity known, motioned to her to leave her seat. Standing beside the motorbike, she removed her helmet.

Before she could ask him anything, the motorcyclist climbed off the bike. With a haste that scared her, he pushed it towards a shed leaning against the building. She followed him. Once they were inside, he turned off the lights of the motorbike. It was so dark that she could no longer see even his outline. If he wasn't who she thought he was, he could end her life here and now, and no one would ever know how her body had got there.

She heard the sound of a bag being unzipped. "Michael?"

No reaction.

She held her helmet in front of her, ready to defend herself with all her might if she had to. A small torch came on, lighting up the surroundings.

"Wait to talk until we're inside, Gaelle," he whispered. "It's safer there."

She lowered the helmet and followed Michael – it had to be him – who opened a door in the shed, which led into the adjoining room. It smelt of cat piss and mould. The light of his torch showed the way, past a disembowelled sofa and a dresser from which the drawers had disappeared. The floor was littered with old newspapers and shards of glass, which cracked under the soles of her shoes. They came into a hallway, where Michael turned and headed upstairs. The handrail was broken and there were only a few scraps to show where a carpet had once been.

At the top, Michael turned left and then opened the second door on the right.

The swiftness with which he headed to his goal made Gaelle suspect he'd been here before. They were in a room that had once been a bedroom. There was a double bed with a stained mattress, which she'd never have sat on under normal circumstances, but at least it didn't smell of cat piss. Michael walked to the window, pulled the cord of the wooden blind and let it all the way down. Then he went to the bedroom door, looked down the hallway and closed the door. He threw his backpack onto the bed, took a cube-shaped object out of it and pressed a button on it. The whole room lit up.

Now that Gaelle could see the motorcyclist, a Mediterranean type with gleaming black hair, a leather jacket and a polo neck, she was struck by doubt again. This was not the Michael who had thrown her to the ground in the park – an athletic-looking white man in his forties – and it wasn't the accountant type with the balding head, the goatee and the boring clothes, the one who had warned her to stay in the boat before leaving this morning.

"It really is me," he said.

"Then you must be mad at me."

"If you knew everything I had to do to save my own skin and to get you here…"

He dropped onto the edge of the bed beside her.

"I'm sorry," she said.

He dismissed her words. "Regret is for people with too much time on their hands," he said. "And we don't have that."

"That's exactly why I ran away this morning. I couldn't just sit there waiting for news about Lukas."

"Your actions haven't exactly helped us."

Gaelle looked at him.

"What do you know about that?"

"Everything. Everything the police know by now too. That two people were shot dead at your friend Ebba's house: her sister and your husband."

Gaelle stared at the floor.

"Just before you turned up at that police station, I was planning to turn myself in. I was hoping it might save Lukas's life."

"So I got there just in time," said Michael. "That was pretty much the dumbest thing you could have done."

"I've done other dumb things today. Things I can't erase, Michael."

Hesitating as she searched for the right words, she told him what had happened at Ebba's house.

A shadow moved across the room as a moth flew around the cube-shaped lamp.

"Now I know who the client was," said Gaelle. "But that won't give me back my son. And if I ever get to put my arms around Lukas, I'm going to have to tell him he'll never see his father again."

She bowed her head and brushed away her tears.

Michael turned to look for something in his backpack. He held out a packet of sandwiches.

"You'd better eat something," he said. "I've brought drinks too."

She took the packet and put it down beside her on the bed without opening it.

Michael handed her a bottle.

"When I saw you weren't on board, I wanted to go and look for you right away," he said.

"So why didn't you?"

"They were monitoring the area around Kastanienallee. I think there were at least two of Scorpio's killers circling around. Everything indicated that you'd left of your own free will, so I thought you'd turn up again. I just hoped you'd interpret my warning correctly."

"I left when I saw you'd hung the flag at half-mast."

"So at least you did one thing right today."

Gaelle took a swig of water. It tasted so good that she downed the whole bottle.

"So what have you been up to in the meantime?" she asked.

"Sorting things out, like this place. And getting hold of a motorbike."

"When I saw your boat was gone, I thought you'd abandoned me," she said.

"You aren't rid of me yet," he said.

"And I don't want to be rid of you. Not until we've found Lukas," said Gaelle.

She paused.

"Is there any hope?"

Michael nodded slowly.

"Everyone has their weaknesses, even people like Dolores. I think I've found a way to track her down. And if we find her, she can bring us closer to Lukas."

Gaelle whipped her head around to look at Michael. Their faces were so close that she could feel his breath on her skin.

"But how?"

"I'll tell you tomorrow. We really need to get some sleep now. We're leaving for the Netherlands at four in the morning."

"The Netherlands? Is that where Lukas is?"

"No idea where they're holding him, but a man who lives there can lead us to Dolores."

Before long, the light was off and they were lying next to each other on the mattress, Michael on the side nearest the door, his hand on the gun. She doubted she'd dare to sleep for anything more than a nap.

"If you're prepared to go to all this trouble, then you must believe Lukas is still alive," she said.

"I do."

"Why would Scorpio's killers keep him alive when they've been paid to kill him?"

"My answer isn't going to reassure you."

"Just tell me."

He waited for a moment.

"Because a dead boy is useless as bait."

Michael sat up in the dark room and listened to Gaelle's regular breathing. He'd often listened to Bellefleur's breathing in the same way, having conversations with her in his mind about things he thought one day he'd be able to say out loud. He was planning to wait until he was almost certain she wouldn't leave him.

He'd waited far too long. Those conversations would never happen.

He'd wanted to tell her how scared he'd been, that night in the forest, after he'd shot Nowak dead. And that he'd soon realised he couldn't return to the detention centre. He'd gently closed Janek's eyes and folded his arms across his chest before running away.

After days of running, he'd found a place to stay with people who didn't ask him any questions and, in exchange, he did some jobs for them. Over the years, he'd climbed his way up from drugs courier to nightclub bouncer to debt collector. During one of those jobs, when he was working with someone else to change the mind of a stubborn defaulter, his partner's actions had resulted in a death. He'd managed to make it look like an accident. Since then, people had started calling on him whenever they wanted to get rid of someone in such a way that it looked as if there was no foul play involved.

Until, finally, he had been recruited by Scorpio.

Since that night in the forest, it felt as if he'd always been on the run.

Maybe most of all from himself.

62

S HE HAD NEVER SUSPECTED she would fall asleep. In the silence of the night, the events of the previous day kept running through her mind. She saw the hate in Lore's eyes and the determination as she'd aimed the gun at her. Again and again, she felt her own helplessness when Bernd had slipped away in her arms – and the emptiness that followed. She thought about Lukas, and her uncertainty about his fate grew into rage, an intense rage targeted at everyone who was involved in this whole business. A few days ago, she'd been complaining about cups that Bernd had forgotten to put in the dishwasher, and now she'd lost her husband forever and she didn't even know if she'd ever see her son again or what condition he was in.

She killed Lore over and over again that night, in far more gruesome ways than in reality, in a futile attempt to find peace. Finally, though, fatigue had got the better of her. She awoke with a start when Michael said it was time to get up.

Her head hurt and the lack of sleep made her want to vomit. Michael was standing in front of her, holding a laptop. His appearance had undergone another little change. He still looked Mediterranean, but he was wearing glasses now, had a trimmed beard and his cheeks seemed fuller.

"Everything's ready," he said. "We're leaving in a few minutes. There's a bathroom down the hall, but don't expect too much. As you'll have noticed, this isn't exactly the Hilton."

Gaelle soon returned. She'd hurried to leave the filthy bathroom as quickly as possible. When she entered the bedroom,

Michael's laptop was on the bed, with the screen facing her. She saw a close-up of a rosebush in bloom.

"What's that supposed to be?" she asked.

"Dolores's virtual fingerprint," said Michael. "This rosebush is unique. We can use this variety to track her down."

He explained briefly how he'd got hold of the picture of the rosebush. During the rare webcam conversations Dolores had had with him, she'd made sure she was never on screen and she showed hardly anything of her surroundings. But the last time she'd been a little less careful and when Michael had analysed the images, part of the garden had been visible through the window of the room where Dolores was located, with the only plant a rosebush that was specially illuminated. He'd had the images enlarged and consulted various experts, but no one could identify the specific variety of rose by its characteristics.

"One of the experts said it was a cross between two exclusive varieties of rose: the Gladiator, the rose with the largest thorns in the world, and the Grande Dame. Both varieties are patented and were originally cultivated by a Dutch grower, Paul de Groot."

He closed the laptop.

"And we're going to pay him a visit."

Lukas had had a bad night's sleep. He hadn't dropped off until late and he'd dreamt his mother was standing by his bedside and that she woke him up to take him home. But when he opened his eyes, he saw the doctor standing there. She was holding a needle in her hand.

Lukas rubbed his eyes. It was probably very early in the morning. He still hadn't woken up properly. He yawned and felt for his glasses on the bedside table, but they weren't there. He sat up.

"Where are my glasses?"

"You won't be needing them today."

"I can't see properly without my glasses."

He gave her an evil stare.

"Aren't you supposed to take care of people in hospital? So why can't I wear my glasses?"

The doctor just tapped the syringe.

"And why is the door to my room locked all the time?"

She looked at him and told him he'd better go to the toilet before they left.

He slipped out of bed and suddenly felt a lot happier at the thought that they'd be leaving this nasty place and taking him – where else could it be? – home. As fast as his shaky legs could carry him, he dragged himself to the bathroom. As he peed, he had to lean on the wall, so that he wouldn't fall. The accident, or whatever it was that had brought him here, had clearly weakened his body. He yawned, looked in the mirror, smoothed down his hair and decided, as a protest against the silent doctor, not to brush his teeth.

"Ready!" he said cheerfully. "Where are my clothes? Then I can finally take off these nasty pyjamas."

"Just lie down on the bed for a moment," said the doctor.

"Why?"

"So you don't collapse."

"I'm a bit dizzy, but if I hold on to the bed with one hand, I can put on my clothes without falling."

He stayed where he was, crossed his arms and thought about how proud his dad would be that he was behaving like a real man.

The doctor looked over her shoulder as the door opened and her male colleague appeared.

"He's being a bit awkward," she said. "I could do with some help."

"Help with what?" asked Lukas.

"You're being transferred to somewhere else today," said the man. "To make sure it goes as smoothly as possible, we're going to give you a sedative to send you to sleep."

"I don't want to sleep! I just want to go home. Can't Mummy come and fetch me?"

"We have your best interests at heart," said the woman.

"Then why can't I go home?"

"We're not allowed to tell you. Now calm down."

A few minutes later, Lukas felt like anything but a real man. He began to wail as the doctors grabbed him and held him down on the bed. The wails turned into screams, and he struggled to get free as the man held his arms and made sure that his colleague could jab him with the needle.

Through his tears, he saw the two doctors slowly dissolving, followed by the rest of the room.

63

PAUL DE GROOT walked through the huge greenhouse of his rose farm, as he – and his flowers – listened to Mozart's Piano Sonata No. 11. There were few certainties in life, but one of them was that plants grew faster when exposed to classical music. It was never pop music that boomed from the speakers on the steel frame of the greenhouse, like the noise that came, far too frequently and far too loudly, from his fifteen-year-old sons' bedrooms. The greenhouse was filled, night and day, with the gentle vibrations of string quartets or piano concertos, usually works by Vivaldi, Beethoven, Chopin and, of course, Mozart. No matter what other people might say and how often his relatives laughed at him at family get-togethers – his sons were the worst offenders – he knew that these sound waves were good not only for people, but also for plants. The evidence was irrefutable. In recent years, he'd won no fewer than eight international awards for his roses, like the Grande Dame, with its large flowers, a new variety that he'd patented so no one could grow it without his permission.

Pausing, he leant forward to another of his most remarkable patented roses: the Gladiator, which had the largest thorns in the world. That had been officially verified by a panel of experts, and he'd made the trade press with it. Since then, various growers had expressed an interest, but he'd never taken them up on it. The Gladiator was his long-awaited designer baby. It had taken years to achieve this result. This variety of rose had his DNA and his stamp on it, and you don't sell your children, although he'd recently suggested exactly that to his wife when the twins had been up to their usual teenage tricks.

He smiled, slowly running his fingers over the thorns of the Gladiator. It was a fitting name for a plant that thrust out its thorns like swords. Once again, he thought of his sons. Even though he never said so, he loved Lennert and Louis, and he would much rather they showed some interest in his company instead of playing those soul-destroying games.

Maybe one of them would follow in his footsteps one day, just as he'd learnt his own father's profession. Time would tell.

He looked up and saw a shadow walking past his greenhouse. He couldn't see who it was because of the matte glass, but the only people who were allowed to enter the greenhouse in the daytime were his wife and their two sons. The shadow was now coming along the walkway to the entrance, as Mozart's eleventh piano sonata entered its final movement.

He tried not to think back to the moment when he'd sold his soul, or at least a part of it, by betraying his principles and agreeing to cross the Gladiator with the Grande Dame. After a few unsuccessful attempts, he'd succeeded in cultivating a unique variety of rose with the largest flowers and the largest thorns in the world. But that news had never reached the trade press. No one knew about it, not even his wife. If he ever blabbed about the ridiculous sum of money he'd received or told anyone that this unique hybrid existed and that he'd been invited to plant the bush on unknown territory in very strange circumstances, his sons would never celebrate their next birthday. That was what the driver had told him, on behalf of the anonymous client.

It had been the previous November when he'd been transported in the back of a truck to the client's residence, and since his return he hadn't spoken a word about it. After the threats to his sons, he'd felt guilty for allowing himself to be persuaded to take part in something so shady. He'd used the money to buy a climate-management computer, a magnificent purchase that perfectly regulated the temperature in the greenhouse, along with the humidity and the amount of light. He'd certainly paid the price for it though, and the threats had given him many sleepless nights.

The shadow was almost at the entrance now. Through the matte glass, he saw the figure approaching, and the fear that something had happened to his sons pushed the last notes of Mozart's sonata into the background.

Gaelle had hidden behind a tree and was pulling the black balaclava over her head as Michael had told her to.

She'd asked him why it was needed.

"It's safer if De Groot can't give any descriptions of what we look like now," Michael had said. "Both for us and for him."

"That means you're planning to let him live," Gaelle had said.

"It mainly means I want to get away from here as soon as possible, without having to change our appearance or worry about De Groot informing the police."

Michael had left the motorbike behind a bush, close to the dirt road they'd driven along to reach De Groot's business premises.

Gaelle saw the door of the greenhouse opening and a man appeared, probably no taller than one metre seventy, wearing a gardening apron and rubber boots. The man, presumably De Groot himself, had no time to recover from his surprise. Michael dived on him and held him in a strong grip. Then he looked at Gaelle and beckoned her with a nod of his head. He wanted to make sure De Groot didn't have any company first. She hurried towards the greenhouse, glancing back and seeing no movement around the large white villa nearby.

Then she headed into the greenhouse, closing the door behind her.

Michael had forced the rose grower onto his knees and was holding him at gunpoint. The man's body was shaking all over and he seemed to be in shock.

"I don't have any money here," he whispered.

"We don't want your money," said Michael.

Standing there, dressed head to toe in black with a balaclava and his gun ready to fire, he terrified even Gaelle.

"Then what do you want?" asked De Groot.

"Information," replied Michael.

"What kind of information?"

Without lowering his gun, Michael took a print of the unique rosebush from his inside pocket and held it out to De Groot.

The man looked at it in silence. Gaelle had the impression that his hands started to tremble even more.

"We know you're the only one who can grow this variety. It's a cross between two of your patented roses: the Gladiator and the Grande Dame," Michael continued. "Where is this bush? What do you know about the client? We want to know everything, right down to the smallest details."

The rose grower blinked.

"Is this a test?" he asked. "Then all I can tell you is that I've never said anything about it and that I'm not planning to do so now."

Gaelle felt sorry for the man. Michael had warned her in advance that he was going in hard.

"Maybe we should bring in your wife to refresh your memory," said Michael.

"Leave my wife out of this," said De Groot.

"Is that how they got you to stay silent?" asked Michael. "Did they threaten to do something to your family if you told anyone about your special commission?"

De Groot's bottom lip started trembling, and Gaelle couldn't hold back any longer. She stepped forward and pushed Michael's gun down a little, so that the weapon was no longer aimed at the rose grower's head.

"I'm sorry it has to be this way, Mr De Groot," she said. "But the information you can give us is vitally important. My son's been kidnapped on the orders of the woman who owns that rosebush, and you're the only one who can lead us to her."

De Groot was still on his knees. He dropped his hands and his arms dangled helplessly by his sides.

"Do you have children?" asked Gaelle.

De Groot nodded.

"That's why I can't tell you anything," he said quietly. "If I do, they'll kill my sons."

Michael cleared his throat.

"Maybe the first impression was a little misleading," he said. "But I'm not one of the bad guys."

Not anymore, thought Gaelle.

"The woman we're looking for is at the head of a dangerous organisation. We want to put an end to their practices," said Michael. "If we find her, she'll no longer be a threat to your family. I promise you."

"And you'll be saving my son's life," said Gaelle.

She dropped onto her knees next to De Groot, took him by the shoulders, helped him to his feet and looked at him.

"As a father, you must know how I feel now," she said.

He swallowed and looked over Gaelle's shoulder at Michael.

"What guarantee do I have that you won't mention my name and that I'll never hear anything else about this again?"

"I give you my word," Michael said. "And this lady can confirm that my word is worth something."

"Without him, I'd never have come this far," she said.

The rose grower hesitated for a few seconds and then began talking so quickly that he stumbled over his words. He told them that the anonymous customer had underestimated him by assuming that transporting him in the back of truck would be enough to keep the destination a secret. Since he was a boy, he'd built up an encyclopaedic knowledge of flora and fauna, which, combined with the length of the journey, had allowed him to deduce the region where the bunker-like house was located.

"You need to go looking for a safe house, more like a kind of bunker, somewhere in the Knyszyn Forest, in the east of Poland."

64

FOR TWO DAYS AND TWO NIGHTS, Ludka had been standing like a statue at the entrance gate of the safe house. During the daytime, she wore an army cap to protect her from the sun. Under her camouflage clothing, she had a bulletproof vest, and there was a sub-machine gun over her shoulder. Three hours of sleep in the morning were enough for her, and she kept herself going with energy bars. The forest stretched out in front of her like a dark ocean whose floor she couldn't see. Dusk was falling and maybe another deer would appear, as had happened the previous day. Out of boredom, she'd briefly considered blasting the creature's brains out with her sub-machine gun, but her boss wouldn't have approved.

Although Dolores had never shown her face to her and Ludka had received all her instructions from the blind butler, who had introduced himself as Cédric, she knew only too well that she'd end up like Zoltan and Jorge if she slipped up. As if that was going to happen when she came face to face with the man who killed her brother, she thought. It wasn't a certainty that he'd turn up here, Cédric had said, but she had to be prepared.

Something rustled in the nearby bushes.

She grabbed her gun, turned towards the sound and listened closely. A bird flew out of the bushes, and she lowered her gun.

It had been hours since she'd had anything to drink. Her body was trained to function with a minimum of fluids. Drinking more meant more toilet breaks, and although she tried to waste as little time as possible, she had no choice but to listen to her body now and then.

A glass of water and an energy bar, followed by a visit to the toilet, and she'd be good for the whole night to come. Dolores wanted her to catch up on her sleep during the daytime, as she felt the night was more dangerous. When Ludka was given this security job, she'd found to her surprise that she was the only one Dolores had brought in. On the one hand, she'd thought that unwise, but Dolores's faith in her abilities had also been encouraging.

She watched as the forest was slowly enveloped by darkness, the leaves rustling and the branches creaking. As some animals retired to their sleeping places, the nocturnal creatures emerged from their homes.

Her mouth was bone dry and she thought about the bottle of water Cédric had left for her on the table in the hallway, close to the toilet. She'd stay away for a maximum of ten minutes.

Turning around, she placed her finger on the glass of the fingerprint sensor and waited for the green light to go on and the gate to open automatically. She hurried inside – the gate would close again in a few seconds. Then she walked across the lawn to the front door of the safe house and used the same method to let herself in.

Michael silently climbed down from the tree where he'd sat watching the woman who was guarding the gate. Something about her seemed familiar, but he couldn't quite put his finger on it.

He expected her to take up position again in a few minutes, for the whole night. Although the entrance was unguarded, trying to get inside Dolores's compound now would be a bad idea. The whole place was surrounded by high walls with motion sensors. It would be impossible to climb over them without setting off an alarm inside. Getting through the automatic gate wasn't an option either. Without the right finger scan, he stood no chance.

For what he was planning, he needed the woman. Or at least part of her.

Leaving his vantage point, he walked towards the spot where he'd pitched his tent in the middle of the forest. Gaelle was hiding there, about three kilometres from Dolores's safe house. Since they'd left the Netherlands, he'd been searching satellite images on his computer, looking for a bunker in the vast Knyszyn Forest. This morning, he'd finally managed to identify the location and they'd arrived here at around midday, after a trek through the forest that had proved tiring for Gaelle. He'd used the rest of the day to observe the safe house, while waiting for darkness to fall.

When he reached the tent, he gave the whistle signal they'd agreed on, and stooped to unzip the tent. Gaelle turned on a torch, holding her hand over it to dim the light.

"I'm doing it tonight," he said, taking a hand grenade from his backpack and attaching it to his belt.

"Let me go with you," said Gaelle.

He shook his head.

"Your presence could put the whole operation at risk. You have to trust me."

She said nothing.

"I won't come back to this place. It's better if I take a different escape route."

"What about Lukas?"

"I'm not going to leave until I've found him or I've discovered where they're holding him."

He took a device from his backpack and gave it to Gaelle.

"What's that?"

"I've set this GPS so it'll lead you out of the forest to an address in a Polish village not far from here, where there's someone who'll help you to get away."

"Why can't I go there now?"

"It's still too soon. Everything needs to happen at exactly the right moment. Wait for me to give you the signal: your GPS will ring briefly and your screen will light up. Then you need to leave as quickly as possible."

"What do I do with the tent?"

"Just leave it here."

She nodded and rested her hand on one of the two guns he'd given her before he left.

"And what if it goes wrong?" she asked.

"If there's no signal within five hours, you can't stay here any longer. Then you need to leave right away and follow the GPS to your destination. The people there will know exactly what to do."

"This could be the last time I see you," she said.

He didn't reply, just turned around and unzipped the tent.

Gaelle had turned off the torch.

"See you, Michael."

65

WHEN MICHAEL GOT to Dolores's safe house, he saw that the guard had taken up position again, as if she'd never left. There was a light on the first floor. He suspected that was the office from which Dolores had been speaking to him when the rosebush had come into view. The illuminated windows had shutters beside them, over a metre thick, like all the other windows of the house. He assumed she had a system that would allow her to close her bunker off from the inside. Once the shutters and gates were shut, throwing a grenade at the walls would have about as much effect as throwing an apple.

He looked again at the woman standing motionless at the entrance. She was almost one metre eighty and solidly built.

As she turned her head and he saw her profile, he suddenly realised where he'd seen her before.

It was the face of the policewoman he'd passed in the hallway at Bellefleur's apartment complex, the day he'd arrived too late.

The curve of her nose also reminded him of someone else: Vasili. If they were related and if Dolores had told her what had happened to Vasili, it seemed she had a score to settle with Michael too.

Then he'd better make the first move.

He looked again at the bunker. The images from his infrared camera told him there were only two people inside the house. So Vasili's sister couldn't expect much backup.

She stood at the entrance, unmoving. If he distracted her so she moved a few metres to the left, he'd be able to get fairly close to her from the bushes on the other side. Then he could eliminate her quickly and silently.

He crept across the ground and lay behind a fallen tree trunk. Feeling his way, he looked for a branch that would be suitable for attracting her attention. His fingers closed around a V-shaped stick. He stood up a little from the bushes, without revealing his presence, and tossed the piece of wood into the bushes.

Instantly, the woman's posture changed. Her body tensed and, sub-machine gun at the ready, she turned to look in the direction of the sound.

She didn't move a step.

Just as he was about to look for a bigger stick, she walked slowly away from him with her back towards him. Like a panther, he made his way through the darkness, climbed over the tree trunk, keeping close to the ground and moving closer and closer to his target.

When he was about one and a half metres from his prey, he dared to pounce.

This endless waiting makes time lose all meaning, thought Gaelle. She was lying on the thin mat Michael had put in the tent, her right hand around the gun and the other on the GPS. He'd assured her the signal would be loud enough to wake her if she fell asleep. Although her body was exhausted and her mind was begging for rest, she still hadn't slept a wink. Her fingers clutched the navigation system as if it were a lifebuoy.

She thought about the last time they'd been together as a family, during that rainy weekend in Altensteig. If she'd known then that it was the last time, she'd have held on to every second for as long as possible.

*

Michael was pressing Vasili's sister to the ground, his hand over her mouth.

He bent down and whispered, "This won't bring back Bellefleur, but at least you'll never cause anyone else to grieve."

She tried furiously to struggle free.

"Say hi to Vasili," he said. With one swift movement, he twisted her neck. Michael heard a quiet snap, and she went limp. He dragged the body into the undergrowth, hid it there, along with the sub-machine gun, took a knife from his backpack and expertly sliced off her right index finger. His surprise attack meant that the fight had been a short one. Otherwise she'd have been a serious obstacle and might have managed to sound the alarm. That problem was out of the way now.

He turned around and walked to the entrance gate. Holding the amputated finger to the sensor, he waited for the light to turn green and then put the finger into a plastic bag, which he dropped into his pocket. As soon as the opening was big enough, he slipped inside and hurried along the path to the front door of the safe house, recognising, on the right, the rosebush that had shown him the way.

From the gutter, a spotlight was aimed at the rosebush. Bathed in light, it had an air of mystery, with its flowers and powerful thorns. He struggled to take his eyes off the rose and suddenly he understood what had inspired Dolores to keep this unique rose in her vicinity: it must be a powerful feeling to know that she was the only person in the world who could enjoy it.

He walked on, avoiding the light around the rosebush.

When he reached the door of the safe house, he saw the same scan system that was used at the gate. Taking the finger from the plastic bag, he pressed it to the glass and waited for the steel door to open.

Gun drawn, he headed inside.

66

THE FIRST THING he noticed about the interior was the sterility. It was like being in a hospital corridor, or worse, a mortuary. As he entered, a light had automatically come on and he'd taken in the surroundings, listening for any sounds. The concrete floor was immaculate, as if no one had ever walked over it. The white walls were bare, and the steel staircase had no handrail.

At the end of the hallway, there was a glass door, which he'd almost shot at when he'd thought he saw someone moving behind it.

He lowered his gun and saw that it was because he was so tired that he hadn't immediately realised it was his own reflection. He was now halfway up the stairs and waited for the light in the hallway to go out automatically before creeping upstairs in the darkness.

In this place, in the cold heart of Scorpio, he couldn't help but think of Dolores. He'd just killed Bellefleur's murderer, and now he was going to kill the person who had given the order for that killing.

The light went out and he focused on his footsteps. When he was almost at the top of the stairs, he heard a loud noise from below. It sounded like someone was stacking plates.

Maybe it was the butler, whom Paul de Groot had described as a quiet man. He'd been unable to look into his eyes, as he always wore sunglasses. It was only later that the rose grower had realised the man was blind.

The fact that Dolores hid away in this bunker with a blind butler made her even more mysterious in Michael's eyes.

More dangerous too.

She made him think of a spider waiting patiently in a dark corner for her web to vibrate. He was upstairs now and trying to orient himself. The room he suspected was Dolores's office was at the front of the house. A strip of light could be seen coming under one of the doors on that side, and he moved slowly towards it. When he was beside the large wooden door, he put an ear to it and listened.

He heard nothing. No voices, no quiet music in the background, no footsteps. And yet he felt her presence, which once again made him think of the spider.

The designer desk in Dolores's office was positioned so that she sat with her back to the door. During the daytime, she could look out through the glass wall. Although it had been dark for some time, she hadn't activated the lockdown system yet. That was because of the illuminated rosebush, which wanted to be looked at, like a beautiful woman who apparently just happens to stroll past a sidewalk café wearing a floaty summer dress. Now and then her gaze moved to the right-hand wall of the office, taking in the frame with the yellowing newspaper article, which she'd carefully preserved behind glass. It did her good to keep all the things she'd achieved in her life close at hand – what she had destroyed and what she had created.

She looked at the screen. She could use her laptop to follow Cédric's movements in the kitchen. She found it pleasant to observe someone who would himself never be able to set eyes on her.

She was about to switch off her laptop when she felt a movement of air, barely perceptible, as if someone had come to stand behind her. Cédric never entered the room without knocking, she thought as she turned around.

She knew immediately who he was, the black-clad man standing in her office and holding her at gunpoint, the one who had succeeded in penetrating her safe cocoon, who was so invisible that her hitmen had been unable to kill him and who had taken everything he'd learnt over the years and used it to find her.

The look in his eyes left her in no doubt about his intentions.

"Hello, Michael," she said, her right hand slipping slowly towards the alarm button on the underside of her desk.

She didn't look anything like Michael had imagined. In front of him was a frail woman in her early sixties. She was dressed simply, in a grey blouse and black trousers. Other than her watch, she wore no jewellery. She had a short haircut that you wouldn't find in any modern glossy magazine. It was almost as if she was too shy to look at him, as she sat there in her desk chair, eyes averted, so that he could see only the right side of her face. If he didn't know who she was, he'd have suspected she spent her days gardening, looking after the grandchildren and knitting hideous scarves that no one wanted to wear. She was the sort of woman who would melt into the crowd in a busy shopping street, the sort of woman who'd be warned by well-meaning passers-by to be wary of pickpockets.

"I underestimated you," she said, staring at the floor.

The metallic sound of her voice didn't fit the image of a grandma who knitted kiddies' socks.

"You know why I'm here," said Michael.

She shifted a little.

"Keep your hands where I can see them," he said.

She put her hands on her knees.

"I didn't expect you to get past Ludka," she said "Vasili's sister was one of the best. Even better than Vasili."

"Don't forget I'm particularly motivated, thanks to you."

"How did you find me?" she asked.

His gaze moved over her and outside, to the rosebush.

"Even people without hearts have their weaknesses," he said.

The desk chair creaked as she turned to face him fully, and he looked in horror at the mutilated left side of her face.

67

H ER FACE MADE HIM THINK of a plastic mask that had been thrown into a fire and had partly melted. Where her left eye had once been, there was now just a socket. Her skin, an unhealthy shade of grey, was rippled and pitted. Her left ear was missing. He knew what had caused the damage. Years ago he'd had a target with similar facial deformities. That time it had been a soldier who had fought in Afghanistan and been badly burned in an explosion. After several failed skin grafts, the man had fallen into a serious depression and someone – presumably his younger wife – had decided to get rid of him for good.

Dolores looked at him with one eye.

"Did I startle you?" she asked. "You're not even trying to hide it."

Still holding her at gunpoint, he walked over to the laptop. On the screen, he saw an empty, almost clinical kitchen.

"You're good, Michael. Very good, in fact. Maybe we should start over and forget what's happened between us. What would you say to running Scorpio with me?"

"I'm not after a promotion, Dolores. And no one can erase what happened to Bellefleur."

"I know your file in detail, Michael. We have more in common than you think."

She nodded at the yellowing newspaper article on the wall.

"Like you, I committed my first murder at the age of fourteen," she said. "At the time, everyone confused the role of the perpetrator with that of the victim."

Michael read the headline: *Fourteen-year-old only one rescued from burning house.* He saw a movement out of the corner of his eye. Dolores's hands were no longer on her knees. He grabbed her arm, pulled her from her chair and threw her onto the floor. Only now did he see the button under her desk, which she'd kept hidden with her body all that time.

There was a movement on Dolores's screen. A man in sunglasses appeared, most likely Cédric, the blind butler. The man hurried across the kitchen, opened a cupboard that clearly concealed a safe and tapped in a code.

Whatever was hidden in there, it was obviously important enough to warrant a safe.

Dolores began talking again and he realised that her only intention was to gain time.

"Goodbye, Dolores. I owe you this."

He aimed his gun and pulled the trigger.

Her body jerked, her head falling to one side, with the good side up, as if she wanted to die beautiful. He wasted no time checking for a pulse. If she wasn't dead yet, she would be in a few seconds' time.

Just before he left the room, he saw Dolores's butler take a USB stick from the safe and slip it into his pocket. Then the man picked up a remote control and appeared to set some kind of timer.

Michael walked out into the hallway, down the stairs, and headed for the room where he'd heard plates being stacked. As he pushed open the kitchen door, all the lights went out.

68

MICHAEL IMMEDIATELY KNEW that the blind man had the advantage. He must know every centimetre of this house and could probably hear where Michael was now, so he'd be able to take aim perfectly, as if he were a sighted person with a target in broad daylight.

Michael walked into the kitchen, his free hand searching for the torch in his inside pocket, but before he could take it out, he heard something click to his left.

He automatically dropped to the floor and rolled away under a hail of bullets. One of the bullets went through his left leg and another went straight through his right shoulder, almost making him drop his gun. He fired in the direction the shots had come from, in an attempt to hit his invisible attacker.

His hope grew when his bullets went unanswered and a silence followed. Michael tried to ignore the pain, pulling himself up on a steel table leg, which he suspected was part of the kitchen island.

It was still silent.

It could be the silence of a calculating opportunist who was standing half a metre from him, ready to finish what Dolores had instructed him to do.

Or perhaps Michael had just killed him.

Soon enough he'd be able to see for himself. He tried to shift his weight onto his good leg, biting back a cry as a flash of pain shot through his body, and then pulled out his torch and turned it on.

The kitchen was just as minimalist as the rest of the house. There wasn't a single piece of furniture for the man to hide behind.

On the opposite wall he saw a sliding door that was not completely closed. There were splashes of blood on the door, suggesting that the blind man had also been injured and was in a hurry to get away. The image of the timer came back to Michael. Whatever Cédric had started, he was running out of time. At that moment he heard a thundering sound from outside. It felt as if the whole house were shaking on its foundations. He thought about the metre-thick concrete panels he'd noticed beside the windows and the front door, and he realised where the sound was coming from. The bunker was being hermetically sealed. Once all the shutters were closed, it would be impossible to get out of here.

He laid his gun on the counter, took out his phone and sent the code to start the navigation system that would guide Gaelle safely out of the forest. Then he put away his mobile, took his gun and his torch and opened the door all the way. He entered a room that reminded him of a garage, but there were no cars in it. On the outside, a steel gate was slowly descending. Meanwhile, on either side of the gate, the concrete shutters were slowly moving towards each other. His route to the world outside was becoming smaller and smaller. He had just a few seconds to escape.

His wounded leg was a dead weight.

Suddenly his knees gave way. He fell and lost hold of his gun, watching as it slid across the floor. No time to grab it. The shuddering was coming to an end – he was almost out of time. He crawled to the opening, dragging his damaged leg, tasting the blood that was flowing from his body. Just one more metre.

He smelt the forest air, the scent of life, and with the last of his strength, he squeezed through the opening that was now just big enough to let a grown man through. As soon as he was outside, he turned his head to see the concrete shutters closing behind him like a steamroller.

He gave himself a moment to recover. Then he stood up, stumbled across the lawn, took the finger out of the bag to operate the gate and looked back one last time.

All the shutters of the bunker were closed. The solid block of concrete no longer resembled a house in any way.

Dolores couldn't have wished for a finer grave.

He took out the knife that had been strapped around his ankle and ran into the forest, thinking about Gaelle and what was in store for her. Even though he wouldn't be able to tell her personally, he hoped she'd understand why he'd done it.

When he was a couple of kilometres from the bunker, he heard a loud explosion, louder than any explosion he'd ever heard before.

He turned around.

In the place where Dolores's safe house had stood, flames and debris were shooting into the air, lighting up the night sky before slowly dying down. It gave him the courage to pull himself together, even with his seriously injured body, and to believe that every ending was also a new beginning.

69

GAELLE SAT IN THE BACK of the Mercedes, which was driving at a leisurely pace through the rolling landscape of Tuscany. Her driver, a muscular man called Cibor, had barely said a word during the entire journey. When, two nights ago, she'd arrived at her destination, after trudging through the Knyszyn Forest for an hour and a half, she'd thought at first that the GPS had sent her to the wrong address. She'd knocked the door of a sort of gamekeeper's hut that looked uninhabited. The door had swung open and in the light of the wood-burning stove, she'd seen a man she instinctively wanted to run away from as quickly as possible. He only came up to her shoulder, but was three times as wide, and he had a scar on one cheek.

"Cibor," he said.

His voice sounded as dark as the rest of the surroundings. She asked him if this was the address Michael had meant to send her to, but he didn't seem to understand a word of what she'd asked. He banged his fist on his chest and then pointed at her.

"Cibor. Gaelle."

With those words, he let her in. The simple wooden furniture was like something from a century ago, and there was no electricity, but it was nicer than the exterior had led her to expect. There was only one source of light, a battery-powered standard lamp. A pan was bubbling on the stove, and the smell reminded her of her mother's cooking. Without asking if she was hungry, Cibor dished up a generous portion into a bowl and slid it onto the table in front of her. She ate it all up and when he took her bowl away, he'd managed a weak smile. Then he'd led her to a room with a bed and a suitcase of clean clothes. On the bedside table was a passport, in which she recognised her photograph, but not her identity.

In broken German, he made it clear to her that she should try to sleep, because they'd be leaving in a few hours. They would be driving for two days, with a stop in Austria before heading to their final destination in Tuscany. When she asked if he knew anything about Michael and if he'd managed to track down Lukas, he made a brief dismissive gesture that said more than words.

It had still been dark when he'd woken her the next morning. They'd walked some way through the forest together before reaching a main road, where the Mercedes had been waiting. She'd gone to sit in the passenger seat, but he'd insisted she sit in the back. When she climbed in, he'd passed her a telephone and indicated that Michael would call her.

Clutching the phone, she stared outside. Although the hotel in Austria was equipped with every comfort, and she'd finally been able to shower, she'd barely slept more than a couple of hours.

For a day and a half, no message had arrived on the phone that Cibor had given her. Her fear that something had gone seriously wrong grew as the hours went by. And Cibor made no attempts to ease her mind.

She looked through the window. It was five in the afternoon and the sun was shining over the green hills of Tuscany, the vineyards and the houses with their terracotta tiled roofs. It could have been a photo from a holiday album if her own reality didn't feel quite so grey. She wondered where they were driving to and realised that she didn't want a new life if there was no place in it for Lukas.

The car made a sharp turn to the left and as they emerged from the bend, she saw in the distance a white house surrounded by olive trees.

"Nearly there," said Cibor.

Just then the phone rang, startling her so much that she nearly dropped the thing. She answered and recognised Michael's voice straightaway, even though he sounded pretty weary.

"I'm sorry I made you wait," he said. "But there were a few things I couldn't put off, such as having two bullets removed from my body."

"You were wounded? But what about Lukas? Where is he?"

"Thanks for your concern. I'm fine. As for Lukas, Cibor's just informed me that you're now approaching your new home."

Gaelle looked out at the white house.

"Isn't it beautiful?" Michael said quietly. "The view, the sense of infinity as the sun sets behind the hills in the evening."

He paused for a moment. "The name of the house is Bellefleur."

Gaelle looked down at her lap.

"Without Lukas, I won't ever have a real home again," she said.

"He's waiting there for you."

For a second, she thought she hadn't heard Michael properly because of the crunch of the tyres on the gravel driveway.

"What did you say?"

"Lukas is there, Gaelle. Scorpio never got their hands on him."

"WHAT?"

She yelled so loud that Cibor turned to look.

"Let me explain, Gaelle. Just listen."

As they approached the house, she listened to what Michael was trying to tell her. On the morning she ran from the boat, he'd made all the arrangements for Lukas to be taken from the hospital in a fake ambulance, so that Scorpio didn't get there before him. He'd had Lukas moved to a place where excellent doctors would take care of him. As soon as Lukas's condition allowed, Michael had arranged for him to be taken to the estate in Tuscany. The boy was now recovering nicely, and he knew that Gaelle was on her way.

"All that time you were lying to me," said Gaelle. "All that time you left me in the dark about whether Lukas was alive or dead. Why the hell didn't you just tell me?"

"To stop you running off to look for him. You'd already endangered the whole operation and put your own life at risk by being impulsive. It gave you a reason to stay with me, which meant I could keep an eye on you."

"But you could have just told me, couldn't you?"

"Then we'd probably never have got that valuable information out of Paul de Groot. I knew that I needed you, that the honest despair of a mother who was looking for her son would be more likely to persuade him than pointing a gun at his head."

"You have no empathy, Michael."

Tears ran down her cheeks.

"Maybe one day you'll see it differently."

The car stopped in front of the villa. She could see the wooden sign next to the front door with the word *Bellefleur* written on it in elegant letters.

"I'll let you go now, Gaelle. I think you have more important things to do."

"Wait."

She opened the car door but didn't get out yet.

"Am I ever going to see you again?" she asked.

He waited for a moment.

"One day I'll just turn up at the door," he said. "I can't say exactly when. It depends on a few things I still have to sort out."

She stepped out of the car and closed the door.

"Thank you, Michael."

She hung up, handed the phone to Cibor and ran straight to the front door. Calling Lukas's name, she pressed the doorbell. She didn't take her finger off the bell until the door opened. An athletic young woman appeared, dressed in beige shorts and hiking boots, with sturdy calves and bright-pink socks.

"Hello," she said with a smile. She held out her hand and introduced herself as Fabienne. "Lukas couldn't sleep all last night after I told him yesterday that you were coming."

Gaelle shook her hand and quickly let go as she stepped into the hallway.

"Where is he?"

"Mummy?"

Lukas was standing at the top of the stairs. He was wearing dark-blue pyjamas and looked a little paler than usual, but his smile lit up his face as they fell into each other's arms halfway up the stairs.

"Finally!" said Lukas. "I've been waiting so long to see you, Mummy."

They walked upstairs and sat close together in an armchair with a view of the olive grove. Gaelle was incapable of speech. All she could do was stroke his head, feel the warmth of his small body in her arms and listen to his heartbeat and to everything he was so eager to tell her.

"I was really scared, Mummy. When I woke up, I was in a bed and I didn't know where I was. You and Daddy weren't there. The doctors wouldn't tell me anything. And the door of my room was always locked."

She stroked his cheek.

"As soon as I got here, everything was a lot nicer. Fabienne made pancakes and vanilla custard, but it's not as good as yours, obviously. And when I'm all better, Claude's going to take me for a ride on the tractor, through the olive trees."

Then he looked at her seriously, as if he'd forgotten he was a child.

"Fabienne explained to me that the doctors weren't angry with me, but that they just weren't allowed to tell me anything. It was all for my own good, Fabienne said. The door being locked too."

He placed his hand on hers.

"Fabienne told me I just had to wait here for you. She said you're the only one who can explain to me what happened."

He wiped her tears away.

"Don't cry, Mummy. You're here now, aren't you?"

He looked out through the window.

"And where's Daddy?"

MICHAEL WALKED ALONG the narrow forest path that led to the graveyard on the edge of the Polish village where he'd grown up – and where his childhood had ended so abruptly. It was mid-August. The sun was burning the back of his neck, and clouds of mosquitoes were buzzing around the trees. The wooden gate squeaked as he opened it and set foot on the soil he hadn't walked on since he was thirteen. Closing the gate, he paused and looked around. There were dozens of rows of new graves, much more modern than the ones in the older part of the cemetery, where his father's grave was. It would have disappeared long ago if the family hadn't paid a fee, a task he'd taken care of years before.

First he visited his father's grave and then he looked for his mother's. He stood in front of the simple gravestone. After all those years, the moss had covered half of the letters. No one had been left here to clean the stone.

He coughed. In his head, he'd already repeated the words a thousand times, but now that he was standing here, he didn't know how to begin. His eyes wandered to a nearby plot, where a woman was placing flowers on a child's grave. He hadn't brought any himself. He'd never understood why people gave gifts to the dead. They should have done it while they were still alive. Glancing in his direction, the woman nodded a greeting. He nodded back and turned away. He assumed the woman didn't know who he was. Maybe she was wondering why this man – well dressed, in his forties, with blond hair and sunglasses – was visiting the cemetery on a nice summer's day. She probably thought he was recovering from some sort of accident or an illness, something to do with his left leg, which made him walk a little awkwardly.

He bent to touch the cold gravestone.

It took longer than I thought. I'm sorry I didn't come back sooner. Maybe one day I'll be brave enough to tell you why. Let's just say for now that I lost my way a little. But I'm back, and I wanted to come and tell you personally.

He said farewell by running his fingers slowly over the moss and over the name hidden beneath. He left the cemetery, got into his car, keyed his destination into the navigation system and drove away, heading for Tuscany. And even when, hours later, the sun went down, the feeling of summer did not let him go.

Somewhere in a place no one will find, in a house where no one ever calls, a blind man is sitting in an office. He can hear the rapid typing on the keyboard as his secretary puts his words online. As he thinks about the valuable information on the USB stick Dolores entrusted to him, he feels a flicker of regret when he remembers all that's been lost: the safe house, the rosebush and Dolores herself. But then he smiles. How naive is it to believe that a plant will die if you pull off its leaves and petals and leave the roots intact? He leans back in his desk chair and, even though he'll never see it with his own eyes, an image appears in his mind: of a woman somewhere, in a perfectly ordinary street, in a perfectly ordinary family, waving goodbye to her husband this morning, knowing for certain that she'll never see him again.

Afterword

Fiction writers are expected to take a creative approach to reality, as I did in this book with actual locations in Germany, France and Poland. For example, I took the liberty of giving the German town of Altensteig a hotel that suited my purposes and placing a souvenir shop directly opposite a bistro. Other than that, nearly everything in this story exists for real: the illegal part of the tunnel system under Paris is explored by people known as *cataphiles*. Something like the Dark Web really exists, the dark depths of the internet that lie beyond the reach of the general public. I descended into those depths only as far as necessary for informational purposes. And Dolores Bartosz's bunker-like safe house was inspired by existing designs. Those minuscule transmitters you can use to trace someone are also products of our modern society and not my own imagination.

There was enough information out there about all the subjects, except for one: contract killers. During my research, I did come across some public websites written in poor Dutch, with hitmen praising their services and offering to do away with your mother-in-law for a nice price. Firstly, you might wonder how seriously to take such things. If a writer can find it within a few minutes of Googling, then the police can find it even more quickly than that. Besides, I wouldn't want to give them my money if the quality of their services is on a par with their language skills.

Those are not the real contract killers. The real hitman or hit-woman moves silently through society. It could be the man sitting across from you on the train or the cyclist who skims past you on a dark road. It could be the woman who follows exactly the same route as you on your daily run through the woods.

The real contract killers are invisible.

And that was the most chilling discovery I made when researching this book.

Acknowledgements

Thank you

My special thanks go to the Italian producer Walter Iuzzolino, who selected my book *Scorpio* (*The Scorpion's Head*) for the new 'Walter Presents' series, published by Pushkin Press in London. Someone who really believes in you can make a huge difference – this has become an important theme in my writing career.

I would also like to thank Peter Bouckaert of Eyeworks Belgium, who acquired the film rights to my thriller *Stille Grond* in 2016. I found this so motivating and inspiring that I owe a great deal to Peter for everything that has happened since then. This includes my thrillers *Schemerzone* and *Pas op voor de buren*, as well as plans for new international film projects, which may already have come to fruition by the time you read this.

I have had a long and happy working relationship with the Dutch publishing house Volt (part of Singel Uitgeverijen). I'm grateful for the enthusiasm and excellence with which my manuscripts are published and marketed. Thank you, Bart, Eduard, Merel, Esther, Jolijn, Michele and also Inge from L & M Books.

I'd like to thank everyone at Pushkin Press, especially Adam Freudenheim, Daniel Seton and Rory Williamson, for their exceptional care and attention in finding a home for my book at their publishing house. *The Scorpion's Head* is in fine company there. Many thanks, too, to Nathan Burton for the outstanding cover design.

I also knew my book would be in good hands with translator Laura Watkinson. We met once at a party held by a literary organisation, where we had a good conversation, and I knew I would suggest her name if a book of mine were translated into English. I'm glad she was so keen to translate this book, and I appreciate her dedication in searching for the right words.

Sometimes it comes down to meeting the right people in the right place. I first met my husband Patrick more than twenty-five years ago. If he'd known then that he would be my First Reader for at least twenty years, he might have thought twice. It's not always easy to have an author in the house. Our two daughters know all about that.

Finally, I would like to dedicate this book to everyone who has inspired me, so that I can in turn inspire others.

—HILDE VANDERMEEREN

FOLLOW THE AUTHOR ON:

www.hildevandermeeren.com

www.facebook.com/Hilde-Vandermeeren-558550840908376

ALSO AVAILABLE
IN THE WALTER PRESENTS LIBRARY

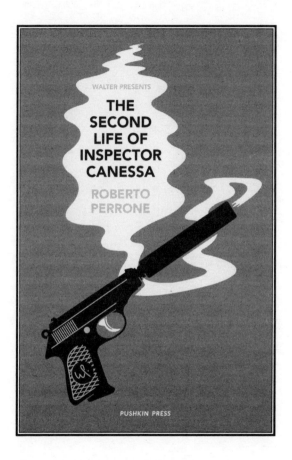